Heads Carolina

Heads and Tails: Book 1

Grea Warner

Heads Carolina
Heads and Tails: Book 1
Copyright © 2021 Grea Warner
All rights reserved.

ISBN: (ebook): 978-1-953335-32-6
(print) 978-1-953335-33-3

Inkspell Publishing
207 Moonglow Circle #101
Murrells Inlet, SC 29576

Edited By Yezanira Venecia
Cover art By Najla Qamber

OTHER BOOKS BY GREA WARNER

COUNTRY ROADS SERIES:

Country Roads

Almost Heaven

Take Me Home

Teardrop in My Eye

The Place I Belong

STANDALONE:

Every Mile, a Memory

COMING SOON:

Tails California

Whiskey Girl

GREA WARNER

DEDICATION

Bethany's unique apartment complex was inspired by a place where I once lived. This book is for every woman pursuing their dream in the big city.
You can do it!

And for my family. It is because of their support, encouragement, and love that I was able to venture out and follow my own dreams.

GREA WARNER

CHAPTER ONE

"You're just too raw. You don't have the maturity. There are others way ahead of you. It's definitely a no."

The group of young women gathered with me in the upstairs lounge booed and threw napkins at the television screen after those cruel words about me were broadcast. They were shocked, but I knew it was coming. After all, it had been three months since the show had been recorded … three months since I had stood there in front of the three people in charge of my fate. Under television contracts, though, I hadn't been able to reveal the outcome to anyone until after the show aired.

I had known the slim probability of succeeding going in. Heck, all of America knew what to expect when trying out amongst thousands for *Singer Spotlight*. And now, after the actual broadcast, all of America knew I hadn't even made it through to the first round.

Compared to other cruelties in the world, my non-advancement on a televised talent show didn't make any lists, though. It wasn't a natural disaster. It wasn't an incurable, spreading disease. I just wasn't going to be the next singing superstar and, most likely, neither were any of the other women in the room, despite most of us coming to Los Angeles for exactly that reason … to be in the entertainment business. Some had entry-level jobs and internships in the industry. Some hadn't even gotten that far. And *my* fifteen minutes of fame, I guess, was going to be right there on that screen—rejected by a stone-faced Ryan Thompson on national television. At least the other two judges had said sorry and gave supportive smiles.

"Maturity, schamurity." Willow grumbled. "You are more mature than most of us. Responsible, considerate—"

"I don't think he was talking about me as a person."

"Well, he better not have been complaining about your body." Only a model, having been repeatedly judged by her shape, would have made a comment like that.

I shook my head. "No. I don't think that was it, either." A pushup bra helped, but I was pretty lucky with my hourglass figure on a five-eight frame. "It was my voice. I never had the training some of those people do. I just like to sing and write lyrics and was half-decent in local theater. It was a pipe dream. I can't regret it." Nevertheless, a resigned, semi-depressed state had still found home in my heart.

I was fielding an I-just-saw-you-on-TV text from a coworker when another of my fellow housemates asked if I was following my Twitter feed. I hadn't been. It wasn't something I did constantly—maybe once or twice a day—but, I guess, right then I should have been.

When I pulled it up, there for the world to see—or at least the thousands who followed *Singer Spotlight* or Ryan Thompson—was a tweet mentioning me, and it was from the TV show judge/music manager himself. *@Bethany_Lenay beautiful song, heartfelt words, real potential as a songwriter. #DontGiveUp*

I checked Twitter. I checked Ryan Thompson's website. I double-checked both. It was legit. The real Ryan Thompson, blue checkmark and all, had just posted those words alongside a clip of me performing my original song on the show. I breathed in a few times and, despite protests from my apartment mates, exited to the quiet hallway. I needed to react to the tweet. But I didn't know how. Those beautiful, heartfelt words Ryan Thompson claimed I had, completely escaped me.

I wrote something quickly, though, so he didn't think I was ignoring him. It was short and not lyrical at all. *@RyanThompsonMusic For real?*

When he didn't respond, I tried not to wonder why. A litany of possibilities raced through my head, though. He wasn't going to respond because … a) I blew it with my stupid insecure reply, b) he thought he'd done his one good deed for the year by throwing poor little me a bone and didn't want to get caught in a Twitter dialogue, c) he was too busy answering all his other social media sites, d) it wasn't really him replying but an assistant who needed permission on how to respond, e) he was too busy making out with his gorgeous rock star wife, or f) all of the above.

I walked back to my room. I had to use the bathroom for one thing. Plus, I needed a quiet spot to think in case he actually did answer.

It was when I placed the phone on my bed and flopped next to it in exasperation that his response came through. *For real.* It was quickly followed by, *If you have other material, would like to see it.*

That shot my body back up to a sitting position. Holy … wow! I waited how long? And my possible break was happening right then? I wanted to look around to see if I was being punked. Get it together, Bethany, I encouraged myself. Reply before he disappears. Reply before your second chance opportunity blows away in the westerly winds. Reply correctly and confidently. And remember, the whole world is kind of watching again. Oh, geez!

@RyanThompsonMusic I definitely have songs.

His response that time was immediate. *Maybe we'll find a time to meet.*

Before I knew it, there was a multitude of comments and likes on our conversation. A lot of people were supportive, saying I deserved a second chance. There were a few others who suggested that other people who were let go were better than me. And there were, actually, a few restaurants that said they would send food if I was interested in writing something with their brand attached. I laughed. Jingle writing was not my aspiration or talent skill … at all.

As I was scrolling through the tweeting fest notifications, another came in from Mr. Thompson. *I will DM you. Hope you're hungry with all these sponsors.*

I clicked on the heart symbol to like and end our public conversation. And then I ran to the bathroom before I had an I'm-too-darn-excited accident. Did all of that just happen? And what did it mean?

***

It was a week later when I was sitting in the sleek, modern lobby of the talent agency that Ryan Thompson ran. I had gone over every song in my repertoire, seemingly trillions of times—making sure every line flowed to the right beat, and the meaning and even spelling were absolutely the best. Willow had told me to quit picking … I was making it worse. She had then played fashionista and decked me out in some of her clothes before sending me on my way. I was fiddling with the crepe, pale pink, button-down top—which she said personified innocence and femininity, along with a touch of cleavage—when the man himself bustled in.

"Sorry … running behind." He spoke to his secretary sitting at the desk in front of me. "Something's gotta give. She didn't show up yet? That's not good."

The middle-aged woman, sporting a dark pixie haircut, corrected him. "She's been here. Twenty or twenty-five minutes now. Early."

As she pointed her finger toward me, the exec turned my direction. His deep blue eyes found my brown ones as

I sat on the broken-in leather sofa, which was not complimentary for either sitting with correct posture or ladylike. It was also not good for getting up gracefully, as I tried to do then. Thank goodness I had on simple black slacks ... with zippers because Willow said they looked "rock star."

I held out my hand, hoping the deodorant I had put on them earlier absorbed any nervous perspiration. "Mr. Thompson."

Dressed in dark slacks, a white shirt, and royal blue tie, he shook my hand in return and apologized. "I'm so sorry. I didn't recognize you. Your hair ... it's different."

"Since the audition? Yeah. It was much lighter a few months ago ... a bunch of bleachy blonde streaks." My hair was back to its natural dark brown color ... almost as dark as Ryan Thompson's.

"It's longer or something, too, right?"

That was also true. I hadn't had it cut until I had someone at my apartment complex give me a trim a couple days before. Plus, at the audition, it had been pinned up to look almost bob-like.

"Yep. I keep pulling at it ... helps it grow." I was pretty proud of myself for coming up with the quick, non-boring response. But then I immediately wondered if it came across as disrespectful or, possibly worse, an old-man joke.

What I did not expect was his reply. "Really?"

I tried not to laugh, but I think a soft snort may have come out. "My brother used to fall for that. I didn't think you would."

"I should try that trick on my kids when I don't shave." He acknowledged his dark beard. "But they would probably pull too hard on my face."

My mind scrambled quickly to recall all the information I had researched online about Ryan Thompson during the week. I had concentrated on his professional side as the owner of a talent agency, which had seen a good number of stars rise in the singing ranks. But I also made sure to know a little about the man himself. Making small connections, I knew could easily help any meeting. Originally from Iowa, he was married to his chart-topping, contemporary rock wife. Both in their low to mid-thirties, they had two young kids. The girl was five years old, and the boy was four.

"That's a fun kid age," I offered and then internally cringed. I wondered if he would catch on that I had done some behind-the-scenes research since he hadn't mentioned their age nor were there any photos present in the lobby area.

But he seemed more focused on the content of my words rather than the source. "I can't say I disagree." Was that a smile on the face that had been so rigid at my audition?

"I guess going the California blonde direction didn't work." I backtracked to our original conversation while playing with a few strands of my hair.

"It wasn't your looks, Bethany." Although, I swear he did a slight grimace. "I know all this is hard to understand, and it's a huge blow." He stopped his train of thought and started again. "Look, sorry. That wasn't how I wanted to get this started."

Geez! Me, either. I didn't want to talk about the negatives. There was going to be a positive, right?

"So, what's first, then? Coffee from California Hut? Tacos from Mexican Mindset …?" I joked, thinking of the companies that had chimed in on our initial public Twitter conversation.

"Yeah, that was a little crazy. Come on in." He started walking toward his office just beyond the secretary's desk. "I *can* get you some coffee if you want."

"No." I internally chuckled. "Thank you. Already had enough." I picked up my purse and guitar, which had been resting to the side of the sofa, and followed him into the next room.

"Good deal. I think I am going to need an IV of the

stuff. Have a seat." As I sat in the straight-back chair, he did so on the other side of the desk, decorated haphazardly with papers. "I usually have things in much better order. Two full-time jobs and …" His voice trailed as he began straightening the materials on his desk. "It's a bit much."

"The reason for the coffee?" I offered while examining the rest of my surroundings.

The all-glass wall behind him hosted a view of numerous buildings in downtown Los Angeles. The others were filled with either awards or photos of famous people … most with him in them, too. It was a little intimidating—the world of the elite percentage who had achieved the dream of what I wanted. But it was also empowering, knowing I had gotten that far. I was actually a step—or a desk—away from possibly joining one of those walls. I didn't want to get too far ahead of myself, though. I had, after all, read and reread what he had told me in the initial tweet. I was a good songwriter. My talent was in my words … not so much my voice. If I was honest, I would agree.

"Exactly." He settled more completely into his chair, and I had to remember he was talking about coffee.

When nervous, I tend to be oddly bold. "So, is this legit, or is it like a publicity stunt?"

"What? You being here?" He drew his dark eyebrows closer together.

"Yeah. I mean, do you pick one contestant or person and put it out there so you don't come across looking so mean?" My boldness probably went a bit too far that time.

But he vibrated his lips in an appreciative burst of air. "Uh, no. I thought I answered the 'real' question with the tweeting last week."

"You did. Just wanted to make sure." I was trying to ease myself back into a respectable conversation.

"When the show actually aired and I was able to focus a little better …" He hesitated and then continued, "I picked up on your songwriting side. I'm kinda regretting it, though …" The expression on my face must have sunk as low as my stomach suddenly dropped because he quickly amended with, "No, no … not regretting meeting with you. I'm regretting making the request public. I'm afraid I have gotten a lot of other people wanting a second chance, too."

"Oh." So, it really was legit.

"This is new to me—the judging thing." It was his first year on the show, which had been around a handful plus. "I thought it would be easy. I mean, essentially it is what I do for a living—weed out talent. And it would be nice to say 'yes' to everybody, but you can't."

"Because they're too raw and people are way ahead of them."

"An exact quote?" He lifted his eyebrows.

"I have it painted on my wall," I teased.

"You do n—" He was starting to catch on to my sarcasm.

"It would be kind of good inspiration, though."

"Just so there isn't a dartboard with my photo on it."

"No, I took that down after you sent the nice tweet."

He laughed, but the funny part was, I had actually considered putting up a nasty Ryan Thompson picture right after the audition. "All right, Bethany, you got spunk. You didn't show it so much on your audition, but I could feel it in your words."

"Thanks." Assuming that was a compliment. "I appreciate you reaching out and asking me to come in. I'm not sure what it all means, but—"

"It just means I want to hear and see more of your original songs. And then we'll see where it goes from there."

"Okay."

"Whatcha got?"

I unzipped the soft, but secure, black guitar case and brought the instrument into my hands. Dark mahogany with fake gems encircling the soundhole, the guitar was a hand-me-down from one of my father's parishioners, and I couldn't love it more. In both the darkest and happiest of times, it was my trusted companion and revealer of truths.

After warming up with a few chords, I started playing and singing some of my original tunes. I wasn't sure if I should make eye contact with him or not. I knew it was important during the show auditions, but his office seemed more intimate, and I found it harder to look into those eyes, which were closer yet just as hard to read. He didn't say a thing during or after any of the individual songs. Although, I did see him scribbling some notes on the lyrics and bio info I had provided him. I tried to nonchalantly look at the papers, but his handwriting had something to be desired, especially from my upside-down point of view.

"So …"

One word was all he provided after I finished. I was going to have to invest in adult diapers when it came to communicating with him. My nerves and bladder didn't work well with anticipation.

"I like some things. Let me … let me play around with it a little. I, unfortunately, have another meeting. It's my fault for arriving late in the first place. But I'll be in touch." He stood as I put my guitar back in the case.

"Um, okay. Thanks."

The sassy, outgoing personality of Bethany Lenay evaporated. In its place was the more legit, insecure girl from North Carolina. I knew a brush-off when I heard one because I had heard one or two or seventy before.

"Thanks for the opportunity, Mr. Thompson." Thankfully, I did manage to maintain good manners as I stood.

"Oh, God. It's Ryan, please. Hadn't we covered that?" He took a few steps to the side of his desk and, with his body directly across from mine, I estimated him to be an even six-foot height.

"No. No. I don't think so. Anyway, thanks." I stuck

out my hand, which he shook softly but cleanly, and then he showed me out the door.

***

On my walk back home, I thought of a billion things I could have, and probably should have, said. I scripted our conversation a lot of different ways—one where I was less sarcastic, one where I was more professional, one where I dared to look him in the eyes, one where I asked questions, and one where I told him more of the background for each of the songs I had written. My walk in the refreshing early March air was just short of forty-five minutes, so I had plenty of time to have alternate endings.

When I entered the building where I lived, I was greeted by the front doorman. He always seemed half-asleep. But at least he was more pleasant than the nasty woman porched at the front desk. After checking my empty mailbox—which was better than a rejection—I took the elevator to my eighth-floor shoebox apartment. I turned the key and started to push the door when Willow swung hers open.

"God!" my next-door neighbor exclaimed. "I've been so waiting for you to come back. Tell me. Tell me all about it."

I laughed. "I'm hungry."

"Geez! Hold on. I got some illegal contraband." She raced into her room and flashed back into mine with a box of miniature chocolate graham crackers. "Here." She shoved them at me.

I scanned the box and then started devouring the secret stash. We weren't supposed to have food in our rooms because the residence provided us with breakfast and dinner daily in the main floor dining hall. Plus, the owners were afraid of fire hazards in our extremely small rooms, which had no kitchen area. There was only enough space for a bed, dresser, desk, sink, mirror, and closet. The bathrooms were shared between two women. It was basically a hard-to-get-into dorm setting but not co-ed. No men were allowed ... even for visits. That was the only thing my dad—a minister by trade—liked about me moving to La-La Land.

"Take it easy, T-Rex," Willow teased. "Your digestive system is going to go all cray-cray."

"You models don't need yummy stuff like this. I thought you only ate lettuce," I countered.

"Ha! Now ... tell me about Ryyyan." She sounded like one of those teeny boppers infatuated with the latest YouTube sensation. But I knew better. Willow was just an upbeat, positive kind of girl. Besides, she was totally into her boyfriend, Tilman.

Besides my parents, Willow was the only person I had told about the actual date of the meeting. Of course, after the whole Twitter escapade, a lot of people who knew me were asking. But I didn't want to jinx or explain anything, so, I kept it private. And sitting there on my twin-sized bed made me glad I had.

"He hated me." I pretend pouted.

"What!"

"He said ... Are you ready ...?" Her eyes fixated on me, I worked hard to sound legit. "He said, 'What the heck kind of clothes are you wearing?'"

"Oh. My. God! I am going to kill that son of a bitch." Her arms started to flail as she paced, obviously offended since they were her clothes and her life was fashion. "Who does he think he is? He may think he knows music. But how dare he chime in with his fashion sense—or lack of. He is—"

She was on such a roll moving up and down the limited square footage that she didn't even notice I was on the bed laughing so hard tears were coming out of my eyes. I had said the little fib just because it was me ... because I liked razzing people either when I was nervous or when I really got to know them well. I was glad I did. It definitely helped me unwind from the experience of Audition Round Two.

"Bethany Opala, I hate you!" Willow bellowed, catching on. "You are meaner than mean Ryan Thompson."

"He's not that bad," I admitted. "And pulling out my real last name? You're like a parent when they're mad at you!"

"Ahhh," she scoffed at the comparison, but she was one of only a few people who knew my real last name versus my stage/pen/California name. "Are you seriously going to tell me?" Willow managed to sit on the desk chair after spinning it around to face me.

"Seriously," I mimicked. "I don't know. He doesn't seem so mean, but I think he's going to crush my dreams again."

"Yeah?" she asked in a softer and kinder tone. "Then I'm back to hating him. Mr. Mean—that is his name," she said with finality.

"No." I shoved the box of treats back at my friend. If I ate any more, I *would* be sick. "I sang my songs. He took notes. He said he'd get back to me."

"Well, that's good."

"Willow," I blew out her name.

At age twenty-three, just like me, she already knew rejection, too … from the modeling world. While she was tall and pretty, it was in a plain, simple kind of way. Willow's features—mousey, thin, straight brown hair, and similarly hued eyes—were not distinct enough to set her apart from others … certainly not in a money-making, cover model sort of way. Hopefully the fashion degree she was about to get would provide her with something promising.

"You never know." The native Bostonian kept positive.

"You never know," I repeated. "Do you want me to throw this outfit in my bag? I'm gonna go do laundry. I need clothes for work tomorrow."

"No, I'm sure it's fine. Besides, it might have Ryyyan's scent on it."

"Oh, geez." I rolled my eyes.

"Does he smell as good as he looks?"

"Better," I teased.

"Nu-uh? Like what?"

"I don't know, Willow! I wasn't there sniffing the guy! The only thing I smelled was my deodorant working overtime."

"Throw the top in the wash then … yuk!" She smiled. "I'll meet up with you at dinner. I read it is couscous night. I love hearing Andre"—she spoke of one of the dining hall servers/maintenance workers—"say that. I order it just to hear him say 'couscous … couscous.'" We laughed together. "I think he likes you. He's always trying to give you two desserts even though we're only allowed one."

"He doesn't know I already partake in my neighbor's secret stash," I offered, trying to get off the topic of Andre.

"You buy next time. I'm craving M&Ms."

"You got it."

"Caramel flavored."

"Sure thing."

When Willow left, I threw her outfit in my overstuffed laundry bag, put on a comfy pair of pants and a coordinating shirt, and started the journey to the basement. The elevator didn't go all the way down to the exact floor of the laundry room, so I descended the few metal steps to completely make it to the deepest part of the complex. I cringed momentarily, looking to the left where maintenance workers stored things and sometimes took their breaks. Then, with a shake of my head, I turned right and entered the dry heat of the laundry area. There were usually sufficient washers and dryers, but they looked like they were manufactured in the 1970s. There was also a place for ironing and a wooden bench. But I had never seen someone actually stay during the hours it took to do laundry. I did, though. I liked the silence the area provided—minus the monotonous sound of the running machines. It was the perfect space to compose lyrics since—even though we had our own rooms—the residency still hosted a variety of sounds and bustle.

After adding the detergent and starting the machine, I sat with my notebook and pencil on the bench. I liked writing things out the old-fashioned way first. It was interesting to see Ryan do that on the papers I had handed him, too.

Before I wrote any choruses or verses, though, I wanted to compose a follow-up thank you to the judge/talent manager. I'd heard plenty of stories where people said they hadn't hired someone because they didn't have the common courtesy to send a "thank you" of some sort. My dad also delivered numerous sermons on being courteous and thankful, and we kids listened.

Once I was happy scripting out my message, I entered it into my phone and DM'd Mr. Thompson. *Thank you very much for the opportunity to meet with you and share my passion for writing music. At the very least, it has inspired me to continue writing. If you are interested in anything I gave you today or additional material, please let me know … hopefully before my hair gets much longer.*

I debated, but I liked the sassy, personal ending to my thank-you message. It showed creativity. It showed a willingness to joke. It showed being fearless. Ha! I pressed send.

I tried to write lyrics then, but I couldn't get my mind to focus. Not only had I just experienced one of the most thrilling moments of my mediocre career, but I also couldn't stop thinking of the last time I was in that laundry room. I had been at my lowest of lows—knowing my *Singer Spotlight* show episode was going to air soon and seeing no future in the music business or even in the city itself. It was amazing what a difference a couple of weeks could make. And any regrets from that time, I was going to have to live with and hopefully learn to forgive myself for.

***

Couscous spit from my mouth clear across the table. I rose from my chair and started apologizing to Nell who had the unfortunate seat in the line of fire. "Sorry, so sorry."

"It's all right. I needed a shower, just didn't expect it to be with food," she replied.

"I'm sorry," I repeated.

"What made you do that?" Willow, who was sitting next to me, asked as I sat back down. "There isn't a bug or hair or something in the food, is there?"

"Ewww." Nell stood. "I'm gonna get some more napkins."

"Sorry. I shouldn't have my phone at the table. My parents brought me up better than that." Nevertheless, I peeked at the just delivered DM again.

It was nice to see you. Don't put up any dart boards or pierce any voodoo dolls. I'm swamped, but I will get back to you. Keep writing.

I had been waiting for it—a reply from the music manager to my thank-you message. And it hadn't even taken him too long—just a load of laundry and partway into dinner. I flipped my phone upside down.

When Willow ever so slightly leaned her head toward me and squinted her eyes, I promised, "I'll tell you later."

From across the room, I could see Andre handing Nell some napkins. She was shaking her blonde head of hair and laughing, and I could only imagine the story she was telling him since he then glanced in my direction. Eternally golden from being raised in southern California, he had that cat-ate-the-canary kind of grin on his face. But I didn't care. I didn't care about anything else but that promising message from Ryan Thompson. The moving papers I was set to turn in were going to have to wait because I was pretty sure I was in Los Angeles to stay.

CHAPTER TWO

We were sitting in the same seats from a week before, and I should have felt more comfortable considering I was back ... back there ... back in the music manager's office. The hard part was over. I had sung and revealed my original work. I had bled out my written heart the last time I was there. But right then ... it was harder somehow.

"You didn't have to shave to prove it hasn't been that long since our last meeting," was my ice breaker.

Mr. Thompson shook his head in amusement. "I much more prefer the no scruff, especially with the show now airing. I was being recognized out and about. Not into that. But your idea works."

I think I liked the clean-shaven look. He definitely appeared younger without the beard. He looked like someone I would have hung out with a couple years before ... before I graduated from college and things seemed so much more carefree and achievable.

"You know, you should work some of that wit into your lyrics sometime. It's a totally different style. For a songwriter, it will make you easier to sell to a wider variety of artists and genres."

"People have told me that about my sense of humor

before. It's not my writing style, though. I kind of become a different person. It's hard to explain."

"So, here's the thing, Bethany ..."

Oh, dang, there was a "thing." I had thought if he asked me to come in, it would be good news. No one lets someone down personally, especially in today's world of electronics galore. But when I thought about it, I guess that's what doctors did for terminal patients. Otherwise, it was good news on the phone. Oh, man, I was dying a slow death.

"You all right?" He interrupted my internal lowering of my career casket.

"Yeah. Yeah. What's the thing?"

"I like your stuff. I do."

"Good. But ...?"

"I can't take any more on."

He paused at the same time as I said, "Oh."

If he knew that, why did he taunt me from the beginning? Men. They were all the same. It didn't matter if they were a college co-ed or a charismatic stud in the base—

"After your songs. I would like to try working on some of the material with you. If you're willing to do that." Pause. "Bethany?"

Backtrack. Backtrack. What did he just say?

"Did I get you on that?" he continued. "Was the dart heading straight for my forehead on the—"

"You did that on purpose?" I expelled.

"I grew up with three siblings. I'm the youngest. I had every trick in the book played on me. I was their personal 'Ha! Ha! Let's fool Ryan.'" I didn't realize I was actually getting teary until he pointed it out. "Oh, geez, I didn't mean to make you ... I thought with your sense of humor ..."

I wiped at my eyes as he handed me a tissue. My meeting with the music exec was going down as the worst job opportunity ever. I was probably going to be shunned from the entire industry.

"You did say you wanted to help me with my songs?"

"For real." He seemed to smirk, and I realized he chose those words to mimic mine when originally tweeting him.

"I think we can use some of your wit, too, Mr.—Ryan." I remembered at the last moment to call him by his first name. "That was good. You got me."

"Mmmm-hmmm." I think he actually smiled. "So … here's my offer. They still need work, but I'll invest my time and people to help make these the best they can be so we can pitch them."

"Great. Yeah, great." Yeah, like a thousand smiley and celebration emojis exploding out of my head great.

"Good. I was hoping you'd say that. I already started passing a lot of the day-to-day stuff off to my associates and need to concentrate on *Spotlight*. And hopefully before that ramps back up with the live shows, I can work on writing with you. This isn't normally how things are done, but the show has really inspired me to get back to why I chose music as my area of specialty … the artistic creativity. I haven't had a chance to do that in years. You have the talent. Together I think we can get you to the next level. I'm looking forward to it." It *was* a legitimate smile. Go figure.

I knew there wasn't a clear path on how to break into the music industry. The one Ryan was proposing seemed more mentoring than a sign-on-a-dotted-line deal. But he was the owner of his company and had that flexibility. And I couldn't be more thrilled.

"So, what's your schedule like?" he asked. "Work?"

"Uh, pretty free since I quit my job."

"Quit? Because …?"

"I am moving back to Carolina?" It came out as a question because I most definitely did not want it to be true. I wanted him to actually refute it.

"You what?"

"I've put my time in here. Nothing was happening. It's

too expensive. Time to face reality. Tail between my legs and all that."

"Would you … you'd consider staying now, though? I mean, I suppose—"

"Yeah. Yeah, of course."

"But your job."

"Well, I haven't turned in my official notice yet. My boss knows my intentions, though. She has been avoiding thinking about a replacement since it is a lot of training and, quite honestly, I am a good employee. She keeps trying to change my mind."

"What do you do?"

"Coffee barista." I grumbled. "I know. It's not an overly-desirable job … like the head of a lucrative, headlining company," I snarked, alluding to his business and feeling a little more confident again.

"But a very important one, and it sounds like you're good at it."

"I make a good cup of joe. And they let me sing there sometimes." That doubled the tips I had coming in from the coffee counter, which helped me be able to barely make my low-rent living situation.

"I know this is asking a lot, but could you see if you can get the end of this week and next week off or at least during the days? That's when my schedule is a little more open, and it would give us an intensive block of time to work."

"I'll see what I can do. Maybe if I say I'm staying, it would be a good bargaining chip."

"Negotiating … I appreciate that." He nodded in regards to something I'm sure he did quite regularly in his business.

"And I haven't turned in my moving papers to the apartment. So, that's not a problem." The probability of it had spread throughout the residence, though, that was for sure. As much as I hated some of the old-fashioned rules and regulations, I would have missed most of the people in the place I had come to call home.

"Good," Ryan continued. "I'm looking forward to the creative stuff—writing and composing. Let the business do the business. Besides, the show is taking up a lot more time than I thought."

"Yeah, I wouldn't know."

Yikes! Maybe I shouldn't have said that. But it was true.

He slightly shook his head before asking, "Are you watching at all?"

"Yeah," I admitted. "My own personal train wreck."

"It's harder as you get deeper in it. Believe me. Honestly, though, the top ten or even the winner … the chances they make a career out of it aren't really good."

"Great. You just told me to stay in town."

"You. Yes. Because you have a talent. It's songwriting, not singing. Not that—"

"I get it." I did.

"A lot of the singers sound a dime a dozen. The few elite—"

"Your wife." I glanced at the photos of blonde-haired, brown-eyed Kari Thompson, which were scattered amongst the images of him and the famous faces.

"Kari, yes, her voice is gold. But without the right words behind them …" He changed his train of thought and said, "All right, check with your job, and let's set a time to meet and work on some of these songs. Then maybe we can get some kind of better theme or branding together."

I almost laughed—it wasn't like I had one. Obviously, he had checked out my social media accounts and knew they were sparse on content. While I looked at them daily, I posted infrequently. And that consisted of just quotes about music or audio clips of me singing to the lyrics on the screen. I didn't show my face. The music was what I wanted everyone to focus on … not me.

"So, how does that sound to you?" he asked.

"Like a dream." That time my internal happy

monologue actually escaped my mouth.

***

Ryan was serious. He wanted to get started right away and had legitimately cleared most of his schedule for the rest of the week and the following. I couldn't have been happier. It was a lot better for me to dive right into something than to allow time to think and be nervous. I mean, after all, I was going to partner up with a nationally known talent manager to work on my existing songs and create new ones. A songwriter. This. Was. It.

So, only two days later, we sat in his office once again. We scanned through the music I had given him, and he talked about some of his notes. He made me choose my top three favorites, and then he revealed his. Two of ours were the same, which was interesting. I thought the one he chose for the third was too mushy. I didn't think I did sentimental very well. But he thought I had. We agreed to work on those three songs first and then see about others or new ones next.

But it wasn't easy. There were so many interruptions. He didn't have a huge staff, but those who were there were bouncing in and asking questions on a fairly regular basis. And the secretary had a number of calls that required Ryan's attention. Some he managed to delay but others he took.

We were struggling to slightly change two lines in a song when the secretary interrupted again. "I'm sorry, Ryan. I know you don't want any more calls, but it's the school about your daughter. They tried your—"

With wide eyes, he looked at his personal phone, which he had silenced. "Put it through."

"I'll wait in the lobby," I offered and got up.

He hadn't asked me to leave on any of the other calls, but his daughter's school was personal, and I figured it was the polite thing to do. I pretended to admire the expensive-looking art hanging on the lobby walls while hoping the call wasn't anything bad. By the initial look on his face, I knew it wasn't a regular occurrence, but from past experiences with my parents, I knew sometimes calls from schools meant emergencies.

"Hey, Bethany." Ryan dipped his head out of his office. "Come back in. We're gonna have to wrap up. Sorry," he concluded as I reentered the room.

"Everything all right?" I wasn't trying to be nosy … just concerned.

"Yeah. My daughter, Sallie, got sick in kindergarten," he said as he was gathering papers. "The school nurse says it's probably an ear infection and the pain made her throw up. I feel bad, though, because she said her ear hurt this morning, and I played the whole 'tough it out' dad routine."

"You didn't know," I offered.

"I should have. She usually doesn't complain at all."

"Tough little girl."

"She is … until she isn't." He sighed. "I'm sorry. I have to go get her, and since she threw up, she'll have to stay home tomorrow, too. So I know we were supposed to meet again tomorrow …"

"Not a worry. Your kids come first."

"They do," he said with straightforward confidence. "Not everyone understands that. And with being a single parent … temporarily—Kari's on tour overseas—it's up to me."

"Go. We can reschedule. My long-awaited music career can wait a day or two longer. My dreams have been crushed before."

"Oh, brother." He shook his head, and I smiled, picking up my guitar. Ryan's fluttering eyes and little twitch in his cheek clued me in that he was contemplating something. "Would you consider coming to the house? My house? Tomorrow?"

Oh. "Uh …"

"She's a good kid. She won't bother us. Joel, though, if he was home … My folks say he is payback for how I was when I was his age."

I laughed, picturing a little Ryan. "You sure? Your house?"

"Yeah," he said more succinctly that time. "If that's all right with you. I'm on a bit of a tight schedule with the show, and I know tomorrow was free …"

"Yeah, I guess."

There was a tiny part of me that was leery of being at a man's house alone … with the exception of his young daughter. But he was nationally known, and it was very obvious it wasn't a setup. Besides, in reality, I put myself in just as perilous of situations every time I took a taxi by myself.

That—transportation—was my real concern. "How far is it?" I asked.

"Depending on traffic … a little more than fifteen minutes north."

"By car?"

"Uh, yeah." His eyebrows gathered.

"Oh."

"Why? Do you have a private jet I don't know about?"

I was enjoying the sarcastic side of Ryan Thompson. It perfectly matched my sense of humor, and I was already discovering how the ease in conversation was helping us as collaborators. It was just so darn different from the version of "Mr. Mean" on TV.

"Yeah," I played along. "But the jet is at my private airport getting refurbished with the latest technology." Ryan's belly shook in laughter as I continued with the truth. "No, I'll need to tell Uber. I walked here. Probably can't walk to your place, though."

"You walked here?" His voice rose in shock.

"Yeah. Don't have a car." I repeated an answer I had been used to giving since moving to LA. It seemed to shock and awe every time I gave it, especially in a world of rush-rush and instant gratification.

"At all?" he asked in the same tone.

"Uh, it's not like … Is it *The Price Is Right* where they have the half-image of the car, or is it *Wheel of Fortune*?"

"I don't know." He shook his head again.

"Nope, no car," I continued. "Really haven't needed one. Everywhere I have to be—stores, work, restaurants—I can either walk, take public transportation, or friends drive."

"Oh. Okay. Well … so—"

"I probably could get one." With years of payments. "Not a Tesla or Porche or anything. I kind of wanted to make sure this was going to be home."

"Hopefully we're one step closer to that?" He had everything gathered in his hands.

"Help me sell my songs and we will be." I smiled.

"Deal." He started toward his door, causing me to follow. "So, how about if you give Anamaria"—he stopped at his secretary's desk—"your address, and we'll arrange transportation."

"Oh, no, that's all right. I told you, I can—"

"Look, I'm inconveniencing you. It's not a biggie." Before I could refute, Ryan told his secretary what was happening, and she said she already had my address on file. "Great. Get her set up with a ride back to her place now, too."

"It's like a forty-five-minute walk. I'm fine."

"Forty-five! Definitely … ride." He nodded at Anamaria, who immediately got on the phone. "See you tomorrow, Bethany. Sorry. Gotta run. Poor Sallie."

***

The Thompson house … oh, my stars. A personal security guard for the exclusive neighborhood, a newer paved private road, and another gate in front of the residence were the security measures in place for an award-winning singer and talent manager couple. But it was the beauty and features of the house itself that made me go weak. Sprawling best described the two-story wood and stucco home from the outside. And once Ryan invited me inside, I almost needed air. It was so breathtaking.

"Thanks for coming, Bethany."

"No problem." I think I got the words out, but my mouth was jarred open, looking everywhere from the soaring ceiling with wood beams to the light oak floor below. "This is so beautiful."

"Thanks. We custom built a few years ago."

"Yeah, I can tell it's newer, but it has such old-world charm."

"Ah, you like that? That was my doing. When you see the kitchen, that's Kari. She's all about the modern stuff. Although, it's kind of ironic. She's not … she's not much of a chef. Anyway, I figured we can work in the living room. The piano is in there, and I brought a couple of the guitars, too."

"Okay, let me—" I started taking off my shoes, glad my feet were relatively attractive and I had recently painted the nails … a weird green color, but nonetheless.

"You certainly don't need to do that because of the house. This place has two young children in it. Finger and feet marks are everywhere. Unless you're like an undercover cable repair person who is mandated to wear those baggie things on their shoes."

I laughed before asking, "Do you *mind* if I take them off? I promise they're clean. Not stinky."

He chuckled back. "Neh, go right ahead. I hardly wear shoes around the house. Only put them on because you were coming." He kicked his off dramatically and left them haphazardly near mine.

"How's your daughter?"

"She's fine," he answered, and I had to take my eyes off the magnificent curved staircase in order to follow him down the hall and past the dining room showcased by an enormous oval table. "She could have gone back to school today—actually wanted to—but it's a twenty-four-hour-policy thing. Joel, on the other hand, begged to stay home. But I didn't let him. Two opposites as opposite can be. So, Sallie is in the family room. Let me introduce you so she knows you're here. She might pop in every so often. But she is pretty self-contained."

"Whatever she needs. It's fine." Upon approach, I had to make a comment again before we entered. "Pocket doors. Geez, I love pocket doors."

Ryan seemed amused as he looked from the partially opened doors to me. "Until the wood swells a little in the heat and they don't slide. But yeah, me, too. Sals," he called to the little girl coloring at a table, "I want you to meet Bethany. I told you we'll be working in the living room if you need anything. Do you need anything now?"

A bright smile emerged as she gave a thumbs up. "Nope. All good, Daddy."

With blonde hair closely resembling her celebrity mother's, the little girl stared at me as I said, "It's nice to meet you, Sallie. What are you working on?"

"A book," she said nonchalantly. "I'm the author *and* the illustrator."

"Very cool and very talented. What's it about?" I asked, impressed by the kindergartner.

"Unicorns going to school!" She literally bounced in excitement.

"Ah, I'd love to read it sometime."

"Okay. When I'm done."

"Daddy gets first dibs, Tink," Ryan chimed in.

"All right, Daddy," she agreed. "Then Miss …"

"Bethany," Ryan reminded.

She looked again at me. "Yeah, she can read it."

"All right, baby. Come get me if you need anything," he directed, but the little girl was already back at work.

As we started out the room, I noted, "I guess ambition and creativity runs in the family."

"She's gonna outshine both her mother and me," he agreed.

"Maybe we should have her be a part of our session."

"I don't think you're going for the unicorns-in-school album, though."

"No, probably not." I laughed.

"Okay, Bethany, let's see what we can get going."

***

Ryan and I were able to get so much done. It was amazing and exhilarating. I admired and respected his talent and wanted to soak in all of his knowledge. But because I was also me, I freely offered my thoughts and ideas as we continued to work on the songs we had selected from my repertoire. We were a really good team— truly bouncing ideas off each other and making things work almost magically. I had partnered up with other musicians and lyricists before, but in none of those cases were we so instantly compatible with ideas and thoughts.

It was nice watching Ryan in a more relaxed state, rather than his office. Fewer interruptions absolutely aided in that cause. Of course he did have to tend to his daughter, but her dramatic interpretation of the book she wrote was a welcomed break.

And there were still phone calls he had to take, too. It was during one of those when he wandered off in the house that I called Willow back. She had left a message to call her as soon as I could. And although it sounded somewhat urgent, I was not about to interrupt my career-changing session.

"Bethany, where are you?" Willow asked as soon as she answered her phone.

"I'm at Ryan's," I replied.

"All hell is breaking loose here."

"What? Where? The house?" I always found it funny that the residents in my skyscraper apartment building called it that. I guess because it sounded homier that way.

"Yeah, yeah," she continued in her gossipy voice. "It's Andre. He's—" She halted her story. "Wait, what? You're at Ryan's? Mr. Mean's?"

"Yeah. Yeah … Mr.—" And I stopped myself, realizing he was close by somewhere.

"You mean his office?"

"No. His house." I hadn't told her that. We didn't see each other daily, despite being next-door neighbors—literally a couple of feet apart.

"Wha—" she started.

But I interrupted. I really wanted to know what was going on, especially since she had mentioned Andre. "Never mind. It's about Andre?"

"Yeah, the cops were here. He got hauled out."

"What? What's going on?" I felt my arms get suddenly warm as the news kickstarted my blood pressure.

"Something about him stealing stuff. They suspected it. So, they were watching him, and then they also caught him drinking with Nell."

"Drinking-drinking?" I knew Andre was twenty-three since the residency had recently celebrated him working there for five years and he started right after high school. But I also knew Nell wasn't.

"Yeah, it was outside but on the property. And we know little miss innocent Nell is underage. And I guess that wasn't all they were doing."

"They were …?"

I didn't say "having sex." I didn't want to say "having sex." I never wanted to think about other people doing it. But Andre? It wasn't that long ago …

Thank goodness I was able to tune back into Willow's voice. "Not yet. Nell's upset, and there's all kinds of stuff being said about how he's a serial Casanova and has been with a number of girls in the house."

Well, there you go. My stomach jumped and turned. I had some regret after the thing with Andre and me happened. But after listening to Willow, I felt downright sick and a little violated. Even though it had been mutual and a no-strings, one-time deal, I thought it was more special than that.

"He's getting in trouble for that, too?" I asked a little more quietly that time.

"I don't think so. That's all girl gossip, you know. Everyone here is at least old enough to get it on. But his contract said he was not permitted to interact socially with the tenants. Kind of sounds like he was being discreet— loving the ones who were ready to leave, probably so he didn't have to deal with them anymore or get found out. He's gone no matter what." She paused for a split second. "Hey, good thing you decided to stay and not turn in your moving papers. You might have been the next little concubine."

My stomach retched once again. Thank goodness no one knew of my indiscretion. Thank goodness I had asked him to use protection. And thank goodness I wasn't going to have to look at him anymore. I should have never let my body rule my heart. I would never make that mistake again.

"Yeah, good thing," I managed to say.

"He is a cutie, though. Although, I am kind of a sucker for men with curly, wavy hair. I'll stick with Til's and not some … What's a good word for men like Andre?"

"Bastard. I'm going with men are bastards."

"Whoa!" Willow's voice came out extra loud since she wasn't used to me using a word like that.

Some of the heightened volume, though, was because there was an echo to her exclamation. I spun around to discover Ryan. As he reentered the room, he said the same word as Willow did at the same exact time.

"Sorry," I apologized to Ryan more than my neighbor.

"Uh-huh, sure." He shook his head with a glimmer of a smile.

"Is that Mr. Mean?" Willow chimed in from across the

line.

"Willow, I'm gonna go. I'll talk with you tonight. Let me know if anything else hits." Before she could question, I abruptly hung up. After all, I wasn't at the Thompson manse to gossip. I was there to create and grow as an artist. "Sorry," I repeated to Ryan. "That was meant about a particular guy—not in general."

"I'm pretty sure I heard the plural version of the word depicting the male species."

"Sorry," I repeated. "No."

"Song material?" he tried.

"Probably. Open a vein and all that. At least it's not my heart." It most definitely was not.

"I can work with that. But how about after lunch?"

"Sure," I agreed, wondering what the plan was.

"Sallie wants mac and cheese. But there are a lot of variations we can add to it—chicken, bacon, on a bun …"

"It all sounds good besides that last one." I chuckled, hoping he was teasing. "Can't wait to get a better look at the kitchen. Put me to work."

"Oh, I didn't mean you had to help. You're the guest."

"I'd love to … seriously."

I loved to cook. I considered it another creative art and a stress reliever. And after getting the news about Andre, I needed that for sure.

CHAPTER THREE

The next day was not only a Saturday, but it was Saint Patrick's Day. Since the coffee house manager was giving me time off during the week to work with Ryan, the holiday meant an extended workday for me. And a busy one it was. Because on March seventeenth, everyone is Irish, and everyone wants Irish-flavored coffee and/or lots of caffeine to keep them up for all the green beer drinking.

Being on my feet all day, I couldn't wait to get home, strip off my shoes, and wiggle all the little piggies around. First, though, I wanted to grab some dinner at the apartment's dining hall. I had just about enough time before dining hours were done to do that.

As I was about to enter, Willow—coming in the opposite direction—pulled me aside. "Grouchy Ms. Ratched is serving today." She rolled her eyes at the behind-the-scenes nickname for the woman who normally ran the front desk. "I guess they're taking turns until they find a replacement for Andre. And then it will probably be an old schoolmarm. They don't want to risk another brothel." Hopefully she didn't notice my cringe as she laughed. "Anyway, a few of us are going out later. Wanna join?"

I blew out an extended breath. "I'd love to. I'm just exhausted."

"I know. I'm gonna need more deets on Mr. Mean."

"Willow." I *tsked*. "He's remarkably not. He's actually quite down to earth." I had briefly filled her in the night before on the hows and whys of meeting with Ryan at his house. "And you promised to keep it on the low, right?"

"Yes, Bethany! Although, you are not going to jinx anything. This is really it. You are going to have a record deal or whatever a songwriter gets."

Gosh, wouldn't that be something? "Well, everyone can know *then*. One grand humiliation on national television is enough for me. I gotta go. I'm starved. I only had a green bagel and some candy at work. What did you have for dinner—the fish and chips or the stew?"

"Go fish and chips. The stew looked like they put in all the leftovers of every meal from the past week."

"Ewww." I scrunched my face. "Yeah, better stay away from that, anyway."

"The pudding was surprisingly decent, though," she mumbled while running toward the elevator. "Hey, hold that."

I opted for the fish on a salad bed for dinner, and, yes, the pudding was delicious. Perhaps because it was dark chocolate and not anything green. It made me think of Sallie and the chocolate cake she had requested for her birthday, which was the following day. Sallie had invited six of her friends—one for each year she was alive—to their house for a paint party. Afterward, of course, there would be cake and presents. It gave me an idea, and I couldn't wait to get started on the surprise.

***

I was able to map most of it out that night. But it was only after coming back from church the following morning when I had a finished product. It was never going to make a greatest hits album and was actually quite laughable, but it was meant to be that way ... especially to a newly crowned six-year-old.

I forwarded the video of myself to Ryan, but I didn't let him know what it was. Instead, I told him I had worked hard on it and thought it was my best stuff yet. Then I added that I seriously hoped he would take it into consideration.

I expected an LOL or even a thank-you back. But what I got later that evening was a different video response. It was a recording from the Thompson abode staring little Sallie Thompson. And it wasn't via direct message, it was a text.

"Hi, Bethany! Thank you!" She bounced as her teeth and light blue eyes shined while speaking into the camera. "Thank you so much for my birthday song. My friends loved 'Unicorn's Birthday.' I played it hundreds of times. Daddy says I can have it be on the movie soundtrack for my book. Bye!"

I laughed so hard and played her response nearly hundreds of times, too. Well, maybe just a few times. Knowing my song brought such innocent happiness erased all the critics who along the way had told me otherwise.

A text from the number I then knew as Ryan's came in shortly after. *Thx. U made her day. It was the only thing she could talk about. For real.*

I texted back. *The smile on her face made mine.* And weirdly so did the fact that he used "for real."

Private #, BTW. Please don't give out.

Understood. See you tomorrow, I wrote of our next lyrics-writing session.

How bout if we meet @ my house again? Feel like we got more done here.

I thought so, too. It was more relaxed, allowing better creativity. And there were definitely fewer interruptions ... even with Sallie. Although, she would be going back to school.

I texted a much-amended version of my thoughts. *Yeah, sure.*

I'll order car service for U.

I was brought up to be a giver, not a taker. Admittedly, though, having someone else set up the transportation, never mind the cost, was a godsend. After an internal debate, I accepted with a simple thank-you text. I was just going to end the conversation that way. But I still felt as if I wasn't doing my part. So, I decided on a compromise and added, *I'll bring lunch.*

His reply came back in what I was quickly learning was sarcastic Ryan style. *What … U don't like my mac & cheese?*

Very gourmet ☺ I'm sure he knew I was being equally sarcastic, as adding precooked chicken, tomato, and avocado to boxed macaroni and cheese wasn't exactly gourmet, but at least he made an effort. *Just my turn.*

U R going to B a hard negotiator Lenay. C U tomorrow.

Even though he didn't know it, I appreciated Ryan's use of my name. My formal name was Bethany Lenay Opala, but I chose to use my middle name as my last name professionally … as a lot of hotshot stars did. But also because I always liked my middle name. As Southern tradition, it was a maiden name from a grandparent—my father's mother's. I didn't mind Bethany, but I hated the abbreviated form of Beth. It sounded so blah and matronly. Besides, I hadn't moved to Los Angeles for that. I wanted to live life to the fullest. And for the first time, I think Bethany Lenay was.

***

"Song which describes your low point." Ryan's eyes intently watched mine, and when I didn't say anything, he urged me on. "And … go. Don't think too long about it. You know you have one. Say it. What is it?"

"'Landslide.' I was blasting 'Landslide' on repeat for

days on end right before the show aired."

I hated to keep bringing up the show because I was realizing how right Ryan had been about his comments that day. But still, not making it on *Singer Spotlight* was my lowest point. And "Landslide" was the song I had found solace in.

"You asked," I said.

"Classic Fleetwood Mac. Multigenerational love for that song. It's a good choice, and I see how it fits."

"Okay, you …"

We had just said our top song for getting pumped up or motivated. Now, we were on the opposite side of the song spectrum. Ryan said it was a way to think about how the song connected to us personally and how we could use those feelings to create new, additional songs. It was an interesting idea. I was definitely willing to play.

"'Under the Bridge,'" he said plainly.

"'Under the Bridge,'" I repeated. "I don't know that one."

"Yeah … Chili Peppers."

"Hmmm." I went for my phone.

"No searching. Think." He had changed from a judge to a mentor for sure. "I don't ever want to feel like I did that day," he recited part of the lyrics.

"It's about depression, right? And about living here in LA."

Instead of answering, he immediately went to the next song. "Song which describes your childhood."

I wanted to think more about Ryan's response, but I knew he didn't want me to by the change of topic. So, I appeased him with an answer. "Ha! I actually have one for that. I used it for a college paper. It's an oldie—'Sheltered Life.' Yours … go!"

"'Old F-ing MacDonald Had a Farm.'"

I couldn't help but laugh, knowing of his roots in Iowa. "I don't believe there is normally an expletive in that song title."

"There is in my version." He seemed as enamored by his upbringing as I was mine. "While on topic, how about your favorite kid song?"

"Um … I used to love 'There's a Hole in the Bucket.'"

"Good one. Do you know why?"

"I think because it is kind of a story."

"Exactly."

"What's yours, farm boy?" I jested a teasing name at him. "Can't do 'Old Mac' again."

"'Unicorn's Birthday'… yep."

My laugh equaled my previous one. "That is so not. Geez!"

"Not changing my mind." When I shook my head, he continued, "Song when you were most in love."

I was waiting for that one. I was dreading that one. "Why do I have to go first all the time?"

"Bethany … song which reminds you of when you were or are—whatever—in love."

"Nope."

"Nope? That's a song?" he teased.

"Nope. Don't think I ever was."

"Really?" He looked extremely doubtful.

"'Every Rose Has Its Thorn,'" I decided on. "There you go."

"No, I don't think that counts."

"Not changing my mind," I echoed back to him.

"How do you manage to take my words and use them against me?"

Ryan's eye roll started because of my comment but then continued when glancing at his ringing phone. Remarkably, it had been pretty silent up to that point, or he had ignored it. Apologizing, he answered it and immediately started sounding more like the businessman persona I had originally met. His phone to his ear, he walked out of the room, and I couldn't help but think I was glad the interruption had put a halt to our being-in-love talk. After all, how depressing would it be to discuss my failures with a man who was so happily married?

***

"I think these words are crisp … spot-on now," Ryan spoke of our fourth rewrite of one of my originals.

"Yeah, I'm glad we let it sit." Playing around with new song ideas the day before was a perfect way to let "Somewhere" rest and hear it cleanly.

"It's missing something, though. The words are too powerful not to add more of a powerful piece of music behind them."

"Okay. What are you thinking?"

"That's just it, I'm not sure." He sat in silence for a moment and then suggested, "Close your eyes." When I did so, he read the lyrics like poetry instead of singing them. When done, he asked, "Did you visualize anything?"

I opened my eyes. "I know this doesn't have anything to do with the lyrics, but, actually, I saw us kids in my dad's old Firebird at the summer drive-in."

"Your dad has a Firebird? The classic car?" That's what Ryan got out of the vision exercise.

"Yeah. Late seventies. He's a little classic-car obsessed."

"Sweet." Ryan got up, moved across the living room, and sat at the piano. "Sing. Sing it for me, but see if you can go with what I am playing. Keep in mind, I'm just tinkering … trying things out." He started with multiple keys that were quick, and I even pictured my brother, sister, and me laughing. "Sorta? Maybe?" he asked, stopping midway. He didn't seem altogether sure.

"Absolutely. Start from the beginning again." I picked up my guitar and matched the piano for the next round.

"God, that sounds good together."

We still went through some modifications and had to settle on an intro, but the end result was out of this world. I honestly didn't care if any artist liked or bought it. It was beautiful to me. Of course, I didn't tell Manager Ryan that. No matter how much I could see he was enjoying making music, his bottom line had to be making something else— money.

***

Ryan and I continued to create music over the next couple of days at his house. After finalizing "Somewhere," we really got into a groove of getting new songs down. We realized our individual strengths and how they complemented one another. Ryan was great at having the story starters and general idea of the music style to accompany it. Then I would pick it up and make the words actually flow into lyrics ... with a little switching done by him along the way.

When the kids bounded in from school that Thursday, we hadn't realized we had worked that long. I had left before Sallie and Joel had come home the other days, so it was my first time meeting Ryan's son, who had the same light blue eyes and blond hair as his sister. Joel had more energy than Sallie, for sure, but he was a four-year-old, after all.

Since we were on a roll and I wasn't scheduled for the coffee house that evening, Ryan and I continued for a little longer as the kids found refuge in their tablets. Ryan then insisted I stay for dinner. "Sorry. This is nothing like your meals." He was making simple sandwiches.

"Believe me, I've been geeking out using your kitchen. I miss cooking so much." Not to mention having three marble counters and top appliances to work with in his gourmet kitchen.

The meat ravioli I had brought on Monday was premade. I had fried it up with dried fruit in a sugar and sweet spice mix. There had been so much leftover, we had it again the next day for lunch. And we did the same with the crunchy tacos we had for lunch on Wednesday.

"I can't believe you don't have a kitchen at your place." He shook his head, recalling the story I had told him about my living arrangements.

"I can't believe I'm allowed to make lunch again tomorrow." I gleamed while slicing some fruit and veggies to complement our dinner.

"I think I totally won on the provide transportation versus provide lunch deal."

"Not a chance," I countered and then made a suggestion for the next meal. "I am thinking chips and dip—tortilla and potato chips with salsa, guacamole, hummus, and maybe seafood salad. Are you good with that for tomorrow?"

"It sounds great, but don't make too much work for yourself."

"I'll buy most of it already made, but I'll definitely make the guac. Then, we can snack all day if we get on a roll."

"Like today."

"Yeah."

"Sallie! Joel! Dinner is ready," he called out to his two little ones, who had been pretty well behaved, considering they had to be patient as Daddy finished work.

Staying for dinner at the Thompson abode was unexpected, but it was also refreshing. It had me thinking of home far away … of my sister, brother, parents, and me sitting around the kitchen table talking about our day. With Sallie and Joel, it was no different. They had so many stories about life in kindergarten and preschool, Sallie could have written another book just about that day. It was a nice break from the normal gossipy group of women sitting cafeteria-style at the apartment, or grabbing a lonely dinner on the go when I was on break at the coffee house.

"Bethany, it looks like there is going to be a wait getting someone here to pick you up," Ryan said after we had finished and the kids were in the family room with their electronics.

"What? Why?"

"Maybe March Madness? I hadn't thought about it. But since it's being played here tonight, tons of people are probably looking for rides."

"Oh."

"We can wait, or I could drive you back myself."

"No, I don't want you to have to do that. The kids don't need to be towed across town."

"Or …" He nodded a tiny bit. "You can stay the night." When he paused again ever so slightly, a strange feeling suddenly zipped through my body. "You'll be here tomorrow, anyway," he added. And before I could get that weird sensation controlled, he concluded with, "We have a guest room."

"No. No need for that," I denied. "See what time they can make it, or I can call my next-door neighbor. She might be able to pick me up."

I got all of it out but wasn't making very good eye contact. What was going on? Concentrate, Bethany.

"Are you positive?"

"Yep. When am I going to pick up all the food for tomorrow if I stay?" I smiled quickly.

"I'm sure we could figure that out."

"Should I call Willow?"

Ryan looked at his phone again. "They said forty-five minutes. Not so bad. You'll just have to hang out with us for a bit longer."

"I guess I'll make the sacrifice," I teased, resorting to my usual Bethany wit. He tilted his head significantly to one side, and I heard the same popping sound I had another time when we were working together—possibly when we had been discussing our favorite songs. "What was that?" I implored. "Was that your neck?"

"Yeah." He exhaled. "It doesn't hurt—just sounds kind of bad."

"Uh, yeah. Why? How?" I didn't know which question I really wanted to ask, but I was, admittedly, glad we were steering away from the staying-the-night comment.

"It's just like how people crack their knuckles." Before I could admit to occasionally doing that, he continued, "So, here's the story. I was on the wrestling team in high school." He was well-built, but he didn't exactly seem like the bodybuilding type—a little too lean and tall. "I dislocated my left hip, which kind of threw everything on that side off. Plus, I pushed recovery. So, that shoulder got a little messed up, too … just where I would pop/crack it pretty good. And I think all of that eventually tightened my neck. So, now it's the neck."

"Wow. I thought that was just a cartoon thing… cracking necks."

"Nope. The first time did scare me a bit," he admitted. "But it's perfectly fine. It relieves pressure."

"Like when you're tense or stressed?"
"Uh, yeah." He looked at me for a beat and then said, "I should at least get Joel started with his bath. I swear the kid rolls in dirt during playtime."

I shook my head and squinted my eyes. "Go ahead. I need to check my e-mail and social media accounts, anyway."

"Yeah, you never know who might tweet you." He smirked and called out for his son, "Joe-Joe, let's go, bath!"

* * *

The entire ride back to my place, I had an inner monologue with myself. Actually, it was a bit of a combustive feud—almost like the devil and angel resting on my shoulders. Something had changed … how I felt … about Ryan. It came on suddenly with his innocent offer for me to stay over. But if I thought about it, it was even before that. It was in the way I naturally found myself openly talking with him. It was in the way I felt so comfortable around him. It was in the way our ideas challenged and complemented one another's so succinctly.

But I had to realize that's all it was. It was work and the way creative people collaborated. I was getting excited about a career dream coming true, but for him, it was something he had seen plenty of times. He was simply being nice. He gave no signs otherwise ... and, he was married. Married.

Goodness, first I had a one-night stand with a whore of a guy, and now I was beginning to have feelings for a married man. What kind of preacher's daughter was I? What kind of woman was I? What kind of human being?

CHAPTER FOUR

"So, I don't want to jump the gun." Ryan's deep blue eyes seemingly glistened. "But I'm pretty sure I can get you some interest."

"Us, right?" I spoke of the brand-new songs we had created, as well as some of my initial ones we had tweaked. "We worked on them together."

"For me … just working on the creative side again is worth it. You need this."

"Ryan, that's not our deal."

It had come out a little as a whine, but it was because I was brought up with a strong belief of being fair, sharing with others, and following through with commitments. Greed was one of the seven deadly sins and an absolute no-no in a preacher's house. And even though I was semi-arguing my point in the most lavish home I had ever been in, I did think Ryan's morality was similar. I had read about the charities he and his wife donated to, and I could see the simplicity of how he lived. The house wasn't meant necessarily to impress. It was truly a home. It just had to be guarded and secured for obvious reasons.

I thought he was going to agree, but he was actually

humoring me. "The deal was—you got to make lunch, and I got you back and forth." He took a sip of his water. "I actually should say the songs aren't ready just so I have an excuse to keep doing this."

I shook my head and tried to prompt a more legit answer while also pushing away the emotional pull of the sinful feeling that had emerged the day before. "So, what's next?"

"I'm setting up time with some audio guys. I want you to do a professional recording. Not just the cell phone stuff. And then I can send it out."

"Really?" My voice rose in excitement. I guess, had I thought about it, that would have been the next step, but it was still exhilarating.

"For real." His smile was large as he watched my animation.

"That's ... wow."

And then ... then ... his lips were on mine. Ryan's lips were touching, brushing, caressing mine. He had leaned in from where we were seated next to one another, and he was kissing me.

When I pulled my lips away from his, his face jerked back a little from the abruptness. I knew the harsh ending was the exact opposite of the soft, new feeling our mouths joining had created. But I couldn't let it go on. The Uber was beeping outside his house, and ... the action was wrong. Oh, my goodness, it was so wrong.

"I ... I gotta go." Luckily, knowing the driver was on the way, I had already gathered my things. I just hadn't realized I was going to have to make such a hasty exit.

"Bethany ..." Ryan called out as I hurried toward the front door. "I'm ... let me—"

I didn't hear his final words. I wasn't sure I even wanted to. I scurried down the sidewalk and found myself, once again, in the back of a car with my mind scrambling and my heart jumping.

There was a difference with the day before, though. I

knew the feeling wasn't one-sided. It wasn't only me. I most certainly hadn't been the one to initiate the contact. He had. Ryan was the one who had tilted in, minimized his eyes, and bit his lip for just a second. He was the one whose mouth had found mine and who did the slightest of groans when I accepted our lips together. But he was also the one who was married. And I was the one who, despite wanting and desiring his touch, ran.

***

Ryan called a couple times during my shift later in the day, but he didn't leave a message. And without a message, I was not going to respond. I wouldn't know what to say, because I had no idea what he was thinking. My mind cycled through the possible reasons why the kiss happened … a) it was simply an excited, in-the-moment smooch, b) it was how creative people acknowledge an accomplishment, or c) it was something he did on a regular basis. Ugh! Geez, I hoped it wasn't the latter. How did I keep finding these Casanovas?

After a restless night, I forced myself to go to breakfast the following morning just to get out of my closet of a room. I wanted to see if I could interact with someone other than my bad girl personality because, dang it, if the angel and devil weren't once again residing solidly on my shoulders, whispering all kinds of things. Neither the toast with jam nor my friends at the table helped, though. They may as well have not been there. I couldn't concentrate on anything but Ryan.

My phone rang right as I made my way back to my room. When I looked at the screen and saw Ryan's name, my heart palpitated. But it wasn't a fluttering, light feeling. It was nerves. It was still not knowing what had happened and what was going to happen. And I just couldn't answer.

Instead of hanging up, though, he left a message. When I picked it up, his voice seemed pretty even-toned. It sounded, I thought, like any other conversation we had. Darn it, if I wasn't even more confused.

"Hey, Bethany. Are you free to meet up today? I'd like to go over some stuff. Call me."

My excuse for not calling him back had been that he hadn't left a message, but that no longer held true. I knew I had to reply, and I couldn't lie. My Christian lessons were very well ingrained. I was good at teasing and sarcasm but not breaking the rules ... like kissing a married man. The guilt for that was already too much. I couldn't add lying on top of it.

But I did cop-out in a way. I texted instead of called. *Didn't know we were meeting. At your office?*

Can't, was his immediate text reply. *Weekend—closed.*

My shoulders tensed, and I felt under pressure to respond. *You don't have a key?*

That was the only thing I came up with. At least it made sense. He was the owner of his business. The building that housed the office should be open.

His message back came a couple minutes later. *I do. But there won't B anyone there & I'm pretty sure that defeats your purpose.*

Saturday. Closed. Yes, that meant no one, *no one,* would be there. And he called me out on my ulterior motive to be in public ... to avoid being alone and not have to deal with what happened or let it happen again. That's what I got for being devious. It was almost like lying.

Before I determined how to respond, he sent another text. *Come to the house. We need to talk. The kids R here.* Hmmm, he was providing his own buffer—two innocent young children. And then, immediately after, he added, *I want to explain.*

There was no denying what he wanted to talk about or explain. We both knew. And the fact that he was basically saying it, made my body shimmy with more nerves. I really didn't want to face it. I wanted it to go away. No ... I wanted it to have never happened. Well, there was a little part of me …

Maybe I could simply brush it off, and we could move on. *You don't need to*, I offered.

I do, he typed back. *But I can't do it over the phone especially not text.*

My sigh was strong. I understood. He wasn't going to risk an electronic trail of the deceitful, unholy act we had done, especially in the Hollywood snoops world.

It was going to happen. I was going to have to meet Ryan in person. And I knew it was better to get it over with and not agonize longer and let things fester. I just hoped I wasn't going to have to face another disappointment in my life. I hoped it wasn't going to mar the friendship and professional relationship we had built.

Okay, I agreed. *In about an hour?* I wanted to at least look presentable—put on some basic makeup to cover the dark circles under my eyes and wear clothes that didn't look like I had just crawled out of bed.

That's good. Do U need me to send a car?

No, I answered right away. *I got it.*

He didn't argue or push. He didn't tease that I could just bring some grub in exchange. He didn't say anything at all. And I knew whatever he was going to say once I got there was going to be different than any of the normal, easy-going conversations we had happily been accustomed to.

***

The poor Uber driver probably thought I was a manic drug user. I was as jittery as heck in the car, and I'm pretty sure I was mumbling to myself. Not knowing what I was going to say or what Ryan was going to say, I wanted to vomit right there in the back seat. Geez, I hadn't even been that bad when I auditioned for the TV show.

Luckily, I was greeted by the perfect little ice breaker. "Hi, Bethany!" Sallie opened the front door to welcome me.

"Hi, Sallie." My smile was natural on her friendly greeting.

"We're watching a princess movie. Joel doesn't like it, but I do. Daddy says he has to because it's my turn to pick."

"What princess movie?" I asked.

"Belle," she announced. "You wanna watch with us?"

"Sallie, at least let Bethany in before you bombard her with stories and requests." That was Ryan's voice.

When I lifted my eyes away from the six-year-old, I found her father propped against the staircase banister as if he had been casually standing there watching our entire interaction. He probably had been. But was it because he was a protective father making absolutely sure who was at the door, despite the guard at the gate announcing my arrival? Or, was he doing it to keep his distance from me?

Our eyes only met for the slimmest of seconds before we both took refuge in looking back at Sallie. Yes, it was a good thing we had a buffer. Just spotting his intense deep blue eyes on me was enough to make my body tighten.

"Daddy, can Bethany watch with us?"

"Let her in," Ryan said a little more succinctly that time.

As Sallie stepped aside, I more properly entered the residence and shut the door behind me. I normally would have instantly shrugged off my shoes and started walking further into the interior of the home. But my sandals remained fastened as did my stance.

Ryan, who I noticed was barefoot, answered his daughter's question. "Bethany isn't here to watch princess movies, Tink." Her lower lip stretched out in the cutest little pout as Ryan continued, "You better go make sure your brother doesn't change the show. He's the slyest four-year-old I know."

With her eyes seemingly growing wide at Ryan's suggestion, she belted, "He wouldn't dare!"

My belly bounced at the little girl's dramatic exit. Ryan actually laughed out loud and shook his head. And then … there we were. Alone.

"So … uh, about recording …"

Despite all the conversation starters I had internally scripted on the ride over, that was what came out. It was not even close to being as melodic or smooth as I had hoped. In fact, it was like a stuttering, old vinyl. Although, I suppose anything was better than the silent tension that had invaded the foyer in the matter of seconds.

"Can we deal with the elephant in the room first?"

"There's nothing—" I tried to just move past the fictional, ugly, gray mammal who wasn't only occupying the room but also my brain.

But Ryan denied me. "Bethany, we have to talk about the fact that we kissed."

He looked at me dead-on then, but I couldn't mirror his action for long. I felt guilt. Didn't he? Shouldn't he? He was the married one.

I let go of the air in my lungs. If I didn't then, I think I might have passed out. "I know. I understand." I decided to go with the best of the scenarios I had come up with. "I get that it was simply the excitement of everything."

"No. Yes. But no. I mean …" When he stumbled on his words, I was able to look up again. "Not on my end. Is that all it was for you? I thought … Look, I don't want you to think this is sexual harassment or anything."

I hadn't even considered any kind of harassment. But I guess it happened in the Hollywood world, and both women and men had to be careful. If there was one thing I knew, though, it was that Ryan treated me as an equal … even if I didn't think I deserved it.

I made sure to answer definitively. "Oh, goodness, no. Don't worry about that."

The muscles in his face seemed to ease a tad as if his jaw unlocked before he opened his mouth to speak again. "I'm attracted to you, Bethany. We have a bond, and it's more than just words on paper."

Oh, swish! My brain was instantly fuzzy again … not that it had been altogether clear. Despite my eyes blinking so much I couldn't see properly, I did know I had heard him correctly. And dang it if I didn't feel the same way, and it was what I would have loved to have heard him say, if only …

"I need you to say something, or I'm gonna feel like a total heel." His words managed to get my eyes to refocus.

Ryan's dark brows were slightly pushed toward one another as if he was anticipating my response. His mouth formed a straight line. The look was similar to when I had seen him judge on TV … but not quite. The difference was the soft, almost watery appearance of his eyes.

"It's not one-sided," I whispered, and those eyes of his seemed to brighten. But then I said, "I just can't. I'm not a prude." A flashback of the storage area with Andre definitely solidified my non-prude status. "Ryan, you're married," I cited the obvious. "I can't. God help me, it's not that … I can't." That was all I could say or do—clearly, it was his turn.

And it was agonizing waiting for him. As I wondered what his next words would be … if it would change anything or everything, he closed his eyes and then stretched his neck to crack it. Yes, the tense feeling was overwhelming for both of us.

"I've never kissed someone else since Kari," were the first words out of his mouth when he eventually brought his gaze back to mine.

I'm sure he could see the doubt tattooed across my face. I knew the world of celebrities. I saw the magazines at the grocery stores and watched the entertainment shows as much as anyone else did … besides my parents. But at the same account, I truly felt there was something special … something different … a kind of pull between the two of us.

"Honestly." Yep, he could see my doubt., and it was his

turn to let his breath go. "I want to tell you something, and I shouldn't. I shouldn't, because I made a promise. And I'm a guy who keeps his promises ... sometimes to a fault. Right now, though, it's only hurting you and, selfishly, me, not to tell you." If he hadn't completely had my full attention, he surely did then. "Besides, the other person involved has broken promises to me left and right."

Our short conversation was like being on a roller coaster. It was going fast and had so many curves, but after the initial start of actually getting on the ride, I was easing into it. I think we both were. We were *almost* talking as we normally would.

"Kari." He said the name of the person who had broken the promises and whom I had suspected. He paused again and nodded as if he was reconciling something in his brain. "Bethany, I'm trusting you not to tell anyone."

His request shot up my nerves a tad. "Is it against the law? I don't ... I don't want to know if that's the case." I'm not sure why I went there besides the serious look on his face.

"No," he denied instantly and seemed to relax slightly. "No. Nothing like that."

"Okay," I said, not only because I was agreeing to his request but also because he wasn't saying anything else.

"We're divorced. We actually have been for a while."

I'm sure a GIF of my reaction would have been trending almost instantly had someone been there to capture it. I felt my jaw drop in that exaggerated way you see people do out of absolute, genuine shock. I had no idea, and I was pretty sure all of America—heck, the world—didn't, either. Tabloids and websites and entertainment shows and social media ... the Thompsons, by all accounts, were happily married.

I hadn't vocalized any of that, but yet Ryan seemed to perfectly assess my reaction. "I know."

The word "what" eventually came out of my mouth.

"We're divorced," he said a little more evenly that time but was still peering his eyes at me as if gauging my reaction.

"But—"

"Bethany, do you think we can sit?"

"Uh … yeah." We were still in the foyer … inches from the escape door. As I started to follow him, my legs actually felt stiff from standing so frozen and tense for that amount of time.

We entered the living room—the same room where we worked together all those days and where he had kissed me the day before. I sat on the sofa. Ryan, leaving an appropriate amount of space between us, just as he always had, joined me.

"It's, you know, the stereotypical story." He dove right into the topic we had put on pause in the foyer. "She rose to fame, and things changed between us. At first it wasn't really either of our faults. We were kind of growing differently. But it wasn't working. We tried. Man, did we try. And she had an affair—a fling—and I just couldn't try anymore."

As I listened, I recognized the honesty in his voice. I had grown to know it through our collaborations. His new revelation made me want to go back and look at the lyrics we had written to see how much had potentially been done with his divorce in mind.

"You're divorced … divorced? Not like separated?" With all the new co-parenting and living together arrangements, it did make me wonder.

"Divorced, Bethany," he confirmed. "For many months and not living together for a year. Yes, we have kept it a secret. She has some court connections, and we have managed to keep things hush-hush."

"But why?" It wasn't as if divorce was something new in Hollywood.

"She's on top of her game, especially with this tour, and part of her persona is attached to me—the classic, wholesome singer who is happily married. And when I got the show, they wanted to tie the same image in, too. We thought it was a good idea to let things appear as is until … I don't know … until it's a better time to announce it. For now, it's the way it has to be." When I didn't reply in any fashion, he prompted, "Talk to me. Please."

"I don't know what to say." I felt bad because I could see how much it took for him to tell me everything he just had … to trust … to put his heart and heartache out there.

"I told you because, yes, I was burned, but I want to move on, especially since I have gotten to know you." His soft smile showed his sincerity.

He had stepped up again, and I needed to do or say something to reassure him that he had been right to do so. "Can I see the papers?" I asked.

He did a quick blink. "The divorce papers?"

"Yeah. I know that makes me seem … I don't know. I—"

"I'll get them." He spoke confidently, got up, and exited the room.

I could vaguely hear him talking with the kids, and it made me momentarily push my insecurities away and wonder about them. What did they know? How were they affected? And knowing all that I found out, how was it going to affect me? I had feared when originally coming to the house that everything was going to change, and it most definitely had. Except, it was in a whole different way and direction than I had suspected.

Ryan reclaimed his seat on the sofa and handed me a piece of paper. "There are others, but I'm pretty sure that's what you want to see."

I hardly even looked at it. Their names, the formal signature, the petition date, the final date blurred in my vision, and I quickly handed it back to him. "I'm sorry. I had no right to ask for that. It's personal. It … gosh … Ryan …"

"You've been hurt or deceived before." He said it

calmly and matter-of-factly as he scooted the paper across the coffee table. "I can hear it in your lyrics but—"

But ... I had never said anything directly. I did then. "Yes, hurt *and* deceived ... both personally and professionally."

I felt tears threatening my eyes. They weren't about the past, though. It was more of a relief from all the stress I had been feeling that morning and the night before. The tears were because I could relax.

And since he had been so honest with me, I explained, "Hutch, my college boyfriend, went back to his ex from high school. I thought they were over. Turns out, I was a placeholder."

"Hmmm." His acknowledgment sounded empathetic. "He's not the bastard though, right?"

"What?" It took me a second to understand and rewind to when Ryan had overheard me speaking with Willow about Andre. It was taking me a lot of seconds just to comprehend the afternoon that far. "Oh. No. The bastard was because I was depressed and drinking. I seem not to make the wisest choices after a certain amount of beverages. Andre was a one-time, no-emotions understanding. I had never done something like that, and I don't want it to ever be that way again," I added, realizing I wasn't talking with Ryan in that moment as a fellow music collaborator. So, the last thing I wanted was for him to think I was some kind of slut. "And professionally," I trudged right on, "I was promised a job once. It was actually what got me out to California. I was told to pack my bags and move here because the job was mine. I did, but I didn't have it in writing. I got here, and guess what? I'm sure you've heard this one before. The job was given to some higher up's niece or something." He nodded, and I continued, "So, I quickly learned to wait for proof."

"I get it."

"When that happened, I probably should have just turned around and went back home, but it was embarrassing. There had been a party and send-off. I didn't want to admit I failed."

"I get that, too," he said with even more conviction.

"Do-over?" I asked after a pause.

"Do-over? Do-over what?"

I was the one who bit my lip that time … the one leaning in. But he met me halfway. Oh, and then that kiss … our lips together. It was very mutual and very magnetic. It was soft and sweet and a sense of relief. And that time it didn't end in heartache or confusion.

***

We ended up talking for a while after. I found out a little more about Kari and how it was in the beginning of their relationship. And if I was honest, I was glad to know they didn't meet in a similar way he and I had. They actually met through a mutual friend on a blind date. In fact, she wasn't and had never been a client of his … and she didn't write a stitch of her own tunes.

He also mentioned how the agreement was that he kept the house with the kids since Kari's touring schedule was so demanding and she was away from LA a lot. When in town, Kari had her own condo in a building owned by her record label. Since it also housed recording studios and other apartments for music execs and out-of-town guests, the press was none-the-wiser when spotting her there.

Ryan said he and Kari were on good terms and they spoke … but mostly about the kids. And it was then when it dawned on me that during our entire time collaborating, he hadn't once spoken on the phone with Kari as normal couples did on a regular basis. Hindsight and all that. Ryan didn't necessarily mind talking about Kari, but we did clip the conversation as quickly as we could. Exes, after all, were not usually a good source of conversation, no matter the circumstance.

His kids, however, I already knew were a bright spot in

Ryan's life. He was starting to tell me exactly what they knew about his relationship with their mother when Joel came running in. He was flailing his arms as if he was Batman Junior.

"Daddy, when's the puppy thing? This princess stuff is bor-ring."

"Joel, say hi to Bethany." Ryan always seemed to instill good manners with his children.

"Hi."

"Hi, Joel."

He immediately went back to his mission at hand. "Daddy, when's the puppies?"

Ryan shook his head and rolled his eyes at his son, but he spoke to me. "I promised we would go to this dog event today. Parade, talent show—that kind of thing."

"Sounds like fun," I offered, thinking of our family dog in Carolina.

"Yeah." Ryan ruffled his son's hair. "But somebody has to understand we can't have one." Joel's pout almost perfectly mimicked his sister's from earlier, and Ryan continued, "Maybe once things settle down and someone learns to take care of his room, he can take care of a puppy."

"I can!" His eyes enlarged.

"Said every kid in the world to every parent who ends up walking, bathing, and cleaning up dog poop!" Ryan exaggerated the last word in a comedic way, surely to get his son to laugh.

"Joel, if it makes you feel better, I can't have a pet either."

"Is your room messy, too?" The little boy seemed amused and appalled at the same time.

"No. We're not allowed to have animals in the building where I live. At least you have hope. Keep working on your room."

Ryan winked at me and then said to his son, "Go get your sister. We really do need to get going." When Joel bounded out of the room, Ryan said, "I'll get a car to come pick you up. No arguing." And he kissed me to seal the deal.

"How could I argue that?" I smiled.

"I know this isn't ideal—the secrecy. But it is what it is for now. I want to see you and get to know you more and … kiss you. But if you—"

"I'm good. In fact, so much better than last night or this morning."

He left out a breath of air. "Yeah, geez, me, too."

Our mouths merged a few times, and I said, "And, I'm definitely good with that."

CHAPTER FIVE

Ryan and I talked on the phone that Monday while I was walking home from the coffee shop. In irony of ironies, we weren't going to see one another until Thursday, and it would be at his office. We no longer had the excuse of meeting privately at his home since the songs were written and I just needed to meet with the sound experts and record. I consequently had scheduled more hours at the coffee shop, and he was catching up at the office before the big push of the live *Singer Spotlight* shows.

"You didn't end up getting talked into a four-legged fur baby, did you?" I answered non-traditionally, inquiring about the Thompson's puppy outing.

"No." Ryan chuckled. "Love my kids and actually love animals, but our life and a dog's needs are not a good combination right now."

"I understand."

"I think you do."

I surged forward, asking about a television promo he had been scheduled to do for *Singer Spotlight* earlier in the morning. "How did your interview go?"

"Well, interesting you should ask. That's kind of why I called."

"Yeah?"

"They asked about you."

"Me?" I momentarily stopped my stride. What about me?

"Yeah. It threw me for a second, too," he admitted. "They wanted to know if we ever ended up meeting after the little tweet fest."

Ryan knew I had kept everything quiet about meeting with him because of my fear of failure. And since I hadn't recorded anything yet, there wasn't much for him to be talking about on his end, either. But still, they asked.

"What did you say?" I held my breath.

"I said, 'She's a pretty damn good kisser.'"

"Oh my gosh, Ry—!" I stopped myself. I should have known he was joking, just as we always easily did with one another. But since were talking so seriously right then, it had initially caught me off guard. "Depends on who I am kissing," I spouted back.

"I'll need to keep on top of my game."

"You definitely have game," I reassured. "Where are you, by the way?" I asked, knowing he surely didn't say the kissing comment in front of anyone. "What did you actually say?"

"In the car." That explained the tinny sound of his phone. "I put a little feeler out there for you. It was free promo that I couldn't pass up. I just said we met and there is some potential in the future. A kind of 'one to keep an eye out for' kind of thing." He paused. "Okay?"

"Yeah," I agreed. "Yeah, because it really is happening."

"It is. Who knows if that part will even air? They asked a lot of questions, and the segments aren't too long. Besides, the real focus should be on the show. Watch tonight. Even if that part doesn't air, they might write about it somewhere. Besides, you'll get a chance to see me look like an idiot on TV."

"I'll get popcorn and my dartboard ready."

"But I said something nice," he teasingly whined.

"All right," I conceded. "I can't call you after, though, right?"

"No, the darn sponsors' event is tonight."

His disdain was audible. I knew he didn't want to go to the banquet. It was to honor and appreciate the elite sponsors of a charity he and Kari contributed to regularly. And I was quickly learning that no matter how much Ryan liked to help, he wasn't into praise or formality.

"Sorry," I genuinely lamented.

"Thanks. I gotta run. Talk later?"

"Sure thing. Bye, Ryan."

***

I was able to keep up pretty well with the higher-level music jargon, despite only being a wanna-be singer-songwriter with a simple guitar, pencil, and paper. My classes in college helped the cause. But I was also glad Ryan was there that Thursday. He knew when to clarify and ask questions of the audio tech, Morrison, with whom we were meeting.

When it appeared our discussion had come to a natural close, Ryan—dressed more professionally than I had seen him in a while—confirmed it. "My kids started their spring break today. The neighbor is watching them just for this meeting. So, I'm gonna bolt if you think we're all set."

"Sounds good to me, Ry-man." In addition to having hair like his namesake—Jim Morrison, the audio expert also seemed to have the easygoing attitude of the sixties era. "We'll see you next week, then, pretty lady."

"Great." I stuck out my hand to shake his.

"Oh, so formal. Not a hugger?" the hippie audio guru asked.

When I shrugged and wrapped my arms around the man, I could swear I heard a low grunt from Ryan. I internally chuckled and physically pulled away. "See you next week," I concluded.

"Come on, I'll walk you out."

But Ryan denied Morrison's offer on my behalf. "I still have some things she needs to sign. Catch you next Friday." Ryan opted for the handshake, and I could tell it was a particularly firm one.

"I have to sign something?" I asked once Morrison left.

Ryan hadn't told me that when we had spoken on the phone previously, and we had talked on both Tuesday and Wednesday. Tuesday it was mostly about his interview and them cutting the part about me. And during Wednesday's conversation, he prepped me for the meeting with Morrison. But both days were also perfect excuses for us just to talk.

"Yeah, I'm going to draw up something for you to sign." He finished gathering his things in his folder and then came around the desk to meet me. "A no-hugging contract," he whispered since his door was open. "Come on, *I'll* walk you out."

I kind of liked the little jealous side of Ryan Thompson. It made me feel like we belonged and were connected. The bad part of that, though, was resisting the urge to touch *him*. I knew I couldn't kiss him or even swipe at his hand. I knew the reason why, but it was hard.

As we walked out, Ryan told his secretary to have a good weekend. The entire staff was off Friday through Monday for the Easter holiday. Since there were a few lingering people in the hallway, though, operation small-talk commenced.

"You walking? Do you need a ride?" he asked.

"I borrowed Willow's car. I knew the meeting wouldn't be long."

"Oh, good deal."

"The kids excited for Easter?" The question sounded legit to any bystander, plus, it was something I was genuinely interested in.

"Yeah. This will actually be the first year we are home.

We usually go to my folks' place in Iowa, but things are too busy here right now. I need to find places in the house to hide the baskets."

"You mean eggs."

"Yeah, and the baskets."

"Hmmm. Never heard of hiding the baskets. Of course, we never did any of that," I said while pressing the elevator button.

"No?" He both looked and sounded surprised.

"Jesus is the reason for the season."

"Oh, right." Ryan, of course, through our many collaborations, knew my father was a pastor.

"Yeah," I sulked. "I wanted the darn bunny and chocolate."

He lowered his voice and, changing the subject, said, "I am hoping like crazy the elevator is empty."

When I tilted my head and creased my eyebrows in question, he quickly lifted his. Before I could react again, the elevator doors opened, and, indeed, the car was empty. No sooner had I pressed the garage floor button and the doors closed, did Ryan take me in his arms. The longing to touch one another was over. I felt his arms around my waist and his lips on mine. I lapped his tongue in reply until we heard the *ping* of the elevator. And then the short ride was done way too quickly.

When our fingers brushed exiting the lift, I took a further step away and Ryan grumbled. I knew the situation was a difficult one for him, too, but I kept reminding myself it wasn't as bad as I had initially thought. The Ryan-Kari situation was temporary. Everything would be out in the open eventually.

We walked only a couple of steps when Ryan stopped and said, "This is me, the dad-mobile."

I had never seen his car, but of course it was his. Not only did Ryan have a prime, marked spot in the indoor parking garage, but his car was a BMW—a newer, sleek, luxury automobile. And it was painted a deep blue color, almost identical to his gorgeous eyes.

"Dad-mobile?" I practically shrieked. "It's a freaking BMW. No BMW can ever be considered a dad-mobile." I non-abashedly looked inside the windows to witness, yes, the car seats but also the dark leather interior, the top dash gadgets, the sunroof ...

"It's comparable to your Tesla ... or was it a Porche?" he teased.

I turned and playfully hit him, realizing almost instantly that it probably came across as too friendly. "Sor—"

He wouldn't let me apologize, though. "Tomorrow," he said. "Can you join us for dinner at the house? Dinner—no work-talk."

"Us?"

"The kids and me. Is that okay?"

His voice caught just a bit. But I knew it wasn't because we had an audience. Luckily, the parking lot was filled with cars but not people.

"Sure," I answered, thinking of a more relaxed setting with him. "Yeah. That sounds great. What can I bring?"

"I said this isn't work."

"But—"

"Look, for the time being, this is the best I can do as far as taking you on a date." He spoke more quietly but also more confidently. "Sorry about that. But let me do it right." His sincerity made my heart melt. On my soft smile, he continued, "But you won't have to suffer through my cooking. We'll wait for you and order something, okay? And I will send a car. And ... dang it, if I don't want to kiss you again."

"The elevator might still be empty," I teased.

"Don't tempt me, Lenay."

He wasn't the only one tempted, though. The close proximity of our bodies, recognizing we were essentially alone, knowing how the feeling of our lips together felt, and the fact that I hadn't seen him in five days, were definitely causing the devil's side to think it was going to win. I took a mini-step closer to him.

"I like that," I acknowledged.

"Like …?"

"When you call me Lenay," I admitted. "The hugging contract? It doesn't pertain to everyone, does it? I mean, we do hug a lot in the South."

"There is one exception." He smiled.

I wrapped my arms around him and whispered, "See you tomorrow," before quickly disconnecting our bodies and walking off to the depths of the garage where Willow's small, white Chevrolet awaited.

***

When I arrived at the Thompson house, Ryan answered the door. Dressed in a plain white T-shirt and relaxed slacks, he looked casually handsome. He brushed his hand through his dark hair and stepped back to allow me inside.

"Hi, Ryan."

"Hi, Bethany. You look … you look so pretty. I like the dress."

A dress was something I hadn't worn around him. I actually didn't wear much of the garment in general. I had grown up practically living in dresses and skirts, as my parents thought that was how a lady should dress. But once I had the freedom of being on my own, I detested and very rarely wore them. Only on special occasions … like an official first date.

"It seemed like the perfect weather for it." I spoke of the even seventy degrees, which complimented the material and length of the pink dress.

After I placed my jean jacket on the coat rack, he pecked me twice on the lips and said, "The kids and I are just getting in from playing some baseball. Sorry so grubby. I'll look better by dinner."

"You don't have to. You are—"

"I planned to."

Before I could question if he was just saying that because I was a little more dressed up, Sallie's voice soared through the depths of the house. "Is that Bethany?"

"Yeah, sweetie," Ryan hollered back.

"I need help with my ponytail. It's tangled," she whined.

I touched Ryan's hand and started to walk toward the family room with him at my side. "Hey, I guess I missed a big baseball game," I acknowledged to the kids as I entered.

"I think next time it's going to be Joel versus Tink and me. He's getting too good." Ryan smiled at his son.

"I am going to be a baseball guy like Daddy was," Joel boasted.

"Baseball?" I looked briefly at Ryan while kneeling and helping undo Sallie's hair tie. "I thought it was wrestling?"

"Both," he said, and then admitted, "I only told you about wrestling because it made me sound stronger."

"Meaner," I challenged with a grin.

"Do you like baseball?" Joel asked me.

"I know it. My sister is more of the sports girl."

"You have a sister?" Sallie, tangle-free, seemed enamored, stunned, or both by my sister revelation.

"Yeah. Her name is Ella. She's in college. And I have a younger brother, too. His name is Garrett. Here, I'll show you. I have pics of them on my phone. Let me get my purse."

"I'll get it." Ryan reached for my purse, which I had laid on the armchair when first entering the room.

But just as he did, Joel ran by, knocking the purse from his father's grasp. The boy was truly, constantly in motion. When some of the contents spilled, Ryan reprimanded his son and started picking up my sunglasses and wallet from the floor.

"Sorry, Daddy."

I was a little distracted because I was putting Sallie's

hair back into a proper ponytail, but when I gazed up, the look on Ryan's face was downright chilling. With my small, brown leather purse still in his hands, he was staring at me straight on. And it was ten times worse than the way he had dismissed me and my talent on the show.

"What?" I gasped more than said.

His mouth barely moved, but his one word was distinct. "Rooms." I had no idea what he meant as he continued to stare at me.

But I guess the kids did. "Daddy, I sorry," Joel repeated with a plea. "I didn't mean—"

"Rooms," Ryan said again in that same unsettling tone. "Bethany and I need to talk, and I'll be right up."

"But I want to see the pic—" Sallie started.

"Now."

I swear Ryan's eyes actually darkened on the word. I would have known. They hadn't left mine at all.

The kids scurried up the back staircase directly off the family room. I wondered if the scene was similar to what it had been like at the end of Ryan and Kari's marriage because the young Thompson siblings knew what to do. They knew what Ryan was asking. And I did then, too. I knew he was suddenly upset—very upset—with me. But I had no idea why.

"Ryan? What—" I finally stood to meet him.

"Leave." He took my arm as if to direct me out of the house.

"What's going on?" I was scared and upset and confused all at the same time.

"I don't know how we're gonna … I mean, the songs are all ready. But you … you and …"

"What? What's going on?" I repeated.

"Bethany, leave. I don't want my kids anywhere near this. Take your paraphernalia and leave. I never … I never thought … God. To think I thought … go." And then he shoved my purse at me.

"I don't know what—"

He was walking toward the front door, and I had no choice but to follow. The next thing he practically threw at me was my jacket. "I'll have someone contact you." And he opened the door.

"What?" What! What?

Everything had changed and was going so fast, I couldn't even focus on what he was saying. I needed him and the world to pause and let me think about what words were spewing out of his mouth. But he wasn't giving me time. He wasn't giving me a chance to understand or even question. Ryan had never, ever been even remotely like that around me. What the heck was wrong?

Directing me out, he remained inside and was ready to shut the door. I couldn't help but think of all the symbolism of the scene. I could write a whole song on just those five minutes.

I put my hand up to the door. Darn it if I wasn't going to go out fighting … or at least understanding. "You need to at least tell me why."

Ryan stepped outside with me but left the door open. "You think I'd let my kids around that shit in your purse. You brought that into my house? What? Did you think I was into that? All Hollywood? Bethany, I can't believe … I never thought you …" His voice rose in the beginning and then sounded disappointed at the end.

But I still didn't understand. I still did not have a clue. What had caused his quick change of demeanor? It was about my purse? Hollywood?

"What are you talking about?" I know I managed to keep my voice lower, but I was screaming inside.

"Your f-ing drugs." Although clearly upset, he used a variation of profanity and somehow kept his volume down, too.

As I was wondering if the control of his voice had to do about the precious Hollywood neighborhood or his two impressionable children inside, I realized what he actually said. He thought I had drugs? He thought I was doing …

"Drugs?"

As Ryan started to speak again, I finally made the connection. "You have—" As I went to pull the evil culprit from my purse, he vehemently tried to stop me. "Don't take that out."

But the capped needle was partly out, and I left it just that way. "I'm sorry. I should have been more careful with the kids here. But they couldn't get—"

"They what?" If I wanted to agitate Ryan, the safety of his kids would be the number one trigger, and he proved it in the way his voice rose. "What do you do?"

"Ryan …" I was trying yoga breaths, something I did every morning in an attempt to start my day the right away. I obviously had not done a very good job that morning. My day had been downward spiraling … not downward dogging. I needed to figure out how to pause his anger and have him listen … really listen to what I had to say. "It's not what you think. I have a nut allergy. I have to carry it. It's cheaper than the pen. I already had to use one of those in college, and I still have one in my other purse. I have to have it just in case."

"Uh … what?" I think Ryan and I had reversed roles somewhere during my explanation. He suddenly seemed like the one who couldn't speak and didn't know what was going on.

"I have to."

"You're allergic?" I liked the way his eyes seemed to be allowing a little more light in. Hopefully, his brain and heart were, too.

"I'm allergic to nuts. Peanuts and some tree nuts. I'm sorry."

"Oh. Oh, geez. I jumped to conclusions."

I didn't know what to say. I felt bad for him because he felt bad. But I was also coming down from being so instantly and emotionally distraught.

"I'm sorry." He seemed to be calming, too.

"Everything … okay?"

"Yeah." He breathed in. "Yeah. Why didn't you tell me?"

My sigh surely meant more to me than him because I had been dealing with that question my entire life. "It's so not a big deal," I started. "But my parents made it be one."

"How?"

"First of all, Ryan, I'm totally aware of what I need to do and look for. I am very careful. And besides when I was little, there has only been one incident—reaction. The one in college. And it was because I was drinking and wasn't thinking clearly … just like another poor choice I made when drinking."

"The bastard," he acknowledged, and I found it interesting how he not only didn't forget but had it so fresh in his mind. When I blinked to agree with his answer, he continued, "So, no kind of nut product."

"No—peanuts, tree nuts, and, of course, products that contain those. But I'm very aware. Haven't you ever noticed me checking food labels?"

"Yeah, but you know, I thought you were one of those skinny minnies. Too many of those around here."

It was the first legitimate laugh I had since arriving, and it was much needed. "For real? Ryan, you've seen what I cook. And I work out a little."

"And walk … a lot." He rolled his eyes at my non-transportation lifestyle.

A car drove past, seemingly on route to exit the neighborhood. It was a Genesis or Aston Martin or something equally as pricy as a BMW—most likely an affluent neighbor. Ryan did a half-wave and then looked at me.

Knowing he already felt guilty for accusing me, I recognized he didn't need any more pressure. "We should go back inside," I said. "We shouldn't be seen together."

"You've been here plenty of times."

But had anyone seen me? And … and it was different

now. Even if other people didn't realize it, I knew—we knew—it was different.

"Am I *allowed* back in?" I hesitantly questioned when he didn't speak.

"Beth—geez, yeah." He nudged at the partially opened door, and we walked back inside.

We sat side by side on the second step of his grand foyer's staircase, and I told him the rest of my tale. How, since I could remember, my parents—especially my mom—obsessed and worried and advocated about my medical condition. And I told him how I had worn a medical alert bracelet.

When he scanned his eyes over my vacant wrists, I said, "I hated it. It made me different. In high school my parents agreed that I could get the necklace." I pulled it out from behind my dress and showed Ryan the practical yet decorative dog tag. "I wear this or a similar ring."

"You wouldn't know—"

"But medical personnel do. That's what's important."

"Kids in school … they made fun of you?"

"Didn't have a chance. I had a pretty bad reaction in kindergarten, and I had to be wheeled out on a stretcher and taken to the hospital. I remember it was in February right before Valentine's Day, and I was so looking forward to getting the little cards and things. I never went back to school, though."

"What? Why?"

"My mom freaked. She was neurotic. She blamed the school … everything. She decided to homeschool me then until I finally convinced her to let me go to public high school. By then, though, I was even more of an outcast. It's actually when I started writing lyrics." I saw the sympathy in his eyes, so I continued with, "I don't want that. That's why I don't make a big deal about it. I can handle it. I'm not different."

He asked some more questions—the procedures if an allergic reaction would happen, how to look for and identify potential hazards, and finally about *him* eating food with nut products. I answered them the best I could. But with the last one, I'm sure I had the most incredulous look on my face.

"As long as you're not allergic."

"I meant"—he took his knuckle and softly grazed my cheek right where I knew my little line of freckles resided—"and then kiss you."

The words and his action made me smile. "I don't seem to have that severe of a problem, but the doctors have said it can happen in some cases. Let's just not have you eat a jar full of peanut butter or a chocolate-peanut candy bar and then immediately kiss me. Provided you still want to do that," I tacked on at the end.

"More than ever."

And I thought we were going to right then. But the kids started to make some kind of noise on the floor above us. From the sound of it, they had not taken Ryan literally with his plural use of the word "rooms" because they were most definitely together.

"Shoot, they probably think I am mad at them," he lamented.

"Nope, pretty much me you were mad at."

"Sorry. I … yeah. I was upset but mostly disappointed. I couldn't believe … Thanks for bullying me into listening to you. You really are going to be a tough negotiator." I wanted to tell him that it upset me as much as it did him, but he yelled up toward the kids. "Sals, Joe-Joe, come here! Bethany wants to show you those photos now." And then he leaned in, and I got that kiss.

CHAPTER SIX

"Hey, Mr. All-Pro WWE," I teased Ryan. "I will take you down if we don't order food soon."

He had been checking the websites of restaurants he usually ordered from to make sure they were all right for me to eat. And it was taking too long. And it was annoying. And unnecessary.

"Oh, will you now?" He shook his head.

"The southwest salad with grilled chicken … please."

"O … kay." Even the kids cheered when their dad finally placed the order and informed the guard at the neighborhood entrance.

Ryan then briefly explained to Sallie and Joel about my allergy situation, and he did a nice job balancing how serious it was without scaring them. Joel was nonchalant, saying there was a little girl in his preschool who had the same thing. Sallie, on the other hand, told me not to worry because she had to be careful with what she ate, too. When I looked at Ryan, surprised he hadn't mentioned anything, Sallie explained that she had a sore in her mouth from falling and biting it and, consequently, some foods still caused irritation.

"Yeah, that wasn't a pretty sight for a couple days,"

Ryan admitted.

I scrunched my face. I was not good with blood and medical stuff. I think my mom being so allergy-crazed had a part in that. I decided to change the subject for all our benefits. "So, Joel, you want to be a baseball player when you grow up. Sallie, what about you?"

"I want to be a teacher like Aunt Megan and Miss VanLeer."

I was surprised it wasn't an author. "Is she your teacher?"

"Yeah, she's super funny and plays games with us."

"That does sound like a cool job. Aunt Megan?" I was pretty sure she was one of Ryan's two sisters, but I wanted to clarify.

"My oldest sister," the man himself said. "Same thing my mom was before she retired. She actually became our principal in high school."

"Yikes!" I exclaimed. "That's almost like me being homeschooled. Couldn't get away with anything, could you?"

"Not. At. All. Couldn't skip class, couldn't call the school and pretend to be our parents, *and* she knew all our friends way too well. Plus, of course, we had to be into academics." I could hear the frustration in his voice. "Hence, the honor society."

Ryan Thompson couldn't be more all-American if he tried—large family, married parents, middle of the country farm town, creative, smart, athletic. He had probably been super popular and would have never even looked my way in high school. The attempt to shake the thought from my brain must have been more physical than I intended because Ryan squinted one eye as if wondering what I was thinking.

"Bethany, what did you want to be when you were my age?" Sallie asked. "My friend Yasmine wants to be a vet."

"When I was your age?" I thought back. "Everyone was into gymnastics. You know, cartwheels, roundoffs ...

I didn't have the right body for it, though."

"What?" I swear I could see Ryan's seductive thoughts as he scanned my body.

My cheeks tingled with an instant flush. "Well, okay, balance and strength might have been an issue."

"I can do a summer sauce," Joel proudly announced, and his sister almost immediately corrected the word "somersault."

Papa Ryan followed just as fast with, "Not in the house."

As Joel burrowed his little eyebrows and twisted his mouth in disappointment, I continued, "I always liked music. I sang in my dad's church choir, and the organist gave me keyboard lessons." Then I added something I knew Ryan didn't know yet. "And I thought about being an architect."

"What's that?" Sallie appeared more and more enamored by my life's story.

"They design houses," I explained. "They decide where the kitchens go and the soaring ceilings and the game rooms." I looked to Ryan who, as I suspected, had a slightly opened mouth in shock. "I loved the creative part of it. I could be the singing architect." I chuckled.

"That explains it," he said.

"Explains what?" I took off my shoes, which I hadn't had a chance to prior because of all the drama erupting when I had first arrived.

Ryan, smiling at my action, replied, "Your doe-eyed look the first time you came to the house. I was afraid you were all starstruck—"

"Sorry. This house—the design, the details …" I was still very much in awe of the home. "It definitely gets top billing of all the Thompsons."

Ryan chuckled a bit. "In a weird way, it reminds me of the farm where I grew up."

"Yeah, the rustic wood and the old-world features." I totally saw that.

"Minus the chickens and pigs and horses, of course." He smiled.

I was barely able to agree when Joel piped in with, "Grammy and Pappy have those!"

"That's what we're talking about Joe-Joe." Ryan shook his head. "So, what made you bypass being an architect?"

"Math. There was way too much math involved. It wasn't as creative as I thought." Truth.

"Now you work with Daddy," Sallie seemed to say proudly.

I couldn't see them, but I swore my eyes sparkled. I know my mouth lifted a bit, and I felt at ease when I looked at him and answered, "Yeah, I do. And he knows the stuff in between." Guitar lessons, high school and college musicals, summer stock, radio temp work, and lots of songwriting were details I had listed on my *Singer Spotlight* bio and info Ryan and I had discussed.

Ryan's smile was similar to mine before he turned back to the kids. "Dinner is on the way. Go wash hands." When the kids dutifully followed his directions, Ryan did a little body shake at me. "Singing architect …"

"Who knows?" I laughed.

He scooted a little closer and caressed my lips with a most beautifully sweet and soft kiss. "I don't want to necessarily be shy about doing that around the kids," he said afterward.

But noting he had waited until they left, I wanted him to know I understood. "But you have to be careful with what they might say. I get it."

"That's part of it, but, more importantly, I want to protect how they feel. They really like you. So, I don't think it's gonna be too big of a deal." I was glad he said that because I felt it from the kids, too. "They know Kari and I aren't together. We've talked with them about it. I try to be honest with them even when it hurts. But we've never said the D-word because of the press. If they say anything about us being apart, people think it's because she is on tour and gone so much."

"If they say they saw us kissing, though?" I brought the conversation back to our semi-secretive smooch.

I hated to see his face dip down, but it was reality. "I guess we cross that bridge if it comes to it. I don't want them to have to lie. And I don't want to hide my feelings with them because that is like lying to them. I will not lie to my children. The public? That's something I kind of need to do … for now. But I'm gonna make sure—"

"Mission accomplished!" Joel announced, pouncing into the room and putting his hand up to his head like a soldier.

Sallie was right behind her brother. "I wiped up the water Joel splashed."

Ryan shook his head. "Thanks, Sals. Guys, you know Bethany is my *friend*, too, right?" He put his hand on top of mine. "Not just someone I work with?"

"Like Nico," Joel suggested.

"Yeah, sure," Ryan agreed and looked at his daughter.

Sallie gazed at her father's hand on mine, and it made me a little leery at first. "She's my friend, too," she pronounced.

Ryan looked at his chiming phone and, noting that the food had arrived, asked for Sallie's help getting it. When he replaced my hand with hers and they started toward the door, I was ready to suggest to Joel—who was more zooming airplane than little boy at the moment—that he and I go to the kitchen, but my phone announced an incoming text. So, I grabbed my purse from the safety of the tallest shelf in the family room and pulled out my cell.

Ryan's text, with an accompanying wink emoji, read, *Soooo not like Nico.*

I looked up to see him grinning. "Bethany, can you sort out the orders?" He handed me the bag of food. "That's okay, right? I mean with—"

I knew he meant my allergy, so I interrupted with reassurance. "Yes. It's all good."

And, thankfully, he seemed at ease. "Okay. I'll be back down in a couple minutes. Joel and Sallie, help Bethany, please."

We went on our group mission in the kitchen as Ryan headed upstairs. The kids were pretty sufficient getting their own plastic plates, cups, and napkins. And I served the food onto the respective plates.

As I was assisting a determined Joel with pouring milk, I heard Sallie say, "Daddy, you look nice."

"Thanks, Sals."

I set the milk down and turned in Ryan's direction. He didn't just look nice. He looked downright dapper. His gray suit, which hugged his frame just right, was coordinated with a white shirt and blue patterned tie.

"I told you, you didn't have to," I commented on our earlier discussion about getting dressed up.

"And I told *you* I had planned on it." He must have. He had done it rather quickly. "Come on," he said with a small, satisfied look on his face. "There's something else. Grab your plate." He grabbed his soup and sandwich combo. "Kids, you good?"

"Yeah, Daddy," Sallie said as her brother, with a milk mustache already, gave a thumbs-up.

"Put them in the sink when you're done and then no arguing with the TV," was the dad directive.

"Got it!" Joel exclaimed.

"Bethany, grab your plate." Ryan nodded toward my salad.

I did so but asked, "We're not eating with the kids?"

"They don't want to sit through a whole dinner. They'd rather get done and go to the family room and watch cartoons."

"Okay." I was curious what the plan was as I followed him through a set of magnificent French patio doors and out to a part of the property I had never been in before … the back yard.

"What? You're not disappointed, are you? You want to

watch *SpongeBob*?" he teased.

"No," I started, but the quaint scene in front of me caused a halt in any sassy comeback I could come up with.

A table covered by a white tablecloth set center stage on the patio. On it were two wine glasses and a bottle of some kind of white. In the center was a vase, which appeared to have six red roses. Although, I was a bit too stunned at the moment to count the exact number.

I set my plate on the table. "This is so nice." I took in the horizon and imagined what it would be like in another half-hour or so with the sun setting. "You have a lot of space back here." I noted the expansive yard, which was bordered on both sides by a tall, solid fence.

With his plate on the opposite side of the table as mine, he wrapped his arms around me from behind. "Yeah, it's rare to have the acreage and privacy."

I placed my hands on his, which were perfectly positioned between my ribs and hips. I loved the intimate, new feel. But I also loved still being able to joke around with him. "It's perfect for a dog to run around."

"Oh, don't you start." He jabbed my side with his right pointer finger.

"Just teasing."

"You know what else the yard is great for?"

"What?"

He released me so he could gently turn me back toward the table. "Growing those roses."

"They're beautiful."

"Something special about them, though."

"Besides being homegrown?"

Besides the thought of him picking them? Besides the magical setting they were placed in? Besides the fact that I had never had someone do something like that for me before?

As I was thinking I better not get too emotional on our first date—it had already been a see-saw start as it was—he gave me an instruction. "Pick them up."

I lifted the roses out. As initially thought, there were six. But I didn't notice anything else besides their beauty.

"Every rose does *not* have a thorn, Bethany," he amended the song title of my bad dating history.

I examined them more closely. They, indeed, did not. If he had pruned them, he did a magnificent job. If he hadn't, I needed to research a little because a thornless rose was seriously cool. Ryan Thompson, since the first time I had met him while standing scared on the stage, had brought out every emotion in me—disappointment, anger, nerves, anticipation, excitement, respect, joy, fright … relief. And if I wasn't careful, I knew the next one might be dangerously close to my heart.

***

I felt like I had a little more bounce in my step and a little more beat in my song as I went through my work shift. And it wasn't because of the caffeine simmering and floating its aroma through the air. It was because of that dinner—that date—the night before. The meal, accompanied by what turned out to be an even more spectacular sunset than I had imagined, had been fantastic. With every kiss, especially the goodnight one in the foyer, I could feel the connection deepen. And the fact that it felt so natural, made it even better.

I had been working a few hours straight when I pushed a large Americano with a shot of cinnamon forward on the counter. "Tom!" I called out the customer's name. Without looking when the hand reached for the coffee, I concluded with the traditional, "Have a nice day."

I was already on the next order when Tom answered, "It would be, if you would join me."

Oh, great, a flirty one, I thought sarcastically. I wasn't into one-liners and never really reacted to the cheesy comments. "Can't. Sorry. Too—" I could at least look up and acknowledge the guy—maybe it would aid in him putting a tip in the jar. But when I did, I saw it wasn't Tom. It was "Ryan!" I exclaimed.

"Tom," the tall, built, rose-picker teasingly and quietly corrected.

I smiled and shook my head. "What are you doing here?" I asked while still working on the next beverage. It was a good thing I could multi-task because seeing him was a whole thought-provoking process in itself.

"I was nearby and thought I would check the place out."

"Steele!" I called out to the next customer and slid the latte forward. "Have a good day."

"Do you have time? Can you take a break and have a cup with me?" Ryan asked as Steele—beverage in hand—walked away.

"Uh, yeah. Give me a couple minutes and I can. Where?"

"I'm parked in the lot—pulled all the way through. You know it."

"Okay."

I was due a ten-minute break, and things were slowing down a little bit—or as much as they ever did in a centrally located coffee shop in a town where no one wanted anyone to get ahead of them. I finished a couple of orders, shrugged off my official apron, and went to the restroom to make myself look a little more presentable before exiting the café. I wasn't going to look as nice as I had in the dress I had worn the night before, but he had seen me in extremely casual clothes when we were writing. That, after all, had been when he had first kissed me.

He was also dressed casually in a plaid shirt and jeans, but, yet, he looked downright handsome no matter what he wore. That's what I was thinking as I opened up his passenger door and slid into the front seat. Even the cool, cushioned leather and electronics on the dash couldn't distract me.

"Hi, Bethany."

"Tom." I did a one-nod and smiled while taking a sip of his coffee, which had been resting in the middle console.

"Hey, why didn't you bring your own?"

"You don't share?" I questioned.

He swiped it from my hand, took a sip, and returned it to its holder. "Not when it's this good."

"Yep, what I've always strived for ... being an expert coffee maker." Sarcasm raced out of my mouth. "Hashtag—life goals." I didn't want to be a Debbie Downer, though, especially with such a nice surprise visit. "What are you doing here?"

"The kids are at the stuff-a-doll-or-animal place a couple stores down. It's one of Sallie's friends. Someone always has a birthday." He semi-grumbled, and I made a mental note to text my sister for hers before I went back on my shift. "Anyway, I was the only dad. The moms took pity on me and let me escape for a few."

"Poor Ryan ..." I used my sassy sing-song voice.

"Yeah, not so much," he admitted. "Got to have delicious coffee with a gorgeous barista."

"I don't know how. It was a horrible pick-up line."

He laughed. "Out of practice and, regardless, hoping I don't need one."

And that magnetic pull between us, which was growing stronger every time I saw or even spoke with him, surged. Nope. No lines needed.

But his facial features suddenly grew dark. His eyes closed. And then his mouth sagged downward along with his shoulders.

"What's up?"

He reopened his eyes and looked right at me, obviously upset. "I wish I wasn't stuck in this car with you."

"Thanks," I sassed, but I pretty much knew what he was referring to.

His head shake was slight. "I hate this situation. I want to take you out on a real date." He brought my hand into his.

"Ryan, let me tell you, yesterday was better than any restaurant or movie or whatever. I … That was so nice."

"It was, wasn't it?" The glimmer was coming back.

My genuine answer warmed my entire body. "Yeah."

"Sorry about any of that beginning stuff." He pinched his lips together.

"I know the kids are foremost in your mind. I will keep my purse up high where they can't reach."

"Where I can get it, though."

"Sure." I loved that he was concerned but not overbearing.

"I'll talk with Kari. I think once she's back from tour, we'll figure out when to tell the press … the public." He squeezed our connected hands. "I better go. They don't know what they've got themselves into with Joel. Thanks for the coffee."

"Thanks for sharing," I smirked and let go of his hand.

"I'll see you tomorrow night, right?"

"Yeah. After all the Easter hoopla."

I should have been reaching for the handle then. I should have been opening the car door. I should have been stepping out. But I was still looking at him. And he was at me. We both felt it. We both wanted the same thing—to have our lips on each other. But it was a public parking lot. There were people milling around. It couldn't happen.

Ryan strummed his index finger on my thigh. His half-smile seemed to be a mix of regret and hope. It mimicked mine as I made myself get out of the car and return to work.

CHAPTER SEVEN

Apparently, people need to be caffeinated in order to deal with their families because there were a lot more customers at the coffee house than I expected on Easter. Ryan, I was sure, could have probably used an extra shot of espresso with what his day held. Following the egg and basket hunt, he and the kids were going to church—which he admitted had become only a holiday and special occasion occurrence—and then to dinner with his former in-laws. He claimed he still got along with his ex-brother-in-law, Maks, and Kari's dad was neither here nor there, but her mom was the one who harbored blame for the divorce on Ryan. Regardless, he did it for Sallie and Joel. He encouraged the family bonding even when Kari was away.

After my shift, I called *my* family. My father never liked when I worked on a Sunday. It was supposed to be a day of rest and a day to honor God. I reassured him, though, that I was still going to church ... which I did after showering and having a special Easter dinner at the apartment. I didn't, however, tell them that after church I was going to Ryan's. My family knew, of course, about the great music opportunity Mr. Thompson and I were working on. But the extra? I felt shame, even though I knew I shouldn't. There was nothing wrong with our budding relationship … except that we had to be secretive about it. And no matter what the reason, my parents, I knew, would consider that lying.

When I arrived at the Thompson estate, I got to hear a little about their day before the kids started to get tired. Joel actually crashed on the sofa a little earlier than bedtime, and Ryan carried him to his room. Decked out in a sparkling pink Easter dress, Sallie lasted a little longer, reciting stories from the birthday party the day before. Ryan had just suggested it was her bedtime when his phone buzzed on the coffee table in front of us. He smiled at his daughter and answered his phone.

It was the first time I had ever heard Ryan talk with his ex-wife and, even though I felt a little intrusive, it was interesting to note the even, average tone in his voice. He didn't seem angry or bitter or, on the flip side, excited or in love. All that he had claimed to me, appeared to be true.

"Yeah, they're both wiped out from all the searching and family and the sugar overload crash." He paused to listen to her dialogue back. "I know it's hard with the time difference." Ryan had told me Kari was currently in Australia. "Talk with Sals for a little bit. You'll have to catch Joel another time. We can set up a video chat with both of them later. Tink?" He handed his daughter the phone.

"It's Mommy, right?" Sallie's light blue eyes, which had been sleepy, were open with anticipation as she looked at Ryan.

"Yeah, baby. She wants to wish you a happy Easter. Just talk for a little bit, all right?"

"Hi, Mommy!" She wiggled with the phone in her hand. "Happy Easter," the little girl said, and then, after a pause, "Yeah."

Ryan, who had been watching Sallie, turned to me. "I'm glad she called. I think Sallie, in particular, was hoping … needed it. She's sensitive to the bigger stuff like holidays."

"Heck, I was a little teary talking with my family," I admitted, and Ryan touched my cheek. "Thanks for the basket by the way. That was way too sweet." It was the first time I had a chance to acknowledge my Easter basket, which included a chocolate, nut-free bunny. I didn't want to say anything in front of the kids, because they still believed in human-sized rabbits who hid holiday things.

"What? I didn't have anything to do with that," Ryan teased. "What are you talking about? That was all Mr. Rabbit."

I chuckled, and we both refocused on Sallie's phone conversation. "Yeah, mine was in the laundry basket." She made an exaggerated disgusted face before saying, "Yuk! No smelly clothes inside." She listened again before explaining, "His was in the bathtub. Daddy's was in the closet under the TV. And we found Bethany's behind the guitars, but we let her find it by herself."

I looked at Ryan. Did Kari know about me? If she didn't—which I suspected was the case—surely having an Easter basket at their house would throw out some flags. Ryan just nonchalantly shrugged.

"No. She's Daddy's friend." Sallie confirmed Kari's lack of knowledge, and Ryan twisted his lips but still looked content.

I wished I was completely at ease, too, but I had that same feeling I had about lying. I felt as though I should be diving under something because the wife walked in to find the mistress. Even though I knew that was not the scenario at all, I felt it. Maybe I needed to quit watching those afternoon soaps with the women at the house when I wasn't working.

"Yeah, she's here now." Sallie spoke into the phone. "Yeah."

I'm not sure if it was because of my squirming or if Ryan legitimately wanted Sallie to go to sleep that he ended the mother-daughter conversation. "Sals, I let you talk with Mommy, but it's late. You need to say good-bye."

"Bye, Mommy!" she obliged. "I miss you. … . I know. Me, too. Here's Daddy." She handed Ryan his phone back.

Ryan gave his daughter a soft kiss on her cheek. "Good night, sweetie. See you in the morning." And then, after watching her walk up the stairs, Ryan brought the phone to his ear and spoke. "Hey." He looked almost vacantly around the family room while taking in whatever Kari was saying. "Sure. I'm glad you caught her. Sorry the little guy was zonked. … . Yep. … . It was. It's fun watching them get so excited. I'm not sure how much longer Sallie is gonna—" Ryan stopped talking for a second or two. "I know. Too fast. She's starting to tuck herself in now." Ryan swayed from one foot to the other and then seemed to react to Kari's next thought. "I think you know what she meant." When his eyes found mine, I knew the topic of their conversation had changed to me. "It's time, Kari. We both moved on. Everything is settled with the show and your tour. We can let the public know."

Ryan's voice was still as calm as it had been the entire evening, and it reassured me. Yet, I felt like that part of their conversation was personal. I should definitely give them their privacy. As I started to walk away, though, Ryan gently grabbed my forearm with his free hand and stroked it. He nodded and clasped my hand, asking me nonverbally to stay.

"Yeah. I do." He spoke back into the phone. "Maybe. … . You know I will. I do." Kari must have spoken again because he was silent and then gave an answer. "Yeah, I agree."

Ryan smiled warmly at me. And while I didn't know the exact words she was saying, I knew what they were talking about. And I could hear there wasn't any anger. I could see the ease in his being when he looked at me.

"Good," he said to Kari again. "All right. Once you get back, we'll find a good day to schedule the announcement.

Bye, Kari."

Ryan had to let go of my hand to hang up his phone and place it back on the coffee table. I noticed immediately how his voice was a little different when talking with me. It was as if he was digging a little deeper into his core to explain a truth he probably hadn't openly spoken of before. "The day the divorce was final? It was your audition day."

"Oh." I think I said it out loud. I had not known that little fact. Sure, I had seen their divorce papers, but it hadn't connected. At the time, I was just registering the shock that he was not married.

"It didn't matter that we both knew it was for the best. It didn't matter that the marriage was done a long time before. It didn't matter that I wanted the closure so much. It still struck as though a sword had sliced right through me. I had failed and, honestly, I'm not used to doing that. Today? That conversation?" He looked at the disconnected call from his ex-wife. "It was the opposite. It was like how I wanted it to feel on that day. It … and you …"

His voice faded, but he didn't need to say any more. I hadn't realized it, but there was a part of me that needed to hear that phone conversation—to know the truth was going to come out … to know he didn't harbor any lingering feelings … to know we were legit. *And* that he wasn't going back to her … like Hutch. The phone call did that, but his little soliloquy to me after absolutely solidified it.

I rested my hands on his shirt-covered back and then tilted slightly up to kiss him. I purposefully did it softly so he could recognize my thanks and give him comfort over what he had just revealed. His kiss back was equally as sweet. But the more the mutual bond continued, the more the passion grew. And I really couldn't honestly say whose mouth and mind started the intensity. I know it was Ryan who halted it, though … if only for a moment.

"Be with me." His mesmerizing eyes had never been that direct and close to mine when he spoke. "Stay." He confirmed his meaning.

Those kisses … My body was already saying yes, and my mind only did one little hiccup when I thought back to the last time he had asked me to stay. That had been because of the lack of Uber transportation. This was not that at all. This was him wanting me and me wanting him. There wasn't a doubt. And I couldn't resist telling him in our unique Bethany-Ryan way. I pulled away and went to my phone, which was resting next to his.

"What are you doing?" he asked with the slightest twinge of unease when I started to type. "You're checking messages now?"

I gave him a little smirk, put my phone back down, and then waited for his to chime the incoming message. His eyes squinting at me let me know he knew I was up to something. Ryan coupled next to me and picked up his phone to read the text.

RyanThompsonMusic—for real? It wasn't a tweet, but I made it in the form of one.

Ryan pressed his lips together in a smile, typed something into his phone, and put it back down next to mine. It was my turn to get the message, which read, *Bethany_Lenay—for real.*

I no sooner had my phone back at rest than he scooped me up with his athletic arms. Since I had on my Easter dress, I swung my legs to the side and looped my hands around his neck. He kissed me once and started walking us toward the back staircase. But just as we approached, he stopped, looked at me, and turned around.

Despite the sudden acidy surge slamming into the core of my abdomen, I kept the humor I was known for. "Did you forget what you were doing?"

He pecked me on the lips for reassurance. "Most definitely not."

Staying on the home's main floor, he walked us down a

side hallway and into the guest room. Gently, he brought me back to my feet—shoeless, of course—in front of the bed. As he wrapped his arms around my waist, the passionate kissing session resumed. I pressed my lips and my body as close to him as possible. I knew I was losing my sense of time and space as the need intensified.

Ryan, blowing out a slight breath, said, "Geez, I forgot about ... I haven't had to think about ... having something."

"I'm on the pill." And just to clarify—even though I hoped I hadn't needed to—I continued to explain, "Just because it regulates me. I'm all good."

And in those seconds that we discussed birth control, I realized I had no intention of asking Ryan for further protection as I had with Andre. Ryan was different. I trusted him implicitly. Being with him was different on so many levels.

"Ryan? This means something to me." My words came out with a clip of caution, and I prayed he understood.

"It means so much something to me." He echoed sweet and reassuring.

Ryan found the zipper on my brown dress and carefully leveled it. The garment easily fell to the ground, exposing my lacy, red bra-and-panty set. I was self-conscious but only for a second because his appreciative groan and slight close of eyes made me do a partial chuckle. After Ryan untucked his white dress shirt, I continued his unveiling by unbuttoning it. And then, oh, my stars ... his chest. Seeing the muscular ripples of his bare abs and just a trickle of dark hair made my insides clench. I had fallen for Ryan because of our connection to words and music and how much of a genuine, thoughtful person he was, but, admittedly, his body was an added bonus. I traveled my hands a little further south, and he joined me in undoing his fly. Shrugging his pants off to reveal black boxer briefs, he once again pulled me swiftly to him for another round of sensual kisses while skimming the sides of my body from my breasts to my hips. After pulling down the cream-colored comforter, Ryan lifted and placed me on top of the heavenly bed before planking himself above. When he kissed my hand where the medical alert ring resided, I smiled at the gesture. He cared—everything about him said it. His hands on my bra felt as if he was sculpting … feeling … taking in the experience. The easy front clasp allowed him to first caress with his hands and then his mouth. That was my complete undoing. My body was screaming for his.

But I had to concentrate on his words. He was talking to me, and it was pure Ryan. "You know my song right now?" he asked as if we were in his living room going over song recollections to help with writing.

"Huh?" I managed.

"'Lady in Red,'" he purred out the title.

I thought about the lyrics that told of a relationship solely between two people. There was no one else. And I appreciated it on a whole different level than simply the color choice of my undergarments.

I was more than ready, and I knew he was, too. Hunching back on his knees, he started to snake my panties down my legs, and then took care of his own. Oh, geez, I could hardly wait. I shut my eyes on his kiss. Then slowly I started to feel him inside me. Ryan called out my name and I his as an amazing, harmonious connection of our bodies happened.

***

With my head resting on one of the blissful pillows, I was sighing in that peaceful, content way while coming down from the experience of making love with Ryan. I opened my eyes to see him propped on his side beside me in the bed … just looking. He was looking at me. Those magnificent blue eyes were almost twitching as if he was in deep concentration.

"You're not thinking of a score, are you?" I teased, referencing his television role.

"Wha—?" he started and then understood. "No!" He touched my lips with his pointer finger and dragged it down a bit as I smiled. "No. God, Bethany, we ... our bodies are so—"

I cut him off because I agreed wholeheartedly. "In tune with each other."

"Yeah." He smiled. "I was going to say in sync."

He rolled over a little so he was able to kiss me in that slow, sweet way of his. I was wondering if I would ever be able to get enough of his mouth on mine or our tongues deliciously dancing with each other's. I wasn't sure I was ready to admit it to him or not, but our lovemaking was, by far, the best I ever had. It wasn't an awkward first-time experience, or being young and thinking I was in love, or a regretful hook-up in a basement laundry area. It was real and powerful.

"Daddy?" I moved my head slightly to make sure I had heard the voice. "Daddy?" It came again after a short pause. It was Joel and, from what I could tell, he was still upstairs. "Daddy!" The pause that time was shorter, and the word came out louder and with much more urgency.

"Ryan?" I questioned.

His chest rose and fell with an extended sigh. "I know. He's been doing this. It's not all the time. But more often since Kari has actually been on tour." When Joel cried out again, my mouth dipped in sadness for the little boy, and Ryan explained, "They know they're not allowed to leave their rooms at night. I usually bring him into my room with me."

"Oh," I said, and then it dawned on me where Ryan was ... not in his room ... and not alone. "Oh." It was my turn to sigh.

"Let me go calm him down. I'll be back."

***

I was sitting up, completely covered by the soft sheets, when Ryan returned about fifteen minutes later. Watching him enter with only his boxer briefs on made my heart pitter-patter all over again. It was hard finding something wrong with the man. And it was so ironic that everything I was witness to since our first meeting was the exact opposite of what the world believed, thanks to a persona he was crowned with on TV.

"Dating with kids," he said crawling back in bed. "I never thought about it."

I was glad he hadn't. It even further legitimized our relationship in my eyes. But he was right. There was a lot to consider when dating someone with kids. So far, things were good. But it was new, and those two innocent little ones never had someone besides their mom be with their dad. I wondered how *I* would have handled that as a young child … or even as an adult. I wanted Ryan, but I didn't want to hurt those kids or, consequently, him.

"What are you thinking?" He had that concentrated look on me again. "Bethany?"

"Should I not be here? Joel and Sallie … they already have enough things on their minds, and if they—"

My brown eyes met his deep blue ones when he gently lifted my chin with his hand. "We talked about this. They know you. They like you. I am not keeping you a secret from my kids."

"Just to everyone else."

He sighed before replying, "But you won't be. That's what the whole conversation with Kari was about." He dipped his face closer to mine. "Joel's fine, and I want you to stay."

"I—"

"For real."

I shook my head but eased my shoulders. "I 'for real' would like that, too." I curled once again into his arms. "Thanks for all of my Easter treats, Ryan."

"Back at you, Lenay." He punctuated his sentence with that special name and a tap on my nose.

Easter is all about resurrection. And in the comfort of his arms, I felt a little like I was doing just that. I was being reborn or at least discovering my new, true self.

CHAPTER EIGHT

I did end up leaving before the kids were up the next morning. But it wasn't because of secrets or expectations. It was because I had an early shift at the coffee shop and still needed to get back to my place and change before heading to caffeine headquarters. If Easter was busy, the Monday morning after was going to be even more so.

Most likely, alongside those espressos, lattes, and caps, I was going to have to pull an extra shot for myself after staying at Ryan's. Not because we had stayed up late. We had actually closed our eyes shortly after Ryan returned from consoling Joel. But in contrast to Ryan, who had seemed so content in his slumber, I had trouble falling asleep and then staying that way. I wasn't used to the rise and fall of his body as he breathed in and out … of having his chest be my pillow and his arm as my blanket. It had been a while since Hutch. And even back then, in school, we often wouldn't stay the night because of roommates and small bed sizes. Everything with Ryan was different, and it frightened me to know I could definitely get used to the comfort and security of his body wrapped around mine. And that was the other part that had kept me awake.

Having Willow catch me coming in that morning, still

adorning my Easter dress, did not help matters. "Uh, uh, uh, what is this? Where have you been all night?" Her eyes seemed to glisten with potential gossip.

"Willow …" I couldn't lie. I already felt like I was doing enough of that, even though it was more like dodging the topic.

"Yeah?" She stood at her doorway ready to lock her door as I was trying to enter mine.

"There *is* a chance you will just let this drop, right? Just pretend …?"

"Yeah, right. How long have you known me?"

Long enough that I considered her my best friend and someone I could confide in. But still, I hadn't told her about Andre due to pure regret and embarrassment. And Ryan trusted me not to say anything about us for the time being.

"Aren't you going to be late for class?" I diverted.

"I can afford a couple minutes."

"Well, *I'm* gonna be late for work." I had my door unlocked and was opening it when I stopped and said, "Let's just say I was singing at a sultry dive and crashed in the room behind the bar … alone."

"Uh-huh. Sounds just like you." She shook her head, and I imagined the now *two* extra shots in my future cappuccino.

"Willow, I am going to be late. I'll tell you when I can." I knew she thought that meant when we both had time, but, in reality, it was when press managers of superstars put it on a schedule.

"Fine." She seemed slightly put off but then turned it around. "The daydreamy look works on you, though." She smiled at me. "Going out with Til tonight. So, I won't see you at dinner or probably after. We'll catch up soon, though."

Thank goodness for Til, I thought, as I bustled into my room. I wasn't going to be around for dinner, either. I was going to bring food over for Ryan and the kids, and I was packing an extra change of clothes … just in case.

***

Ryan was amused, and Sallie and Joel loved the creative dinner I made for them that night. Not only was it fun for the kids to help me make it, but it was a great teaching tool for how a food allergy doesn't have to restrict a life. Instead of peanut butter and jelly sandwiches, we had *sunflower seed* butter and jelly sandwiches. Ryan and I chose raspberry jam, but the kids stuck with traditional strawberry. I also sliced up bananas and apples and drizzled them with honey, and the kids got a big kick out of filling celery with cream cheese and raisins for "ants on a log." The best part was, it was easy and quick for Sallie and Joel.

Ryan had insisted he was in charge of dessert, which to me was always the most alarming food category as far as a nut allergy. But he showed me the wrapper of the premade cookie dough and how the three of them had topped it on Rice Krispie treats—a recipe he grew up with. And there were absolutely no nut ingredients. He admitted it wasn't as hard as he thought it would be to live a nut-free life. In fact, he said he was eliminating everything nut-related from their kitchen … which I assured him he did not have to do.

After the kids went to bed, Ryan and I watched the conclusion of that week's *Singer Spotlight*. "What did you tweet?" I asked once he turned the television off and placed his phone back on the table.

"Just how hard it is to let contestants go … and that the makeup people need to hold back a little. It looked like I was wearing eyeliner!"

I laughed because it had a little. "Do you regret it?"

"Regret what? The eyeliner?" he questioned.

"No. Helping me out … tweeting … asking me to meet you in the first place. There are so many others who are way better than me."

"Oh, boy." Ryan's head moved ever so slightly from left to right, but his eyes remained glued onto mine. "Where do I even start with that one?"

"The truth?" I suggested because there was no denying the talent we both witnessed on the show.

"The truth is … first of all, I know you realize all the shows so far are recorded. I already did—saw—all of what is airing before I tweeted out to you."

I did know that. I wasn't really concentrating on that fact right then, though. "Yeah, and you said you regretted doing that because other people thought they deserved a chance, too."

"Trying to use my words against me again, Lenay?" He was serious but added a little smile to also bring some levity to the conversation. "I didn't say I regretted asking you to come in," he clarified. "I said I regretted doing it publicly. You know I don't do a lot of social media, anyway. Are there good singers left? I am not denying that. There are some fantastic artists. It's gonna be hard when it comes down to the live shows, no doubt. But what you are seeing now isn't only makeup as a cover. There are a lot of sound effects to help. Those initial tryouts that you were in? *That* was the real deal. Uh-huh, let me finish." He raised his eyebrows, and I pierced my eyes at him for knowing I was going to say something, even though nothing verbally had emerged from my mouth. "Absolutely no regrets … about any of it." He rubbed his hand on my jeans-covered leg. "I never, in a million years, though, would have thought it would have led to this."

I had arrived to the West Coast a young woman with miles of naivety. And the city of angels had definitely crushed some confidence. In a lot of ways, however, it had also made me stronger and more realistic. Except in little moments, like that one on the sofa in the Thompson family room, when I needed a boost … a reminder of all I had. I was writing, it was going to be pitched, and … Ryan.

"In a *million* years?" I returned to my real self after a blip in the insecure world. "I'm pretty sure that wasn't a compliment."

"Geez!" His eye roll was much exaggerated before he kissed me quickly. "What I'm saying is, I was taken in by your words—your talent for words. And I still am. That's where my mind was set … strongly, by the way. But you changed all that."

"Ry—"

"For … real," he said with determination.

I thought about how *those* two little words were the first interaction between us. It had become our thing, and I loved that. When I smiled, he brought my body onto his lap. I started my finger at his temple and traced down the smooth surface of his cheek to his chin and then finally rested my open palm on his chest, covered by a blue cotton pullover.

Our kissing intensified pretty quickly then. We both knew where it was leading. And the anticipation was even greater than the night before because we understood how incredibly good it was between the two of us.

While working on unbuttoning my girl cut, dark blue top, he asked, "Upstairs? My room?"

I pursed out some air. "Why?" I asked, and then clarified, "Why not yesterday?"

We had started that way the day before but ended up in the guest room. Ryan didn't answer. And any further action stopped, too.

I played off of his machoism with a hopefully snarky remark. "What? Didn't think you could carry me up the stairs? Did you work out today?"

Luckily, he let out an exasperated breath and poked my side. Then he spoke honestly. "I didn't know how you'd feel about being in the room I used to share—" He stopped himself as his eyes darted back and forth, examining mine.

"With Kari," I finished for him.

It had been my guess all along, and I was actually glad we were discussing it. But for both our sakes, I hoped the conversation could conclude quickly. Buzzkill and all that.

"It's my room, and the thing is … I don't want you to feel like you're a guest. You're not. I realized maybe I … It's up to you."

"What do you want?" I asked, thinking maybe he still pictured her in there and that could be a problem.

"Bethany, I'm asking you."

"It doesn't matter." It didn't. As long as he felt comfortable, I wanted him no matter what or where. "You decide."

"Ah, geez." He grabbed at the zipper of his jeans and undid it, exposing his white briefs. "I can't play this your-choice game right now." He pulled off his shirt, flung it behind the sofa, and kissed me passionately before quickly but gently laying me prone.

His actions were definitely intensifying things to the next level, but suddenly a rational thought invaded my mind. We were in a room with open pocket doors. Two very impressionable young children were a floor above us somewhere.

"Kids?" I breathed out.

His breathing pattern was similar to mine as he spilled out the words, "Asleep. Told you … can't leave rooms. Green today?" He had gotten my shirt completely off and was gazing at my bra. And then we took care of our pants and, very soon after, collided most blissfully into each other right there on the sofa.

***

"That was Judge Ryan." I smirked with his face still so close to mine moments after our climax and collapse.

"What? What do you mean?"

"The other judges … they confer with one another and debate. But Ryan Thompson?" I lowered my octave a little to mimic a male voice. "Nope. No. None of this. Sofa it is."

Ryan's stomach bounced in laughter. "You're exhausting, Lenay."

"That's because you're old." I smiled a tease, knowing our ten-year age difference definitely seemed to meet somewhere in the middle.

"Really?" He swiftly and expertly flipped us around so I was lying on his stomach and he on his back.

"No," I admitted. "You proved you're not a few minutes ago."

His smile was genuine before he gave me a kiss and asked, "You're staying, right?"

"Uh … yeah. Okay? Yeah?"

"Don't make me Judge Ryan you," he teased. "No more debate. Yes, you're staying." And then he added, "Upstairs in my room."

"Mmmm-hmmm." I was glad he made the decision. I think when it came down to it, it was truly his to make.

"And I can so carry you up there."

"No doubt."

***

After breakfast with the kids that next morning—where Joel was trying to con Ryan into giving him a Rice Krispie cookie and Sallie was wondering why I was working at their house so early—Ryan got them bustled off to the school van. Then he insisted on dropping me off at my place on his way into the office. I didn't mind. It meant that many more minutes to be with him. And I absolutely wanted that.

"What are you doing today?" he asked as we got closer to my place.

"I'm not sure. Probably resting from my active weekend." I waited for him to look my way so the magnetic, sexy feel could connect both of us.

It had been another night when I hadn't had enough sleep. But that time, it was for better reasons. Noting not even a trace of Kari in the master bedroom—no photos, clothes, double toothbrushes, or anything else—I fell a step deeper. It was me who initiated our lovemaking that second time in his bedroom, but he certainly hadn't been far behind or put up any arguments.

"Mmmm," he murmured in the driver's seat, surely remembering what I was. "Once you recover, look over your bio, double-check your links, and let me know if you have any changes."

"Oh, shoot. We were supposed to work on that."

"I got distracted." He did a short chuckle.

"Funny, me, too. Next right," I noted the street to turn onto. "And then it will be down on the right."

"Sorry my schedule is picking up," he said as we started down my street. "Got those show promos tomorrow. I'll definitely see you on Friday, though."

"Little nervous about that," I admitted.

"You shouldn't be. You were on national television. This recording is nothing."

Maybe it was because of the way the national television gig went, or maybe it was because I knew if I didn't get the recording right, the possibilities of ever making it took a nosedive like the worst day on Wall Street. I didn't say any of that, though. I wanted to push away those insecurities. Besides, we had arrived at the apartment house.

"Right there." I pointed to the building approaching on the right. "Where those women are coming out." Ryan pulled the car up to the curb a little before the entrance, and I internally sighed. "All right." I tried to sound casual. "Thanks for driving me home."

When he didn't say anything in reply, I stopped looking at the apartment building and, instead, glanced over at him. He had a most definite look of longing. It was something we could rectify when it was me leaving his house. I could kiss him before opening the door and going down the sidewalk to meet the car service. *Not* in his car, though … in public …

"Ah, screw it." Before I could respond, he grasped my face in both his hands and pulled me in for a quick but needy—needed—kiss, followed by that deep, stirring groan of his.

My closed smile was huge. "See you Friday." Grabbing my tote bag, I opened the car door while the coast was still clear, winked, and tried not to skip to the front door.

***

Both miraculously having a free afternoon, Willow and I were able to help one another with our career needs. She was my second set of eyes on the material Ryan requested, and I was her amateur photographer. My friend was working on her portfolio for graduation and needed not only photos of her designs but some of her, also. We started out in the building's mid-way lounge, but its dark red décor and limited lighting weren't ideal. The best shots were on the roof of the apartment building. Usually a place where we would sunbathe, the mid-day natural light and blue skyline as its backdrop worked much better.

My next-door neighbor tried to pry more out of me regarding my Easter dress attire, but I kept mum. It was hard, especially because I was once again skimming around the truth without flat out lying. I respected and made the promise to Ryan, though, and that took precedence.

What we did end up talking about wasn't much easier. Since I wasn't around the house as much, I was missing out on the gossip, and Andre Upton was the number one subject. One of our apartment mates found out Andre's aunt had just passed away. Between the obit and the information coming out because of the charges against him, it was uncovered that it was Andre's aunt who had raised him after both his dad and grandmother did stints in jail and his mother was too strung out and having other kids to keep custody of him.

"So, now on top of having to pay back the apartment to keep out of jail, he has funeral expenses," Willow explained.

"Yeah, that's rough." I tried to be sympathetic.

More than anything, Andre's story made me appreciate all I had. I didn't have enough money to own a car or home, but I made by. I certainly didn't have to steal or beg. And I may have been sheltered growing up, but I always knew I was wanted and cared for. That not only included family but also friends like Willow and a certain music manager who was changing my world in so many ways.

CHAPTER NINE

Ryan was there to greet me when I first arrived at the recording studio just down the hall from his office. Almost immediately, though, he had meetings to attend. But that was probably for the best. Although I could have used his support, it couldn't be in the intimate way I really craved. So, having him present probably would have just distracted me.

I had been in recording studios before—first on sight-seeing tours, then on campus where I worked at the radio station, and finally at a temp job I had in Carolina before moving west. But that day it was all about me, and it was thrilling and nerve-wracking at the same time. I was harder on myself than the professional techs were. They kept insisting that with some tweaks in post-production, everything was going to sound great. It made me think of what Ryan had said about the makeup and special effects of the music world.

Before we wrapped, I decided to do an alternate version of one of the songs. I wanted to play around with the tempo by slowing it down at the end compared to the rest of the song. It was just to get another feel ... kind of a different twist on the meaning of the song. Almost like a cliff-hanger at the end of a book. Like, oh, what just happened there?

I wasn't in the booth but in the main room playing around with it, when I heard Anamaria's voice. "Ryan, there's a phone call."

I stopped singing and looked up as Ryan cleared his throat. "Take a message," he said to his secretary.

The way he was comfortably propped in the doorway made me wonder how long he had been standing there. I tried not to smile. But I hoped he could tell or feel it in the slight blink of my eyes.

"It's important," Anamaria insisted.

"Wha—"

"It's about Kari." That time her words made me look down like a guilty party, even though I knew I wasn't.

"Just take a—" he started again.

"It's … something happened. They said it's urgent." I looked first to the woman who said it and then to the man next to her.

"Okay." Ryan's eyes caught mine for the briefest of seconds before he followed his secretary out of the studio.

I was distracted from that point on. Luckily, recording that version was the last thing we were doing, and the guys admitted they liked the final cut better. "Haunting" is what Morrison called it.

Having run a little over our time, they packed up in a hurry, and Morrison alone walked me to Anamaria's desk. Just beyond, I saw Ryan in his office. His door was shut, but it was glass, so I could see how very serious he looked while talking on the phone. Anamaria explained to us that Ryan couldn't be disturbed, which worried me even more. Morrison just shrugged it off, though, and said he would send Ryan the file as soon as he put the magic touches on it. When he started to give me a hug good-bye, I glanced Ryan's way again and instead shook hands with the head technician.

Once Morrison left, I spotted the leather sofa I had

originally sat on before my first ever meeting with Ryan. I couldn't help but think how much had changed since then. It was all good, and it had started right there.

"Miss Lenay." Anamaria—who called me by my California name despite knowing my legitimate last name—seemed shocked I was going to take residence on the sofa. "I told you, he's on the phone."

"I can wait," I insisted.

I wanted to wait. Sure, I wanted to tell Ryan all about the session he had put into play, but mostly, I was concerned. I was concerned for him and whatever the call was about. Anamaria had said "urgent" when she originally told him, and by the look on his face in that office, it appeared it was.

"It's still about that same call." Anamaria confirmed my internal thoughts. "I don't know that he—"

She was interrupted by the intercom system on her desk, which suddenly had Ryan's voice coming out of it. "Send her in," he directed.

Anamaria looked completely shocked, and I was a little, too, especially when I could see he was still on his phone, but she silently waved her hand for me to go into Ryan's office. I picked up my guitar case and purse, did a half-smile at her, opened Ryan's door, and walked in. He motioned for me to shut the door behind me.

As I sat down, Ryan was pacing while speaking into the phone. "My biggest concern right now is the kids. They can't find out." My eyes furrowed in apprehension as Ryan tried a non-convincing smile at me and continued to talk with whoever was on the other line. "I know. I know the school or daycare won't—" As he continued, I wondered if it was actually his ex he was talking to. "I'll call and make sure—" He seemed to either keep losing his thought or was cut off by the other person. "I'm going to pick them up. ... . Yeah. All right. I mean, it's all right. I need to talk with her." He listened and replied again. "I know. I know. Okay." He looked at me. His smile was not any more convincing at all. "Yeah, that, too. Hey, thanks." And with that, he hung up his phone and did the longest exhale I had ever heard from him.

I wanted to stand up and go to him. I knew there was something wrong, and it wasn't just in his words. It was in his mannerisms—the way he jittered instead of standing still and the way his eyes seemed to be zipping all over the room. But I couldn't. Dang it. Not in an office with a glass door. The energy between us was on a different level than when he had dropped me off in his car that Tuesday, but it was definitely strong and palpable.

Ryan walked past me and opened his door. "Everyone gone?" he called out to his secretary.

"Yeah, Ryan," she answered.

"Go. Go home." He was direct but kind.

"I'll stay. There's tons of calls coming in, and I can—"

"No. That's exactly … You haven't been saying anything, have you?"

I couldn't help but turn then so I could actually see Ryan's face. What was wrong? What was happening? He didn't seem angry … just concerned and worn.

"No. Of course not," she denied. "I don't *know* anything. Can you tell me? What happened? The news—"

"I'm still trying to put the pieces together." He was the one who spoke, but it exactly mimicked my internal thoughts.

"Is she all right? She's all right, isn't she?" Anamaria asked about whom I could only assume at that point was Kari.

When Anamaria's phone rang, Ryan insisted, "Leave it. We don't have a comment. Go home. It's … everything is fine."

I didn't believe him, and I'm pretty sure Anamaria didn't either by the way she seemed to freeze and then look at me and back to him. "You're sure?"

Ryan, I guess, had enough. He went out to Anamaria's desk and started handing her the light blazer draped on the back of her chair. "It's Friday. You know we clear out early. You should have been gone already. Go. Have a good weekend."

She grabbed her purse from the bottom drawer. "Call if—"

"Of course," he concluded. "Thanks, Ana. I mean it." And then he started to walk her toward the elevator bank.

When he reentered his office, he still shut the door behind him. Whatever was going on was serious. I finally at least felt all right standing up to meet him.

"What happened?" My voice trembled a little.

"You sounded good. I think I liked what you were doing with 'Pack Tomorrow.'"

"Ryan!" I exclaimed. I didn't want to talk about the new version of the song we had written together, even though it was his talent I had been channeling when making the changes. I wanted to know what was going on.

"Kari was attacked." He sounded defeated.

"What?" My voice jumped an octave.

He blew out another gust of air and spoke remarkably plainly. "After her concert. There was some afterparty thing. Some crazy fan."

"Attacked?" I questioned. "Like what? What does that mean? Is she all right?"

"Hit and pushed … fell. There was a hustle."

"Oh, man."

"I … I guess she's okay, but I haven't been able to talk with her. They're saying she's at the hospital." His pause I think was only because he probably had a million things on his mind. "I need to make sure the kids are sheltered from it. I don't want them to hear about it from the press and be scared." Of course that was his top concern, as it should have been.

"Is there anything I can do?" I offered.

"Just be here. Okay?" He tilted his head slightly and gave me a sad little smile.

"Ryan …"

I could tell he was trying to be brave or hold back or something, and I hoped it wasn't for my benefit. If it was initially, it didn't last. He pulled me into his strong, all-encompassing embrace.

"Geez. Man." He exhaled behind my back, holding on tight. Then after a moment, when the power of my hug hopefully helped, he brought me away, just to arm's length. "Looks like we have the place to ourselves like you wanted before." His smile was a little more legitimate that time.

"That was *not* what I wanted." I did an airy laugh. "But had I known, it would have worked out just fine." I tried a reassuring smile for him because, even though we had a sentence or two of lightheartedness, I knew there were heavy things on his mind.

And his next words proved it. "I've got to pick up the kids, and I'm sure there's going to be a lot more calls. I wanted to spend some time with you," he partially pouted.

"We still can if you want to. How about if I order some dinner and meet you at your place?" I suggested.

"You sure? Cause I'd love that."

"Yeah. So … what? Thai? Mexican? Chinese? Italian?"

"It doesn't matter."

"What do you think the kids would want?"

"Up to you. What—"

"Just tell me. Your choice."

"Oh no, we're not playing the your-choice game again."

I let out a light laugh. I hadn't even realized we were starting similar dialogue. "I kinda like how that game ended, though." I wrinkled my nose in jest while thinking of his body savoring mine on his family room sofa.

"Me, too." He smiled back with a glint in his eyes. "All right, listen, there's a burger and fries place or a deli with salads and sandwiches. They are both in the same complex. I can drop you off, get the kids, and pick you back up."

That was not making it easier on him, which is what I intended the offer to be about in the first place. "That's a lot of juggling around. I'll just meet you at the house."

He stuck his pointer finger up to my lips. "Shush. Judge Ryan has made a decision on transportation." He did a quick smile and continued, "As long as either are safe for you, which eatery will it be?"

Glad he was still attempting to bring some levity to the situation, I offered some of my own. "Let's flip a coin."

"It's always different with you." He shook his head. "People still flip coins? Do you even have a coin?"

"Yeah, probably in my purse. Don't you, money bags?"

He *tsked* at my impulsive nickname and said, "Hold on." Walking over to his desk drawer, he pulled out a quarter. "Heads greasy, tails healthy."

"Sure."

He was ready to flip when he squinted one eye at me and said, "No best out of three or other variation. Whenever I lift my hand, that's what it is … not flipping it over after."

"Okay!" I legitimately laughed. "Your siblings kept changing the rules on you?"

"Just making sure all the negotiations are in order." He smiled. "By the way, thanks for not breaking our no-hugging contract."

"I thought you might have seen that."

"Oh, I did. And I was going to shatter some glass busting through that door had you not stuck your arm out." He flipped the coin. "Heads, it is."

***

Along with the burgers and fries, I bought a pie at the adjoining bakery for dessert. The kids and I enjoyed everything, but Ryan didn't have the time to truly appreciate the food. He was on his phone for most of the evening.

"I'm gonna go," I said after another one of his calls.

The kids were already asleep. And after a full day of a

brand-new recording experience followed by the jolt of Kari's news, I was growing tired, too. Besides, I knew I wasn't much help to Ryan at that point. All he was doing was confirming or denying aspects of the incident to the media and other sources.

"I'm sorry," Ryan offered legitimately.

"You don't have to be," I replied in the same tone. "I'm glad Kari's all right and that you got to talk with her."

And I meant it. Kari, after all, wasn't giving us any grief. I certainly didn't mean her any ill will.

"There's just so much." He semi-grunted.

"I get it. I'm gonna go home. I need some sleep."

"Go upstairs," he stated, as if I had missed the obvious.

"Tired," I punctuated the word to reiterate what my intentions in a bed were.

"I know." He managed a chuckle and admitted, "So am I."

It was *my* phone ringing that interrupted us that time. I was a little shocked, especially since it was getting to be fairly late in the evening. Seeing Willow's name on the screen, though, I accepted my next-door neighbor's call.

"What's up, nextie?"

"Hey, Bethany. Exactly that," she answered back. "I need you to do me a favor."

"Okay. Sure, if I can."

"Could you check to make sure my door is locked? You know how I am, running around last minute. Can't remember if I locked it." She laughed at herself.

And I laughed, too. That was so Willow. She led a very active life … in and out all the time. It was amazing we ever formed a friendship since our schedules conflicted a lot.

"I'm sure it's fine," I reassured, knowing I couldn't possibly do as my friend requested.

"Yeah, but make sure, okay?" she asked again.

"I …" Oh, boy. "I can't."

"What? Why?" I thought her two little question words

sounded a little leading, but maybe that was my paranoia.

"Because I'm not there," I admitted.

"Yes!" she screeched, nearly making me jump. "I know. Because *I* am. Where are you? I'm not being all mother hen or anything, but where are you?"

"Willow!" Dang it, I should have known she wouldn't have really cared if her door was locked or not—she was pretty easygoing. I had walked right into her little trap. "Geez. I'm out … celebrating the recording."

Ryan, who was leaning against the fireplace and looking at something on his phone, shifted his eyes at me. I shrugged my shoulders. There was some truth to what I told Willow, right?

"Yeah, yeah." She sounded excited. "That's why I've been dying to talk with you. How did it go? What did Mr. Mean think?"

My look at Ryan possessed a little bit of guilt … as if he could hear the nickname Willow called him. She was so far off the mark. Those blue eyes zoned in on me again, and I tried a smile.

"It went well, and he wasn't there." But as I said it, "he" was coming to sit right next to me on the sofa.

"I heard his wife was attacked or something in Europe. It wasn't much more than a headline. The article didn't say a lot."

"Yeah, I know." I touched Ryan's hand.

"They make a striking couple." Before I could regurgitate something from my mouth as my stomach wanted to do, she continued, "Where are you? It's so quiet. Doesn't sound like a celebration. And why wasn't I invited?"

"Sorry. Last minute." When she didn't say anything, I felt bad for not inviting her to my fake party since she was the only person, besides my immediate family, who even knew of the recording. I forged forward with the tale that was getting more and more made up as I went along. "It's just a couple of us at a friend's house … from work. I'm probably going to stay over." I did work with Ryan, but I knew Willow wasn't going to think that.

"Oh," she said simply. "What's her name? Gracie? She's the gay one, right?" Willow asked about the manager of the coffee shop.

"Yeah, that's her name, but, Willow, geez, that's not very politically correct."

"Sorry. I didn't mean to offend her or ..." Her pause seemed to have the inflection of realization. "You ..."

"Not me," I tried to clarify, but I could see how she might think that with the vague information I had been giving her recently.

"Then, geez, Bethany, what is up with you?" Her exasperation was very evident.

There wasn't a way for me to alleviate it right then, though. "I'm sorry, but I got to go. Okay? I'm sorry."

"Yeah, okay. Whatever." She hung up before an official good-bye.

"Well ..." I turned to Ryan and laid down my phone. "I just went from offending my best friend by not inviting her to a fictitious party to her thinking I'm gay."

"What?" His eyelids narrowed.

"Yeah."

"Would it help if I told you I don't think you're gay ... at all?" He managed to get a light laugh from me as he rubbed his hand along the side of my shirt-covered breast.

"I think you would be right, and it absolutely works to your advantage."

"Indeed, it does." He kissed me softly on the lips and then looked at his buzzing phone.

"She also thinks you and Kari make a striking couple." I just couldn't let that one go.

His shoulders sagged. "I'm sorry you're being put in this position, Bethany. I know you hate it, and I don't want to make you lie."

"You are worth silence and a little twisting of words, Ry." I also knew my friendship with Willow could withstand a frustrated, confused phone call.

He slowly closed and opened his eyes, indicating his appreciation. "I'm glad you came here tonight. Looking over and seeing you? It helped me."

"You're welcome." I touched his smooth cheek with my hand before kissing him.

"Come on." He patted my leg, grabbed my hand, and stood both of us up. "Screw the rest of these calls. I'm not her press manager. All I need to know is that she is safe, the kids are good, and you are sleeping beside me tonight."

And that's what we did. He changed into a pair of sweats and then gave me one of his tank tops so I could curl into him in only that and my undies. His arm never felt more secure and his gentle kiss good night never more thankful. And shortly after, when I heard his breathing turn to the low whistle I had come to know as Ryan's sleeping, I knew we both had found the perfect ending to our twisted day.

CHAPTER TEN

I was walking around Ryan's custom game room and only peeking every so often at the music manager himself. My feelings were similar to when I received that initial tweet from him and when I had anxiously awaited his thoughts during our first meeting. Ryan and I had evolved a lot since then, but because of that, I valued his opinion even more. I wanted to do right by him. That's why listening to the recording of my demo that Monday evening was like minor torture. To me, that was. Ryan seemed perfectly content sitting and tapping his foot while I paced.

"What are you doing?" His eyebrows intersected while looking at me from across the room. "Come here. Come over here." When I scrunched my nose and shook my head slightly, he lightly admonished me. "Bethany ..." And when I still didn't move in his direction, he got up and playfully attacked my sides before lifting and guiding me to the carpeted floor.

Laughter helped release some of the nervous, anticipatory energy from my body. With him smiling and planked above me, I said, "I see those wrestling skills come in handy."

He pecked me a couple of times on the lips before saying, "If I'd had such beautiful opponents in high school, I probably would have kept up with it."

"Flatterer ... and I think the injuries might have had something to do with that."

"Way to ruin a compliment." He *tsked*. "The songs are good, Lenay. They sound good." He emphasized the last word, tucked some of my loose hair behind my ear, and brought his chest up so he was kneeling in between my legs.

"I think you might be biased at this point."

"Yeah, you're right." I was a little impressed he admitted it until he immediately followed through with, "You mean because I basically wrote them, right?"

Rising, I gave him a swift but light push on his chest. "That wasn't what I meant," I denied with a quick laugh.

He laughed, too. "I might be a bit biased, but they are good. I can't wait to pitch them."

"Mmmm-hmmm." I was still trying to comprehend artists listening to my songs, nonetheless, potentially making them theirs.

I didn't realize my nose had scrunched again until Ryan brought his finger to touch it. "Stop it." He leaned down again to kiss me.

"Joe-Joe, incoming!" I heard the little boy declare before pouncing on his father's back and, with the domino effect, consequently me.

My laughter was much more legit that time. And Ryan's smile was enormous as he pulled his son in between the two of us and peppered him with pokes to his little belly. Suddenly, I didn't care if he was biased if it meant such pure happiness.

***

Despite his reassuring that everything was all right, I couldn't help but feel a little apprehensive while sitting in the cemetery just a few blocks from my apartment. Ryan had texted about forty minutes earlier asking if I could meet him there. While we were solidly in that stage of finding an excuse to text or call one another every day, because of schedules and obligations, we didn't actually see each other at the same frequency. And the last-minute request to meet was surely perplexing, especially since we had planned on me coming over to his place for dinner later that night.

"Hi." His deep voice sounded smooth as he sat on the wood bench next to me.

Ryan was visually scanning the surroundings. I knew it was because he wanted to make sure there weren't any onlookers, gossipers, or, worse yet, press. But we had decided on the cemetery for just that reason. The potential was slim. Although public, it was also secluded and not terribly popular, especially on a Wednesday afternoon. Still, he refrained from sitting too close to me. And I had to resist touching him, even though the strong invisible magnetism was certainly pulling me that way.

"Hi," I echoed with a sigh. "What's with meeting up?" I asked, trying to get my mind off my secret life. "The location isn't foretelling, is it?"

"I hope not," he answered. "There's good news and bad news. What do you want first?"

"Oh, geez. I knew it." I took in a deep breath—of course there had to be bad news.

"Bethany, good or bad first? I'm gonna tell you both."

"Flip on it," I suggested.

"I figured." He shook his head and produced a coin.

"You have a quarter?"

"It's *our* quarter, and I decided to keep it in my wallet just for you—just in case you can't make a decision and go all old-school with determining an outcome." My belly rolled in silent laughter as he named the sides. "Heads good news, tails bad news?"

"Sure."

"Tails," he announced after the flip and reveal.

"Typical."

His mouth curled on one side and he blinked his eyes at my negativity before saying, "I have to cancel on tonight." His lips turned downward.

"Yeah? Why? What's up with tonight?"

"One of my clients is performing downtown in *Charlie and the Chocolate Factory*. He got orchestra seats for me and the kids. They'll go nuts. I couldn't pass them up."

"You should totally go," I agreed and offered an alternative to my plans in the hope he wouldn't feel bad for bailing. "Willow was gone with Til all weekend, and we've only seen each other in passing the past couple of days. So, it will be good to have dinner with her tonight and maybe, you know, clarify some things … without, of course, being specific."

"Yeah, sounds crystal clear." He laughed.

"It'll be fine." I knew Willow felt left out more than anything, and simply spending the time with her to reinforce our friendship was what was most important.

"So, here's the thing …" he started.

"What?" My body automatically tensed. "What thing? I thought you already told me the bad news."

"I did," he said in that exasperating yet calming tone of his. "Why does the thing have to be bad?"

"I don't know," I admitted. "The first time you pulled that on me, you were jerking me around with not being able to take on any more musicians."

"What?" But before I could explain, he remembered. "Yeah, that was kind of funny."

"It was not, Ryan!"

"Okay," he soothed but still had a last chuckle in him. "Listen, I'm not messing with you. Here. This is for you." Out of his wallet, he pulled out a small piece of plastic that resembled a credit card and handed it to me.

It wasn't a credit card, though. It wasn't a gift card or membership card or discount card of any type, either. Very non-descript, it had me completely confused.

"It's a key card," he stated as I twirled it around in my hand. "There is a separate entrance to my neighborhood off of Heritage … instead of Harlan where the main gate is."

"Oh, I didn't know that."

"Yeah, I know. It's not as convenient, but it's only for residents. Everyone else has to go through the main gate with friendly Mr. Dak."

With his chin nodding upward toward me, I knew the adjective he used to describe the man had at least some hints of sarcasm. I would have never mentioned anything to Ryan about the main daytime guard at the entrance of his exclusive neighborhood, but he was a character. Serious and nosy were definitely two words I would use instantly. He reminded me of a hard-as-nails cop the way he questioned time and time again in his monotone voice if I was on the list for entrance.

"He knows it all," Ryan continued. "Sometimes too much."

"Hmmm." The sound brushed against my lips as I revisited Ryan's words and started connecting them to the card in my hand.

"There's no one at the gate on Heritage. You slide the card and the gate opens and allows you in. You don't have to bother anyone … until the doorbell, and then it's me." He gave a small smile at the end of his explanation.

"Hmmm," I said again, and I knew it was even more downtrodden that time.

"What?" he questioned. "What's wrong? That was supposed to be the good news."

"Oh."

"What?" He leaned ever so slightly in my direction.

I wanted real good news. Not something that was another coverup for my personal situation with Ryan. I guess I understood how he thought of it as good, though. We wouldn't have to put up with any questions—at least from a strict guard. I accepted that's how life was for the time being. But it wasn't good news.

"I know." I started to voice my thoughts. "I'm not supposed to be seen. We shouldn't even be sitting here. I know. I understand. I—"

"Crap, no," he interrupted me. "That's not the reason I'm giving it to you. Dang it. I ..." He started to trail his hand toward me but then pulled it away, and I saw the agonizing regret stretch across his face as he did. "Bethany, no one else, besides Kari, her parents, and I have gate access. It's exactly the opposite of what you're thinking. Even though we can't tell anyone yet—yet, Lenay—it was meant to show you that you are an important part of my life. I don't want you to feel awkward coming to my place or that someone needs to validate your presence. They don't. I want you there. That's what I meant by giving it to you."

"Oh." I was processing his words ... and liking and appreciating them more as I did. "Sorta like upstairs ... not the guest room." I offered up an analogy.

"Yeah." He seemed to breathe easier. "Yeah, like that," he continued as we both spotted a young man in a low riding baseball cap putting flowers on a nearby grave. "I know it's not much, but—"

It was to me. "Thank you." I could feel the warmth in my heart escape in the form of a soft smile on my face.

"You're welcome." His lips pursed out a breath and, thankfully, before I thought anymore about kissing them, he said, "So, what do you think about Friday? Try the card out on Friday? Are you free? Fridays are better than midweek, anyway. There won't be school or work the next morning. We can have a game night with the kids if you want ... dinner ... you can stay ..." He smiled legitimately that time.

"Yeah," I agreed while mentally going over my work schedule. "I ... yeah. I work, but Friday evening is free."

"Great. Next up, by the way?" He poked me quickly on

my arm. "Getting you a car."

"Next up?" I smirked back at him, glad to feel like we were legitimately us for the first time that afternoon. "Getting a song sold."

"It'll happen," he said confidently.

"I'm getting a silver Audi convertible," I proclaimed.

"An Audi convertible." He rolled his eyes. "Oh, brother."

"Or a VW bus. I can't decide."

I thought he would chuckle, but he just had that same look as when he first sat down next to me on the bench. And then there was his groan—that Ryan Thompson groan. "I should have probably just called you and given you the card later. I was being selfish wanting to see you, and now I can't kiss you … and I have to leave. This was harder."

"But worth it."

"Uh-huh." And, after a deep breath, he slowly stood up, did one backward glance, and walked away.

I was going to sit for a moment, not only to allow space between his departure and mine but to gather my thoughts for a potential song that seemed to suddenly be singing inside my head. I didn't get too far into the process, though, since the grieving fellow with the ballcap was suddenly in front of me. It was only when he said my name that I looked up.

"Andre," I partially whispered.

He sat without asking for permission. Not that it was mine to give. But still.

"How are you?" I asked the former apartment employee and basement voyeur. Having been caught by surprise, I didn't know what else to say.

"You're doing him, huh?"

"What?" It wasn't that I hadn't heard him. It was that I was appalled by the crude comment and wanted a second to collect my thoughts.

"Couldn't hear the words, but it was pretty obvious,

Bethany."

"Geez, no it wasn't … Andre." I clipped my words.

"Smart suit, clean do … Where'd you meet him? Not in a laundry room, I take it." He smirked.

Andre wasn't acting at all like the carefree charmer I had known. The one who had sat next to a drunk me late at night in the laundry room and said I was special and that everyone was going to miss me when I left, especially him. The one who had convinced me that we both needed to release our emotions through our obvious physical attraction. The combination of drinking too much, not having had sex since college, and knowing if the city of dreams didn't want me but a built man in a basement did, had made me climb onto the recliner in the adjacent caged storage area and grasp onto the momentary pleasure of him pumping repeatedly into me.

The Andre next to me on the cemetery bench could have never convinced me. He was harder … colder. He seemed more like his family members I had recently found out about. I knew it couldn't have been easy with the allegations and things he was going through. At the same account, though, he needn't take it out on me.

Before I could reply, he continued, "I feel like I know him … seen him somewhere. Yeah?"

"No," I instantly denied. "I don't think so." I shifted on the bench.

"I just can't picture—" He stopped dead in his verbal tracks, and my dry mouth tried to gulp down the fear of recognition. "Oh. He looks just like this guy at the gym I go—used to—go to. He's not, though. I think the gym guy's hair is lighter. So, who is he, Bethany?"

"Just a friend. Friend of a friend kind of thing." The lies kept coming.

Gosh, my parents would be so disappointed in me. Was this what the life of a mistress was like? Was it how I had to roll … in secrets and lies?

"Hmmm," he said in a way that I knew I hadn't

persuaded him even one little bit. "You get into doing it around corpses?"

"What?" I practically screeched. "I told you, we're not—" Ugh! I didn't want to defend myself or talk about sex or Ryan anymore. "What are you doing here?"

Revealing his tight dark curls, he took off his cap and used it to point toward a grave. "My aunt."

I couldn't help but soften a little. *There* was the glimmer of the Andre I had known before. "Sorry. I heard about her passing, and I know she must have meant a lot to you."

"She was a good one," he lamented.

"Sorry," I repeated. "Hope things are getting better for you."

"Barely. I don't know how I am going to keep making it with a minimum wage job. I need to find a way to make more money." Before I could agree that we all would like that, he spoke again. "You are one I won't ever forget." He rubbed his hand on my thigh. "If I wasn't already late for work, I'd find a cozy little storage area near a laundromat with you."

I closed my eyes momentarily at the sickening thought and stood up. "That's not gonna happen."

He joined me and, after surveying my chest with his eyes, said, "Hope this guy—whoever he is …" His eyebrows crumpled as he paused as if in contemplation. "Well, I hope he's worthy." And then he walked away.

I breathed. I breathed again. I breathed once more.

After another beat, where the world seemed to finally come back into focus, I considered my options. I had wanted to stay for a little while and play with those lyrics in my head, but the encounter with Andre had muddied them and, for some reason, had shaken me. I wanted to let the conversation with the former housing employee go. I knew I could do it in a roundabout way with any of the women in the house … a "guess who I just saw" sort of thing. But who I really wanted to talk with was Ryan, so I picked up my phone and dialed.

"I'm right here." Ryan's voice pierced my thoughts after the first ring.

But it wasn't coming from his phone. It was his authentic voice, and he was standing right in front of me when I turned around. Scanning his face, I noticed his jawline seemed tight ... so much more strained than only moments before when he was sitting with me.

"Hey, you didn't leave?" I questioned, pressing end on my phone.

"No. I sat down on another bench before I got to the car and was checking messages when I saw ... I'm trying hard not to jump to conclusions like I did with your medicine."

"What?" I was a little thrown. "What? Why?"

"Bethany, you have to realize what happened with Kari burned me a little."

"Uh." It was more of a breath than an actual word as I took in his statement and realized that he must have seen me sitting with Andre. "Oh. Okay," I empathized. "Listen, what you saw? It wasn't what you think it was. So, no ... no jumping to conclusions. I was obviously calling to tell you." I shuddered. "I didn't know it was him until he sat down."

"Him? Him who? Who was that? He seemed friendly," he tagged on at the end ... the surely jumping to conclusions part of Ryan Thompson.

"Andre."

"Andre? Andr—" He stopped himself. "As in 'the bastard?'" Ryan knew everything about my regretful night before him—I had not only told him Andre's name and what had led to my poor choice but why the sweet-talking tramp of a man was crowned with the name "bastard." When I nodded in agreement, he asked, "Are you all right?"

I loved that those were the next words out of his mouth. I knew he had immediately stripped any doubt from his brain about what he had seen and that his concern for me took front and center. "Truthfully? No," I admitted.

Ryan's eyes instantly flinched, and he did the slightest of head nods toward me. "Bethany …"

When he started to look around, I echoed what was surely transmitting in his mind. "I need to tell you what he said, but we can't do it here."

"All right. Let's go to my car." He started to turn.

But I didn't move. "I … I don't think we should. I'm afraid he might still be lurking."

"What?" I had his full, worried attention again.

"It's okay. He's not going to hurt me or anything. We can't be seen together, though. He already has suspicions."

"About?"

"Us … who you are." I felt like I was leaving Ryan down. "Let me get back to the privacy of my place. It will take five minutes. Then I'll call and tell you."

"You sure?"

"Yeah."

"You know how much I want to hold you right now?"

"You know how much I want you to?" I knew the tear was coming. So I tried inconspicuously to swipe it away.

But I must not have done a good enough job. "Dang it." His arms tensed at his sides, as if he was trying to resist bringing them out to me.

"Five minutes. I'll call you," I confirmed, and then *I* was the one to turn and walk away.

***

"So, what I'm hearing right now is all pretty much good."

I turned from the open window and practically yelled into the phone. "What? How can you say that?"

"He doesn't know who I am," Ryan said in a calmer voice than mine, and I imagined him still sitting in the cemetery since I knew the phone conversation was not going through the tinny sound of his car speakers.

"He hasn't put it together, no. It just worries me."

"Bethany, the only thing that worries me is how he thought he could put his hand on—"

"I know." I cut him off for his own good. "But if you were watching, I stood up to stop him, and then he left."

"I guess I was a little too preoccupied with the actual touch to take that part in."

"Well, that's what happened. I denied everything, but he could tell it wasn't the truth." Especially the way I felt about the man on the other end of the line.

"I'm sorry I've put you in this position ... you have to lie about us."

"You don't need to keep saying that. It's my choice."

"I—" he started.

But I stopped him, knowing we had to get back to us— a teasing, easygoing humor. "But when *is* Kari coming back to the states?"

He breathed out with what I determined was a cleansing breath. "Soon. She's coming Saturday to get the kids. And then it shouldn't be much longer until everything is out."

"Good."

"Sorry for almost jumping to conclusions. Hopefully, I'm not earning a bastard nickname for that."

I legitimately laughed. "No, that's not the name."

"Wha ... what? You have a nickname for me?"

"Uh ..." I debated.

"Lenay ...?"

"It's Willow's, not mine."

"What is it?"

"Uh ..."

"Come on, tell me," he prompted.

"Mr. Mean."

"Mr. Mean?"

I laughed at his shock. "Just because of how you

treated me on the show. She doesn't know anything else—the real you or about us. So …"

"Mr. Mean." He seemed to *hmmmf.* "Well, it could be worse, and it is kind of the role they have me playing now."

"You are *so* not Mr. Mean. Thanks for talking me through, Ryan."

"Back at ya. See you on Friday, then?" His voice softened even more, and I heard the car start and the phone change to his car speaker.

"Absolutely." I sat down at my desk. Maybe I could write, after all.

CHAPTER ELEVEN

I have to admit, I did feel a little more special—a little more as though I belonged—using the key card and going through the private gate of Ryan's exclusive neighborhood. Besides that, I was also in a good mood because it was the start of the weekend. That meant Kari was coming home, and pretty soon after we could stop the masquerade. My lighthearted feeling came to an abrupt halt, though, as I approached the opened front door of Ryan's house. The sound coming through its passage did not match my happy heart at all.

It was Ryan's uncommonly raised voice I heard first. "What are you talking about? No."

The second voice I didn't immediately recognize but, oddly, sounded familiar. "We can make it work."

I didn't want to interrupt or even dare enter, because, for one thing, it was a heated discussion. For another, I didn't have a legitimate reason for being at the residence. Of course, Ryan knew I was coming over, but I wasn't sure whomever he was talking with did. I took a few steps and craned my neck around to the side driveway. A sleek black convertible was parked in front of the garage with Ryan's BMW next to it. I couldn't tell the make of the second automobile because of its further away position, but I knew it rivaled the other cars that belonged in the high-end neighborhood.

"No. We've been done a long time now. What are you talking about?" Ryan's voice was incredulous. "We're divorced."

Those words made me peek inside. Sure enough, a few feet or so away was Ryan and his ex-wife. I would not have recognized Kari Thompson had I not heard the words coming from their mouths or been at the house. She was beautiful. There was no denying that. But she didn't look like the images that I, and most of the world, had seen— the polished platinum-blonde short bob, chiseled cheekbones, long lashes, and designer clothes. No. In contrast, her hair was more of a bland blonde, longer, and slightly unkempt. She had little makeup on and wore an oversized white sweatshirt and jeans.

"What did we talk about Easter night?" I refocused on Ryan's voice. "What was that whole conversation about? Setting up a time to announce the divorce. We are not a couple. You said you were happy. I'm happy. The—"

"So glad you're happy with little miss songstress. I can't believe you had the gall to message my people about her stuff—like I wouldn't put it together. I don't want her crap. I'm not going to sing anything she wrote."

That was news to me. I didn't know Ryan was shopping my songs to Kari's team. But, regardless, from what Ryan had told me about their amicable relationship, I didn't think she would come down so hard on my music or even us. I had been a firsthand witness to the Easter conversation, after all.

"Stop it, Kari. What's wrong with you?" His voice escalated even further. "Geez, I'm glad the kids aren't here." It was then when Ryan noticed me. "Bethany ..." He walked to the door and held out his hand.

But I didn't take it. It was weird enough emotionally being in the situation I was in. But to physically be in the middle of the three of us? It was terribly awkward, despite knowing I wasn't doing anything wrong.

"Uh, well, perfect timing. See?" Kari seemed downright spiteful as she scowled her eyes at me—not at all the woman I had been told she was.

"I'm sorry," I immediately apologized, still caught a little off guard. "I didn't realize you would be here." And I silently cursed Ryan for not giving me a heads-up that Kari was coming a day early.

"What kind of bitch moves in on someone else's man when she's down?"

"Whoa! Whoa! Whoa!" Ryan took a half-step toward Kari as his eyes seemingly grew bigger. "She ... What is wrong with you? What are you talking about 'down?' And I'm not your anything."

"I'll let you talk." I met Ryan's eyes more than his ex-wife's. "This is between the two of you."

"No. That's all right." He touched my hand before seething at his ex. "Kari ..." If I thought the whole situation was awkward for me, I couldn't even imagine what Ryan was feeling.

"What?"

I decided to be the bigger person. "I'm glad you're home. The kids will—"

"*My* kids," she emphasized, not letting me finish.

I left out a full chest of air I hadn't even realized I had been holding in. Ryan was worth fighting for, especially since I knew he was fighting for me. But, for sure, I knew at that moment my presence was not helping. Sticking around was only going to set up a scene like one on *Jerry Springer.*

I couldn't escape completely, though, because of the obvious transportation dilemma. So, I hastily made a temporary escape plan. "I'll be ... upstairs." I decided on my destination.

I heard Kari *hmmmf* as I readjusted my tote bag on my shoulder and started toward the staircase. I wondered if her reaction was just a sense of superiority or if it was because, without realizing it, I had chosen to retreat to the room they had once shared. I could have gone to the back yard or a remote part of the house, but I hadn't. Maybe I was claiming my own stake.

Once in the room, I shut the door, placed my quilted bag on the floor, and flung myself onto the bed. Their quite vocal conversation became muffled, and a part of me wanted to spy and hear the rest. After all, I had an invested interest. But the other part of me knew to respect their privacy as exes and as parents.

It wasn't much later when I heard the door shut and a car start. A little wash of relief flowed through my body. I was glad she was gone. I had been nervous about meeting her when I knew it was an inevitable situation—not only because she was a singer I admired, but mostly because she was Ryan's ex-wife … someone he, admittedly, had loved. But I thought I was going to have time to prepare myself. And I most certainly never expected such a tumultuous first scene.

Ryan entered the master bedroom with a most impressive exhale. "I'm sorry." His weary, worn-looking eyes found mine as I looked up at him.

"Did you know she was coming today?"

"No. Not at all. She was here when I pulled up … just a few minutes before you."

"She left, right?"

"Yeah. Thank goodness. She had no right saying anything she did."

I stood up to meet him then. I wanted to hold him. After hearing his commitment to us via his words, I wanted him to know I felt the same. I wrapped my arms around his torso, rested my head on his chest, and breathed in the light scent of his favorite cologne. His semi-relaxed sigh told me he appreciated the gesture.

"I never imagined her to be like that," I admitted after a minute or two. "In the media, she always comes across so wholesome … so mannered … so pure. I guess everything … everyone is fake or make-believe out here."

I felt Ryan's body tighten. I hadn't meant it in reference to him and our circumstances. But I guess, in a way, it fit.

"She was over the top. And we—our marriage—didn't last … and it wasn't nice at the end. But it was never like that. Maybe it was jet lag or something. She just flew in today, after all. That's why she was coming for the kids tomorrow."

"Did she say why she came today?" I pulled slightly away so we could look at each other more succinctly.

"No. She just wanted to see the kids. Bethany, I would have let her, but I'm telling you, she wasn't herself. What she was saying about her and I?" He cocked one eyebrow up as if he had heard the most ridiculous thing. "And then, especially when she went off on you … I made her stick to the agreement. She has to come back tomorrow to get them. She needs some sleep and to de-stress from the extended tour."

"Ryan?" I asked but didn't wait. "I think I better leave tomorrow or at least not make my presence known when she comes to get them. I don't want anything to upset the kids when they see their mom after so long."

"You don't have to." I know he was going to stop with that, but then he continued his response with objectivity, "You have a very kind heart, Bethany Lenay Opala."

"Well, you might not think so after what I say next."

"What?"

"I don't want her to have any of my songs."

There was the slightest of sighs before he said, "I understand. A couple of them would actually be perfect for her. I debated. But I would have never sent them if I didn't think she was on board with everything."

"You'll find someone else."

"I will. I promise."

"And you take your promises seriously." It was the first time I did a semi-smile since arriving.

"I do," he agreed, surely catching my reference.

I kissed him while resecuring my hands around his muscular back. "Mmmm." I rested my head on the softness of his ribbed, powder-blue pullover.

"It feels so good to have you in my arms. I hated not being able to even touch you at the cemetery."

"Daddy! Daddy, we're home!" Sallie's voice vibrated from the foyer that only moments before had been filled with such drama.

"Man, I'm glad they weren't here when Kari was, but Rebecca still could have driven a little slower getting back." He spoke of the neighbor he sometimes shared daycare carpooling duties with. "I wanted some more alone time with you." He looked out his front bedroom window, gave a wave to his neighbor, and then said to me, "All right. We got all night."

"Yeah. I'm looking forward to game night."

"Right hand yellow, left foot blue."

My lips rubbed together with air before I said, "Twister?"

"A classic."

"Ha! My father would have a fit."

"Why?"

"That, young man"—I deepened my voice in a pretend strict dad voice—"is a sex game."

"It's a what?" His belly rolled in amusement.

"Yep. We weren't allowed to play it growing up. Forbidden," I tacked on at the end, dramatically but truthfully.

"Hmmm …" Those deep blue eyes of his took on a mischievous, sexy gleam. "Maybe we'll save that game until right before bedtime. I think I am going to look at it completely differently now."

I smiled and poked him. "I'm so gonna win."

"Game on, Twister virgin."

***

"Perfect," I answered the phone.

"Yeah? Perfect what?" he replied.

It was Thursday … four days since I had seen him. And even though we talked on the phone, it wasn't the same. Especially after that past weekend when, because the kids were at Kari's, Ryan and I got to spend some true alone time together. It was like we were a real, albeit reclusive, couple.

"Timing. Willow just left to turn in one of her final school projects, and I was painting my toenails."

"Everything good with you two then?"

"Yeah. I told you, she knows something's up, but she's respecting my privacy." Although, I knew it wasn't going to stop my friend from trying to examine every one of my comments every which way. "I was thinking of doing some writing using one of our theme starters."

"Good. I want to have a follow-up if—when—there's interest in what I just sent."

Not wanting to get too hopeful or even slightly confident, I changed the subject. "What are *you* doing?"

"Besides talking with you, homework, and then we're gonna make brownies."

"So domestic, Mr. Thompson." I appreciated that he didn't shy away from the kitchen. It, for sure, wasn't a passion of his as it was for me, but he tried things for the kids and always helped me when I was food-creating.

"The Rice Krispies were okay. But you've never tasted brownies as good as the Thompson trios." On the end of his proclamation, I could hear the kids chanting their pride.

I laughed and made my request. "Can I have a couple?"

"Of course. I'll save you some." And then he added what I had hoped my question would lead to. "When am I going to see you next?"

"Up to you. I know your schedule is getting even crazier."

"Yeah." His sigh was quite audible. As the show neared closer to the live airdates, he was getting jammed with more and more things to do.

"Did you get anything clarified with Kari?"

"No." There was that sigh again. "She is gonna have the kids again this weekend while I go on that stupid show retreat. Maybe she'll be more apt to talk after that. She has been either combative or dismissive."

"Sorry," I replied to both the retreat and Kari facts.

"*I'm* sorry because going away means I am not gonna have a chance to talk to or see you. Monday, though. Does Monday work?"

"The day of the live premiere?" Monday was the last day I thought he would suggest.

"Yeah. I don't have to be there until late afternoon." He had already decided not to go into his office on Mondays and Tuesdays because doing the live shows those afternoons and evenings would just be too much. "I'd say Sunday night once I get back from the retreat bull, but I'm already gonna be getting the kids settled and ready for school again."

"I'm working Sunday night, anyway. What are you doing with the kids for the premiere?" I asked, knowing he had been undecided before.

"They're going," he said with a partial grunt. "They conned me into it. They think it's going to be fun. Kingston and Rebecca are bringing their kids and will watch Joel and Sallie, too. I told you I would get you a seat."

"No. I don't think it's a good idea," I reiterated my previous decision to Ryan. I didn't think it would look good, even though we had a legitimate working relationship. "Besides, I have that consolation-prize pass for one live show."

"They didn't give it as a consolation prize." I could hear the grumble in his words.

"What else would you call 'You're not good enough for

the first round, but come and see the ones who are at a later date'? No, thanks."

"Okay, I see your point. *I* didn't mean it as a consolation prize."

"I know," I replied much softer.

"When did kindergarten get so hard, by the way? When did kids even have homework in kindergarten? Ugh."

I couldn't help but laugh at his classic dad statement. "You got this."

"So, are we good for Monday? Can you make it work?"

"I'm gonna call right now and ask for a shift change, okay?"

"Perfect. Good night, Lenay." I swear I could see the smile on his face, although we weren't on any type of video chat.

"Good night, Ryan."

***

Even though I missed spending any of the weekend with Ryan, it was a great couple of days doing other things. After work on Saturday, I joined some of the ladies from the apartment building in the upstairs lounge. Every other Saturday, a few of them organized a movie and craft night. Willow called it the lonely-hearts club and never went. I hadn't attended in a while and didn't regularly, but it felt good to wear sweats and make a spring wreath—the perfect optimistic object to cheer up my door.

Since I didn't have to work on Sunday, I got to spend some quality time video chatting with my family. It was still early in California, but timing the call to Carolina on a Sunday had to be done with precision. The magical window was after they arrived home from church but before they all split to do their individual things. For my mom, that meant cooking the traditional big Sunday dinner. My dad would be going over any information he received during the service and categorizing his week.

Fifteen-year-old Garrett, for sure, would be involved in something tech-related. And Ella should be studying but would mix in some basketball in the driveway, too. I still knew them spot-on, despite living so far away. It was a good thing, but it also made me miss them possibly even more.

When Ryan greeted me at his house on Monday, I was set to tell him about the lyrics I had written the night before. But instead, my mouth gaped open and I said, "Oh, geez, the beard."

Both of Ryan's eyebrows went up as he repeated one of my original sassy comments to him. "Kept tugging at it." It had been just over a week since I had seen him, and while he didn't have a full beard, it was definitely beyond scruff and more than I had seen him with since our first meeting at his office.

Still standing in his foyer, I shook my head. "Hmmm."

"You are gonna kiss me, right? Tell me because I will go and take a kitchen knife to it if I have to."

His comment changed my stunned demeanor to laughter, partially because I think he was serious. "Save the culinary cutlery," I offered. "I was just taking in the new landscape."

I reached out my right hand, touched his cheek, and then tipped up just a tad to meet my lips with his. I had never kissed someone with facial hair. It was different but not as gristly as I imagined. And it was actually me that time who let out a desired groan.

On that action and sound, Ryan tugged me tight into his body and kissed me with more precision—the way we were used to. He then pulled me away and gave me the look that asked for my verdict. I didn't raise a number card or send him away. I just smiled.

No words were needed as our bodies instantly knew what the other's wanted. We didn't even make it up the stairs. We found the family room, instead, and repeatedly twisted and turned in unison in a much naughtier way than when we had played Twister in that same room.

***

"Dang, Lenay." Sitting in his car, Ryan looked over at me in the middle of Los Angeles traffic. "I don't know if this makes me sound like a caveman or what, but I needed today just exactly as it was. Sor—"

I smiled at his sexy thoughts, recalling our morning tryst. "You don't hear me complaining, do you?"

Between him dealing with Kari and nerves about the show, and me, yes, trying to fight off jealousy of his ex, I knew we both needed that incredibly sexy morning. Being with Ryan was so much different than any encounter with men I had in the past. Feeling cherished and free and safe, I trusted my body to his and realized the difference between those words that are often used interchangeably—sex and making love.

When he had said he would drop me off at the coffee house since it was on the way to the studio, I hadn't argued. Admittedly, I wanted to spend every last second with him I could, especially since his schedule was ramped up and we were still a couple incognito. I couldn't wait for things to get settled with the live premiere and for Kari's team to figure out when to make the "shocking" announcement.

I looked at his hands on the steering wheel. His wedding band glistened in the sun. I appreciated that he took it off when at home and that I didn't see it too often. Because even though I knew it was a very false symbol, it still made me feel a little dirty.

I purposefully shook my head, trying to erase that thought from our otherwise beautiful morning. "Not sure about the beard, though," I offered, only half-joking.

"Me, either. I actually prefer not," he admitted. "I never had one until …" He paused, glanced over at me, and then said, "I never had one until things started falling apart, and then it was, honestly, because I got depressed and lazy."

"'Under the Bridge'?"

He nodded, but really no words were needed. We both had our low points. But being in his car with him that sunny afternoon most certainly was not one of them.

"Then, I told you, I started to get recognized, so it had to go."

"Why now then?" I asked.

"The show wants it. It is my"—he momentarily removed his hands from the wheel and put up hand air quotes—"trademark. So ... honestly, no, huh? You don't like it."

"It's not physical. It's mental." He gave me a queried look, so I went on to explain. "Physically, it makes you look in charge and highlights those magnificent looking eyes." On his partially bashful smile, I said, "Truth." But then I said the next part. "Mentally, though, it reminds me of the guy who rejected me."

"Bethany ..." His shoulders sagged on my name. "Oh, geez."

I tried to lighten the instant downer and poked him teasingly in the arm. "But you certainly didn't reject me earlier."

He ignored my tease by remaining his caring self. "I have to keep it, though. You understand, right?"

"Yeah, I guess." I did, and I wouldn't hold it against him.

"Dang it, we're here and there are people." He noted the coffee shop parking lot that I hadn't even realized we were at already. "I can't even—"

I went straight for the car door handle. I knew the reality of the situation. I knew his sentence was going to end with "kiss you" or "touch you." And I didn't want to hear it. I wanted to end on a good, positive note. So, it had to happen quickly.

"Have fun tonight," I offered my encouragement and

made my way to the shop.

***

Even though it had been my choice to depart as I did, I didn't want that to be our official good-bye until I talked with him after the show. So, I waited until I knew he should be at his destination. I did not want him distracted while driving.

I can still smell you, I texted from the back room of the shop.

It was only about a minute later when he replied with a wink emoji, *U should have showered w/me.*

Since his answer was impressively sexy, especially considering there had to be hundreds of people swarming the studio, I continued, *I had to make coffee—strong, sweet coffee & then blow it since it was so hot.*

LOL. I nearly just spilled mine.

I laughed, picturing the image of him with his travel mug of coffee I made him in his kitchen. *Sorry. Not sorry.*

Preacher's daughter. SMH.

I laughed again but knew I had to draw our sexting to a close since both of us had to work. *Ha! Ha! Can't wait to watch the show. You'll do great.*

Thx :)

***

"Willow …" I wanted to scream, but it came out as a raspy whisper. "Willow …"

"Sheez, Bethany, what? Be quiet. I want to hear the singer and see what Mr. Mean says. He should get a negative—"

"Willow …" I couldn't focus on *Singer Spotlight* or anything on the television. I couldn't focus at all. "I don't feel good. My mouth is tingly, and I'm a little light—"

"What? Did you bring Brownie Marys? I'm not feeling

that at all. Although, they are delicious. Where did you say you got them?"

At that moment I was especially glad we were watching the show in the privacy of my room and not in the lounge with a lot of other women. I knew I shouldn't be embarrassed. It's not my fault. It's a medical thing. But …

"Call 9-1-1 and my … purse …" I managed. "I need my purse."

CHAPTER TWELVE

I shifted in my seat, checked the large analog clock on the wall, and sighed at my ringing phone. I cleared my throat and answered, trying to sound as normal as I could. "Hey. How did it go?"

"You're watching, right?" His voice came across the line.

"Uh, yeah, no … change of plans."

Ryan didn't catch my hesitation. He instead threw himself under the proverbial bus with his question. "There's something better to do than watch me make a fool out of myself on national television?"

"The tripping part?" I countered. "Yeah, Ryan, you need to work on the art of an entrance."

I had, indeed, grimaced when I had seen him stumble on his own two feet as he first took his seat at the judges' table. Willow, by contrast, had rolled over laughing. The show hostess, Portia, thankfully provided some quick, witty humor, and then the lights had dimmed and the future stars had taken the stage.

"You did watch." I could hear the chagrin in his voice.

"Not much after that," I admitted.

"Why? Where are you? What is that noise in the

background?"

"So … funny thing …" I started.

"What's that beeping?"

I breathed out, just anticipating his reaction. "Yeah, I'm in the emergency room."

"You're where? Why?" That was the start.

"So, even with the injection, if you had an allergic reaction, you should follow up with a hospital visit immediately."

"You what? Are you all right?" And there it was … he was off to the races. Thank goodness he didn't know about my ambulance ride, with Willow following in her car behind us.

"I—" I started while glancing over at my faithful friend, now sitting next to me.

"What happened?" Ryan's voice soared through my telephone. "Did you eat something? What—"

"Ryan, where are you?" I interrupted, mostly as a way to get him to calm down.

"Home," he answered quickly before asking his own question. "Do you need me to come to the hospital? I can … geez, I can be there in—"

"I'm fine." I think my breathing was becoming labored just through an osmosis of him. "Goodness no, don't come here. Willow is here, and I am fine."

I looked over at my best friend again. Grinning like crazy, her eyes were glimmering as if she knew a secret, and, of course, she then had. It was my secret. I knew I hadn't said anything directly via the phone conversation with Ryan, but just how Andre could tell by the way Ryan and I had looked at each other on the bench, the current intimacy of our phone conversation was surely giving me away to Willow.

"The doctor did an exam. My breathing is under control. I just have to stay here a while to make sure I don't have a second reaction, which sometimes happens. I'll be released tonight with some scripts. It will just be a while," I informed him and that time tried *not* to look at my friend.

"I know you are so careful. What happened?" Ryan at least sounded a little calmer.

"I … uh … might have taken a couple of your brownies. Sorry," I apologized. "I should have asked. I just grabbed some for a snack. You had said you would save me some, and I know how crazy you are with the nut-free house." If I hadn't given our relationship away to Willow at that point, it was surely outed then.

"They're Mr. Mean's brownies?" she whispered wide-eyed, and I smacked her.

"What brownies?" Came the music mogul's voice from across the line.

"The ones you made with the kids on Thursday." Gosh, was he so upset he didn't remember the brownies?

"We didn't end up making them," he denied. "We ran out of time. What brownies? Sallie! Joel! What brownies do we have?"

"Oh, I j—" I started, only to be cut off.

"What? Hold on, Bethany." I could only partially hear him questioning the kids. "You made them with Mommy? Did they have nuts?" The bustling hospital area didn't help my ability to hear Ryan and most definitely not Sallie or Joel's responses. "Didn't you tell Mommy not—?" He seemed to listen before asking another question. "And what did she say?" Again, I couldn't hear the children but only his disbelieving response. "She said what?" There was a shorter pause then before he continued, "No, it's not your fault. Let me know next time, okay? Finish getting your pjs on." There was a slight growl before he more calmly said my name.

"Yeah, I heard." I resisted *my* growl, although there was certainly one growing. "Kari made them."

"I'm so sorry. Are you okay? Can you believe she told them it wasn't that big of a deal?"

Growl! Growl! Growl!

"Some people don't think it is. They think we are just whining." I somehow managed not to call her out directly or suggest what I was trying hard not to believe … the nut additive had been deliberate.

I heard another low grunt before he redirected his focus. "You sure you don't need me to come to the hospital?"

"Totally sure."

"Come here then. Come here after you're completely checked out or whatever."

"I'm fine, Ryan. Willow is here." Willow nodded with a grin as I continued, "And you have enough going on."

"Tomorrow?" he relented.

But that wouldn't work, either. "I have to work from eight until three."

"Call off. You are going to need your rest." What he said about sleep was absolutely the truth.

But I said another. "Can't."

"Why? If you're sick—"

I cut him off with determination. "I am fine."

Surely hearing the frustration in my voice, and maybe remembering the stories I told of my mother, he resigned with a compromise. "Well, then I think I'm gonna need a coffee stop tomorrow."

"You can't see me, but I am shaking my head." I literally was.

"I don't think I need to see you to know that." I was glad he was coming down enough from his initial freak-out to tease me.

"Go take care of the kids and any follow-up you have from the show. I'm sure there is a lot. We'll talk later."

"For real."

A smile warmed my face upon hearing and repeating our meaningful words to one another. "For real."

Willow barely waited for me to return my phone to my purse before she nudged me hard and smirked. "This is no longer coworkers or even friends, is it?"

"That *is* what we are," I tried to continue down the road of denial.

"Someone like Ryan Thompson has lots of coworkers and friends. But he called *you*. And that talky-talky was pretty personal …" Her voice led in that tell-me-it-all way.

"Remember, I know you snuck Til in," I cautioned, recalling how Tilman had pretended to be a delivery person at the apartment complex and insisted he needed to deliver the new television—a.k.a empty box—personally to Willow per store orders.

"That was fun," she reminisced. "But I don't think we're going to try that again after the Andre shit. So, anyway, Miss Innocent … Miss Easter Dress, this is what the big secret is, huh? What kind of blackmail do I exactly have on *you*?"

"I think you already have it figured out." I was trying to stay true to my word and not actually say it out loud.

"Bethany Opala, whoa!" The college-grad-to-be almost bounced in her chair.

I thought about shushing her, noting the abundance of people nearby. Instead, I used a softer voice, hoping she would mimic mine. "Willow … if there is ever something that I need you to keep a secret about, this is it." She didn't need to interlock her smallest finger with mine for a pinkie swear, but when she did, it only confirmed how much I trusted my best friend. Yet, I still couldn't tell her he wasn't married. I told him I wouldn't say anything, and I would honor that. "Just remember, it's not as bad as you think."

"But is it good?" Her eyebrows raised in anticipation.

"It is," I agreed. "It's good."

An immediate, uncontrollable heat blushed my face, and it had nothing to do with any allergies. I was not only thinking about our physical intimacy but how much Ryan cared. His reaction on the phone call solidified it.

***

I traveled the Americano with a shot of cinnamon across the counter and went to call out the name. Had I not been so tired, nor had the customer line not been starting to snake toward the door, I would have realized. I wouldn't have even bothered to start with the T before stopping myself.

"Oh, my gosh, you really did show up." I looked across to those deep blue eyes, which did bear a little sleep deprivation, too, if I was right.

"I told you I was." And Ryan kept his promises. "You all right?"

"I'm tired," I admitted. "But otherwise good." I then went on to explain. "The shock of the med brings my system on a little bit of a roller coaster. Then, going through all the doctor stuff. It was just exhausting. I'm probably gonna crash early tonight. Hopefully, I will get to see any Ryan bloopers first," I teased.

"Mercy." Ryan rolled his eyes.

"You're Ryan Thompson, right? You are. I know you are."

The voice caught me off-guard, even though it was coming from a woman standing directly next to Ryan in line. For a beautiful moment it had been as if we were in our own private Bethany-Ryan world. Now, the blonde, about my age, and the rest of the coffee shop were back in focus.

"God, you're even better looking in person." She wouldn't stop staring at Ryan.

"Hi," was his solitary word response with a quick glance at the initiator.

"I saw Ben Winthrop in here once, too."

I nudged the coffee closer to Ryan and used his alias. "Tom, be careful … it's hot. You don't want to get burned." I know he caught my meaning the way he casually grazed my hand on the cup exchange.

I looked for her name on the next order, laughed at the

irony of her drink choice, and used it fully to my advantage. "Hadley? No more blondes." I spoke of the coffee roast but meant it in a whole other way for the man in front of me.

"What?" She actually managed to look my direction instead of Ryan's. "They didn't tell me that at the register."

"Just happened. You might want to try something else. It's been taken." I raised my eyebrows at Ryan, who I could tell was trying not to laugh before walking off and exiting the shop.

My back pocket buzzed as I was making Hadley's order … somehow having "miraculously" found more of the roast she requested. I normally wouldn't look at my phone when busy at work—it wasn't good customer service—but I pretty much knew it was going to be a text from Ryan. And I couldn't resist.

U seem to B feeling OK.

Blood pressure went up a minute or so ago, I texted back with a snort as I multi-tasked with the drink.

Me or the little minx?

Combo, I replied with the truth.

I enjoyed the quick banter.

I'm sure you did. It's the lyricist in me.

Oh, the lyricist, is it? He called me out on my jealousy.

I wanted to remind him of his almost jumping to conclusions with Andre but, instead, asked, *Does that happen a lot?* I mean, besides Ryan being a celebrity in his own right due to the show, he was a gorgeous-looking man. Maybe I was glad he wore his wedding ring.

I was working on the lid of Hadley's coffee when Ryan's reassuring text came through. *No worries, Lenay.*

Hadley should be the one who is worried. LOL! I teased and then sent, *How does the coffee taste?*

Not as good as U. Ryan was spot-on with a witty comeback.

Right answer. I added a smile and two thumbs-up emojis.

Gotta get to the studio.

155

DO NOT break a leg. I referenced his tripping the night before and finally handed a grumpy Hadley her coffee. *See you tomorrow.*

He replied with, *Not funny. Yes tomorrow.* And added a bunch of smiling, winking, and flames emojis.

***

By the time I got to Ryan's that next day—Wednesday—he and the kids were having a snack before bedtime. Ryan also had a deep glass of some kind of golden-brown liquor. We talked a little about the show—whom he liked, whom I liked, how they differed from each other, and who would probably win. But when it was time for the kids to go to sleep, Ryan had to deal with a resistant Joel. The kids, after all, were completely off their schedule, having gone to the show for the previous two nights and still having school.

"Fine, Joel, whatever, you stay up. When you are miserable tomorrow, there's not going to be any treats." I could hear Ryan—who had to be exiting Joel's upstairs room—all the way from my seat in the living room.

"I'm not tired!" the little boy yelled.

"Fine." And then, a couple minutes later, Ryan reentered the room to join me. "What?" he asked, examining a look on my face I hadn't even realized I was giving. "What?"

"Nothing."

"He's overly tired."

"I know. I think you are, too."

"I just need another drink." He reached for his tumbler on the coffee table. "You want anything?" He tilted one of the red wine bottles up.

"No. Still kinda recovering from the other night." After a grimace, he sat back on the sofa, and I asked, "You all right?"

"It's just a lot."

156

I rubbed his hand. "I know." I brought his hand up to my lips and kissed it—that even felt tense.

"Everything is coming at me all at once. The pressure with the show, work, Kari returning and being so unapproachable, trying to figure out a schedule with the kids … and you."

"Me?" I blurted. How was I a pressure? I didn't want to be that.

He clarified, "You scared the crap out of me on Monday."

My heart skipped a sweet beat on his concern. "Sorry. I'm fine. Please don't think about the food." I had noticed a little extra scrutiny on his part when I had eaten some of the cocoa-flavored popcorn snack with the kids.

"I'm trying not to." He closed his eyes momentarily and then, after reopening, used a directive tone on me. "You really shouldn't have pushed yourself going back to work like that."

"I had to. The ER bill is not going to pay itself."

"That's what insurance is for." When I didn't say anything, his eyes appeared bigger and his face more serious. "You have insurance, don't you?"

"Yeah. But it's not the best, by far. So, the copay and the meds and what the hospi—"

"Let me take care of it. I'll pay whatever."

"No." I halted that idea immediately. "Absolutely not."

"It's my fault y—"

"No, it's not. It's not your fault or responsibility."

"Bethany …" He cracked his neck.

"Come on, stop. You are stressing me out now, too. Turn around."

"What?"

I gently prompted him to move so I could be a little more behind him. I wanted access to his upper back, neck, and the knots I knew were surely tight throughout. And I wasn't wrong.

When I started kneading with my knuckles, I heard an

appreciative moan escape his mouth. He let me continue on my mission for a little bit before turning and kissing me sweetly. I smiled and rubbed my hand along the side of his face, which was definitely more beard than stubble. Gosh, was I trying to like his new facial accessory. I wanted to ask if he and Kari had set up anything regarding the divorce announcement, but I knew it wasn't the time. And from what it sounded like, they had hardly spoken unless passing off the kids. So, instead I went with that angle.

"So, you said the kids' schedule. What's going on with that? Kari's still getting weekends ..."

He took a final gulp from his glass and set it back down—along with my hands, it seemed to be putting him in a more relaxed, sedentary state. "Yeah, it's more stable for them to be in their home, have a routine, van picks them up for school. But these live shows ... I can't keep bringing them. You saw them. They're exhausted, and it lost its appeal halfway into the first show."

I leaned my head onto his side. For one thing, it felt good just to be connected in silence with him like that. For another, I had an idea, and I needed to formulate it in my mind before I voiced it out loud.

"I don't want to overstep ... just tell me," I began.

He didn't move, making me realize he liked the feeling of us, too. "Go ahead."

"I'll watch the kids. I can be here on Monday and Tuesday afternoons if you want."

"You what?" He moved then. "Do you want to do that?" He was looking me directly in the eyes.

"Yeah. Like you said, they'll have some stability. I'll figure it out at work. I usually have early shifts anyway. The kids wouldn't even have to go to daycare. I can be here when they get dropped off after school like they did when we were writing here. But I can only do it for the next couple weeks because I have my trip home for Ella's graduation." I couldn't tell what he was thinking, but whatever it was, he didn't shy away from keeping his eyes on me. "I understand if you don't feel comf—" I started when he hadn't said anything.

"Of course I feel comfortable. And we can make those our days too, then." He smiled peacefully and then added with a wink, "You can stay, and we can catch up."

"We can." I lightly chuckled. I hadn't thought about that part.

"Are you sure you're good with that? They can be a handful. I mean, I could—maybe should—ask Kari. But I … You know what? I don't want to. We have our arrangement."

I most heartedly agreed. "I'm sure."

"And I can compensate you whatever that hospital bill is."

"Oh, no. No. I didn't offer because—"

"I know," he reassured with a soft rub of my arm. "But I would pay anyone who would watch them."

"I'll rescind my offer. I mean it." I was adamant.

"Geez, you are a stubborn negotiator."

I smirked a little and then eased into a smile. "Ry, I'm offering because of you. That's all. Because it will help you and the kids, like you have me in so many ways."

He was quiet again. And he had an even more serene yet intense gaze at me. Finally, he said, "What do you want, Bethany?"

"What do I want?" I repeated the question back, not understanding the context in which he was asking. I didn't think it was accusatory or even in reference to our payment/nonpayment debate, but if not that, then what?

"I mean out of life," he explained. "Life goals … that kind of thing."

Well, that was such a big, almost intense, subject all of a sudden. And one I wasn't sure I even had the answer to. "Well, I …"

I guess my uneasiness showed through because he took my hand and stroked it softly with his index finger. "It's not an interview, Lenay." Just by using that name, he eased my mind.

"I guess that answer has changed a lot. It depends on when you asked me."

"Uh-huh." His non-word was leading me to say more.

"I'm no longer the little girl in front of the mirror with the hairbrush up to her face belting out a song and thinking I am going to be the next Whitney Houston or Taylor Swift."

Ryan's eyebrows crinkled, and I suspect he was thinking of his part of that dream going away. "Betha—"

"I know, Mr. Mean, I know." I used Willow's nickname to lighten the mood. "I'm really okay with not being a star." I touched *his* hand that time. "It's not me. It never was. I don't think I ever truly wanted to be on stage. I just wanted to feel and express myself. I love the idea of the whole thing … the rush of being around it all. But I don't want to be *that* person. That's why I started looking for jobs on crew and such. That's what got me out here. Trying out for *Singer Spotlight*? That was more or less peer pressure. But it was also my last straw. It did hurt to not make it," I admitted, but he already knew that. "But mostly because I knew I had to give it all up here … maybe even altogether. I was thinking of going back home and being a teacher. I don't know how many more credits I would need to teach music or something."

"But now? What about now?"

He was still looking at me intensely … listening to my words, possibly reflecting. It did feel a little like an interview. But most likely the alcohol and unwinding from stress were also contributors to his demeanor.

"Honestly, I don't want to teach. I want to create … behind the scenes."

"No glitz and glamor?"

"No," I answered immediately and saw the look on his face instantly relax.

It was only then when I started to put together the line of questioning. Kari wanted all of the lights … the cameras

… the attention. And look what had happened. Was that what the late evening, casual interrogation was all about?

"No," I reiterated and pushed my head just slightly closer to his. "This is what I wanted all along, and I don't think I ever knew it completely until now."

"Including sitting on a sofa with a divorcee who has two kids?" While he asked it in a joking manner, I knew he did want a truthful response. What Ryan questioned was his weak spot … where he thought he had failed—the divorce.

"Well, the kids are great. Their dad, though? I don't know," I said in an obvious teasing voice, and Ryan rolled his eyes. I left him off the hook fairly quickly, though. "Ryan … absolutely, yeah."

His mouth on mine tasted like the sweet alcohol he had been drinking. I didn't mind. He was kissing me his appreciation. And I was kissing mine back for him asking me those questions … for wanting to know what I wanted and where I wanted to be.

His stifled yawn immediately after, though, led to more of my teasing. "I'm gonna try hard not to take that personally."

He touched my face. "Sorry."

"You're tired. You need to go to sleep."

"I'm not."

I couldn't resist. I made my Judge Ryan face and mimicked him from earlier with his son. "Fine, Ryan. Whatever. You stay up. When you're miserable tomorrow, there's not going to be any treats."

He squinted at me and sighed but was a good dad to the core. "He's probably passed out on the floor. I should go check on him."

When he started to stand up, I pushed on his thigh, urging him to stay seated. "I'll go. Sit. Relax. Okay?"

To my surprise, he smiled, nodded, and let me go check on Joel. And just as Ryan had predicted, I found the four-year-old sprawled out on his bedroom floor. Toys were scattered around and under him. Luckily, the slumbering little boy was already in his pajamas and was easy to coax the couple of feet to his bed and under the covers.

When I got back downstairs, Ryan was not sprawled on the floor, but he was just like his son … sound asleep. "Not tired." I laughed, shook my head, and pecked him on the lips.

"Hmmm …" he murmured.

"Do you want me to tuck you in, too?"

"Without … a … ques … tion," he spat out groggily.

I didn't want to wake him up enough, though, to get him up the stairs or even to the guest room down the hall. He needed the sleep. So, I grabbed the plaid blanket that was draped across the side chair, encouraged him to stretch out on the sofa, and curled myself and the blanket on top of him.

"No place I'd rather be."

I thought I had said that as an internal monologue, but I got an answer along with an extra squeeze from his secure arm. "Yeah. Good night, Lenay."

"Good night, Ryan."

CHAPTER THIRTEEN

The next time I saw him was two days later, and it was in his office. It was a last-minute decision on Ryan's part … and it was a complete ruse. Near closing time, I was pretending to meet with him regarding some kind of business. In actuality, he was going to drive us to an obscure beach location where we would picnic. Ryan really wanted us to have some kind of date that did not involve his house. And since Kari was picking up the kids at daycare and had them for the weekend, it seemed ideal.

When Anamaria told me to go directly into his office, I tried to act all professional, but it was getting harder and harder not to melt when I saw Ryan. Never mind the *color* of his eyes, it was the way they looked so deep into me. It was knowing how he felt that did me in every time.

"Mr. Thompson." I had to clear my throat.

"Miss Opala." He stood up from behind his desk. "Have a seat."

"Okay." I did so, putting my guitar case down … which didn't house an instrument but, instead, a change of clothes.

When Ryan immediately reclaimed his seat across from mine, I was shocked. I expected since he had gotten up that he was going to shut the door as he normally would have. But since he didn't, Anamaria—although a good few feet away at her desk—had the potential of hearing our conversation.

"The reason I called you in today is …"

His mouth and eyebrows rose at the same time, and I scrunched mine at him. Were we playing out the little act? All right. I was game. Kind of fun. Let's just make sure we get to that secluded picnic at the beach soon.

"There was interest in your demo."

"What?" I said, almost not hearing him. Then when I realized I, indeed, had heard him correctly, I spoke a little louder, "What?" When Ryan lifted his eyebrows again, I let down part of my veil and called him by his first name … although more quietly. "Ryan, you better not be messing with me."

"Miss Opala …" He seemed quite amused and was good at keeping up the masquerade. Of course, he had plenty of practice in that field. "I would not mess around … with music or anything else."

I caught his extra little meaning, and my eyes widened on the truth of everything he was telling me. "For real, Ryan? What?"

"Finn Murphy—"

"The country singer?"

"Yes." He let out a soft, short chuckle. "Are you going to let me finish?"

"Uh-huh. Do I need to stay seated?" I wasn't sure I could. That man still made me think I was going to pee my pants!

Ryan looked quite amused. "No, you can stand or whatever you need to do."

I stood up, began pacing, and then managed another, "Uh-huh." So much for being a prolific songwriter if that was the only word I could say.

"Listen, he didn't mention a specific song. He just said he would be interested in hearing anything you have.

Remember when I told you to keep writing?" When I nodded in affirmation, he continued, "You've done that, right?" Ryan knew I had. Maybe "Mr. Thompson" had not.

"Yeah," I answered regardless.

"He is going on his summer tour soon and just released an album not too long ago. So, it might be a little while, but he likes your stuff."

"O … kaaay." I didn't even get a whole connected word out that time.

"Lenay," he let his special name for me slip, but I don't think he cared. The smile on his face told me so. He then continued, "He'll be in contact. Just give it a little time. No commitments on anything. I'm still shopping around. He knows that. It might put a little fire under him."

"Oh. Okay."

"You said that." There was his smile again.

"Is that it?" I think I managed to quit pacing. I was going to have to turn over any profits from a song sale to buy him new carpet … it was going to be so worn out.

"Yes."

"Ry—" I stopped myself, even though I knew I had called him by his first name plenty of times at the office.

"Come on." He stood up. "Do you need a ride? I know you usually walk." He was gathering up his things.

I kept up with the plan. "I … yeah." And I picked up the guitar case.

When we walked out of his office, I guess my beaming bright face wasn't concealed at all since Anamaria questioned me. "Good news?"

"Uh, yeah," I answered.

"Congratulations. Ryan is the best."

"He is." And I resisted the urge to touch his hand.

Ryan directed his comment to his secretary. "You're just saying that so I tell you you can go home for the night."

"It *is* Friday," she noted their unofficial early release

day.

"Then you can also go home for the weekend."

"You are too generous, Ryan." She smirked. "I have a little more to finish up, and then I'm going."

When we were walking to the elevator, I could hardly stand still, and Ryan was shaking from trying to control his laughter. I couldn't wait to get into the elevator. I couldn't wait to be—

"Oh, darn it!"

Ryan actually burst out a vibrating gust of air on my reaction as the elevator doors welcomed us … along with a handful of passengers. He did an upward nod to the group, and we joined them, remaining quiet for the entire passage down to the garage floor. As the collective group scattered to their individual cars, Ryan and I got into his.

"Ah! Ah! Ah! Ah!" I screamed the instant both of our car doors were shut. "Why did you do that to me?" I asked as Ryan let out a full-hearted laugh. "Why didn't you just tell me in private?"

"It was business," he stated.

"It was cruel."

"It was fun." He raised his eyebrows. "What was that comment about when the elevator first opened, Lenay?"

He knew what the comment was about, but I answered in a seductive way, nonetheless. "I wanted to thank you."

"And now?"

When I looked out my side window and through the rear, Ryan understood my reason and concern. His prime parking spot, so close to the elevator bank, meant we could be seen by any potential onlookers exiting the building. He turned on the car, put it in gear, and drove us to a section of the parking garage that had zero cars and limited chance of getting any at that point of the week. The instant the car was turned off again, I climbed onto Ryan's lap, accidentally hitting the horn along the way. My giggling quickly subsided when Ryan pulled me closer to him and we began kissing.

"You're very welcome," Ryan said once we stopped. "But if you sit like this on my lap much longer …"

"Okay." I pecked him one more time on the lips and slid back onto the passenger seat. As Ryan restarted the car, I asked, "Are we really picnicking, or was that the actual ruse?"

"Yes. The beach. Absolutely." He smiled and touched my hand once more before we drove into the natural light of Los Angeles. "Remember, nothing is set. It's just interest."

"I know. It's still good news."

"It is. So, we'll pick up some food and … Shoot, hold on," he said as the car speaker announced an incoming phone call.

Ryan answered and, because it was on speaker, I was privy to the entire conversation. It was the after-school daycare. They wanted Ryan to know Kari was there to pick the kids up.

"Yeah, that's fine." Ryan spoke to the daycare representative. "Of course."

"Mr. Thompson? She's quite … well, Mrs. Thompson is acting very bizarre."

"Oh." He looked over at me—the smile was definitely gone as we listened again.

"We don't feel comfortable letting Joel and Sallie go with her."

"All right." He sighed. "I'm on my way. It shouldn't be too long. Don't … don't let them go if you're that concerned," he directed.

What did "bizarre" mean? It had to be big for someone not to be given their own kids. It had to be *very* big considering who Kari Thompson was. Was she acting similar to how she had in Ryan's foyer? That was my only encounter with her, so I had nothing else to go by.

"Thanks," the person on the other end of the line said. "We'd rather you make that decision."

"Yeah." Ryan ended the call, made three sudden lane

changes amidst horns blaring, and then looked at me. "What the heck?"

"Let's just get there and find out," I reassured.

Ryan tried Kari's cell phone the entire time we were making our detour to the daycare, but he got no response. I know it frustrated him even more. In the meantime, I tried to remain calm and quiet in the passenger seat. He didn't need any other white noise.

I made a similar decision when we arrived, too. Remaining in the car, I watched as Ryan approached Kari. Dressed in a glittery gold and hot pink top with similar wrap, she was talking with two other adults in front of the building.

I couldn't hear the exacts of the conversation, but I did immediately see why the center had called Ryan. Kari looked visibly drunk. She was swaying and was even more disheveled than when I had seen her before … besides the outfit. But who wore something like that to pick up their young children for the weekend?

Because it was getting stuffy in the car, I opened my door to get air. That was when I heard Ryan calmly tell the workers to have the kids come out. Kari looked at him and scoffed dramatically. But before anything else could unfold, Sallie and Joel—with their wide eyes looking from Mommy to Daddy—emerged from the building.

"Hey, kiddos, go ahead, get in my car," Ryan said. And then to the daycare workers, "Thanks for calling me. I'll take care of it now. Much … much appreciated." He shook their hands in that businessman sort of way, and they seemed none the happier to go back into the building.

The kids, obviously knowing something was terribly wrong, started walking zombie-like toward the car. That was the first time, I guess, Kari noticed I was inside the BMW. And she was not at all pleased.

"*She's* with you? You brought her with you?" she screeched.

"Geez. Yes. She was in the car with me when we got

the call. Kids, get in the car. It'll be all right. By the way, Kari, I hope that wasn't intentional with the brownies the other day, because so help me …" Oh, boy! Ryan was bringing *that* up?

"What about the brownies?" She was still swaying. "I'm not allowed to make food with my kids?"

"You know what I mean. Sallie told me she told you no nuts," he said as I got out and opened the back passenger door for Sallie and Joel.

"There weren't any nuts," Kari denied.

"Don't play word games," he challenged. "Peanut butter … whatever."

"It was only a little for flavor and moisture."

The way Ryan somehow suddenly stood even taller, I could tell he was ready to erupt. But he remained calm, especially since we both noticed a car parking a few spots away from his. "First of all, as if you would know baking secrets. And second, more importantly, it landed Bethany in the hospital."

"Sorry," she offered as I shut the door for the kids. "I really didn't think a …" Kari took a couple of steps closer in order to bridge the physical gap between us. "I am. I'm sorry …" She paused when speaking to me and then said, "about that." Kari then turned back toward Ryan. "She still shouldn't be in the car with my family."

Ryan's jaw tightened as a man got out of the newly parked car and started walking past us to the door. "You gave all of that up. Don't start this now," he whispered in a warning way to his ex-wife. "Where's your car? I'll drive you to your place. Bethany, can you take the kids?"

I hadn't thought about how Kari was getting home. I knew the minute we pulled up—and probably the moment we heard the word "bizarre"—that the kids were going to be with us. But Kari? She should have to fend for herself. She was the one who had chosen to be so incredibly irresponsible.

Before I could answer, drunken Kari said, "Is she even

old enough to drive? I mean, Ryan, honestly …"

"Fu—" His temper rose and was, thankfully, aborted instantly. "You know how old she is. *You're* the one acting like a spoiled brat."

"Hmmmf," was her classy response.

Because I was brought up to be kind to others, I resisted anything negative back. "Call her a cab," I suggested. Heck, I could even do it. I had plenty of experience with it.

But Ryan shook his head. "We don't want the publicity. If someone picks her up like this?"

I sighed—that was what it always seemed to come down to. "Okay."

"Kari, you need to sleep off whatever this is. And the kids don't need to be a part of it anymore." He looked at me. "I'm sorry, Bethany."

"Yeah." I shut my door, walked around to the driver's side, and got into his seat.

Before I shut the door and tried to figure out how to drive such an expensive vehicle, Ryan leaned into the car. "Thank you. The garage remote will get you in, but the alarm pad—"

"I know it, Daddy," Sallie piped up from behind me. "It's your birthday backwards."

"Yeah, Tink. You're a smart little girl. Bethany's allowed to know, but no one else, okay?"

Kari did another grunt, and Ryan shut my door for me. I wanted desperately to kiss him or touch him, just so we could have one positive thing from the whole debacle, but I knew I couldn't. I pressed the button to start the car, put on my seat belt, and wondered if I would even get to spend one of Ryan's December birthdays with him. Or would Kari come in between or control that, too?

***

When Ryan returned home, the three of us were in the

170

kitchen eating the dinner I managed to whip up rather quickly, considering I had been expecting to be on a beach with a blanket and some sort of take-out. His royal blue shirt highlighted his eyes, but they were quite the contrast to the cheerful, expectant ones that had shone before our sudden change of plans. He did his best not to let us see his distress, though. He first wrangled the kids' hair and then caressed my shoulder. I couldn't help but think what a beautiful scene that was … the four of us. It was exactly what Kari had, indeed, given up.

"Here." I stood. "I'll get you a plate. I just need to heat it up."

"I can get it. You've already—"

"Ryan, talk with the kids." I met him eye to eye. "They could use that."

He gave me a partial smile, and I went about the business of reheating the skillet that was host to a fajita mix. I watched the three of them at the table. The kids had done all right with me, alone really for the first time. I had kept them busy, helping to make corn muffins and glossing over anything topic Kari. I didn't know what to say or what Ryan wanted me to say.

As it turned out, I'm not sure he did either. As I was setting down Ryan's plate, he was telling them that their mom was just overly tired and needed some rest. Sallie seemed reassured, and Joel said Kari was tired more often since coming home. I flashed my eyes at Ryan as I reclaimed my seat.

I'm not sure how he was going to respond, though, since Joel jumped right on to the next subject. "Can we watch TV now?"

"Yeah. Uh, yeah. Go ahead." He thanked Sallie for clearing their two plates and watched as they ventured toward the family room. "Sorry our plans got ruined," he then offered to me.

"Your kids come first." I remembered and still stood by the statement I first told him when Sallie got sick in

March.

"They do," he echoed his, too. "Thanks for taking them. Kari's such a mess."

"Kind of figured that out." Admittedly, that came out a little snarky.

Ryan didn't comment on my delivery but instead filled in the blanks between the daycare parking lot and texting me that he was on his way home. "She passed out almost as soon as I got her into her place. Thank God the daycare called and she didn't have the kids or drove anywhere else. They or some other innocent person could have been hurt or worse."

I momentarily closed my eyes at that horrific thought. "What was she doing drinking in the middle of the afternoon like that? Does she do that a lot?" I thought of Joel's comment and if the little boy meant tired literally.

"No." He sounded and looked truly flabbergasted. "She pretty much always has control over her alcohol. It just seemed weird … the whole thing. Her manager happened to call when I was about to leave. So, I picked up her phone. I mean, I know Voight. He knows our situation … one of the few who do." He looked at his wedding ring then, took it off, and placed it on the table. "Anyhow, he said Kari was a little off the last few days overseas. So, maybe she is just tired. I mean, she had an extensive time abroad."

"Hmmm …" I hated that it sounded as if he was trying to come up with an excuse for her.

"Maybe it's me moving on. I don't know."

"You're not blaming yourself, are you? She makes her own choices."

"You're right."

"Wise beyond my baby years?" That came out *very* snarky.

And Ryan caught my reference right away. "Don't listen to a word she said. I should have just left her in the parking lot."

"I tend to remember you, yourself, telling me I wasn't mature enough."

"What?" He looked genuinely confused.

"The very, very first words you said to me. They're painted on my wall."

"Bethany." He sighed and put his fork down. "You know that's not what I meant." He got out of his seat and sat in the vacant chair next to me. "You're not really bothered about the age thing, are you?"

"No. No …" I denied. I honestly didn't even see it between us. But I did bring up the real issue I had. "I'm … I feel like she tries to manipulate you, and I don't like that I'm letting her get under my skin." When all I got was a closed mouth half-smile and a little piercing of his eyes, I asked, "What?"

"I'm the only one allowed under your skin." And he smiled and poked me with his finger. "Ryan!" I had been serious, but he was right to try to get us to ease up on the whole topic.

"Let's rewind to this afternoon … my office. How about that? Come on …" He nudged me again. "Whatcha think? A do-over."

I couldn't help but smile at his remembrance of our first kiss. I took a cleansing breath and went with his suggestion. "I'm trying not to get too excited," I admitted.

"You mean more than you already were?" he teased.

"Yeah." I let out a light laugh.

"You can be. And even if nothing happens from this group of songs with Finn Murphy, I know he is going to keep you in mind. He's a genuinely nice guy. He wouldn't have reached out and said something if he wasn't interested."

"Thanks, Ry." I leaned onto him, and he curled his arm around me.

"You know what we were talking about the other day? Life goals?"

"Yeah?"

"I'm definitely where I want to be, too. Exactly." He emphasized the last word.

With those words, I forgot about the sand that was supposed to be between my toes, the wine that was supposed to be in my hand, and the cool breeze that was supposed to be blowing through my hair. I had all I needed. His thoughtful words and then lips on mine were all that mattered.

We both heard the kids' nearby giggle, but Ryan refused to break our lip-lock. "You laugh at me, and you'll find your beds early tonight." He managed to do a half-turn look at Sallie and Joel.

"Mr. Mean," I whispered with a light laugh.

"*You* laugh at me, and you'll find bed real early, too," he warned me in the sexiest of voices.

"Promise?"

"Find out." He started tickling my ribs, getting me to instantly laugh. And Ryan always kept his promises.

CHAPTER FOURTEEN

With a shift at the coffee house and attending Willow's graduation celebration with her family from out of town, I didn't have a moment to myself the next day. I was able to text back and forth a few times with Ryan, though. He said Kari had apologized and wanted to have the rest of the weekend with the kids as originally planned. He told me she had arrived at the house very subdued—far from her off-the-wall self the day before. While he still didn't know what the trigger had been, he, at least, felt better about letting Sallie and Joel be with their mother.

Our busy schedules kept us apart on Sunday also. So, it wouldn't be until Monday when I would see Ryan again. It was my first time watching the kids while he did the live shows. I had babysat during my teen years, and my brother was a lot younger than me. Plus, I had done fine during our emergency Kari-is-drunk test run. But this was somehow different. I felt an enormous responsibility with Ryan's kids. And how the afternoon started out didn't help matters.

"Ryan?" Holed up in his master bedroom, I whispered his name into my phone.

"Yeah?"

"Where are you? Do you have any privacy?" That was important on both our ends.

"Uh … yeah," he answered. "I can. Give me a minute." And in less than that, he continued, "Okay, I just stepped into my dressing room. Where are you? You're going to be there for the kids, right?" he asked, surely knowing it was almost time for Sallie and Joel to arrive home from school.

"Yeah … yeah," I reassured. "I am. I'm at your place." My eyes were fixated on his closed bedroom door.

"Okay."

"Ryan?"

"Yeah?"

"Uh … maybe you should have told me you have a cleaning service."

"Oh," he said and then repeated with a little more recognition of the situation, "Oh. That's today? Are they there now?"

"Yeah." Somewhere behind that door.

"It's only twice a month. I guess you've never been over when—"

I interrupted his dialogue, needing to get my story out and, even more importantly, get a resolution. "I was in your room taking a shower. I didn't hear when they came. Then I was getting dressed, and the lady walked in. Scared me … scared each other."

"Oh, crap. What did you say?"

"She was apologizing like crazy. I told her I was there to watch the kids."

"You are."

I know. I didn't lie. I already skated around the truth enough when it came to him, but … "Ryan!" My voice rose an octave and then lowered again. "What childcare person takes a shower at the house, especially in the master bedroom?"

"Yeah. Uh, I don't know."

"She's still downstairs." I had heard her at least go down the stairs. "What do you want me to do?"

"Stick with it. They're reputable. Lots of policies are in place for what they see in homes. It'll be okay."

"I'm sorry." I somehow felt dirty, despite the shower.

"It's okay. It's me not thinking or having too much to think about. Hold on." His voice changed to a more bro-to-bro one, and I realized he was talking with someone on his end. "Hey, yeah? They're ready? Sure. I just needed to take a quick phone call." And then back to me. "I gotta roll. Everything … everything good?"

Since it appeared he had company at the studio, I made it be. "Yeah, I guess."

"It … yeah." I could tell he wanted to say more, but alas. "See ya."

"Bye, Ry."

***

It was fun being with Sallie and Joel for a couple days in a row. Since Ryan had the East Coast feed set up in his home, we were able to watch *Singer Spotlight* legitimately live. The kids laughing at their dad on the screen was a completely different experience than watching it with the women at my apartment house.

The humor and goodwill ended abruptly, though, with about ten minutes left of the Tuesday show. Kari was the guest celebrity performing right before they announced who was being cut. I had known about it. And I totally got why the show wanted her. Not only was she a vocal genius, but she was also a "spouse" of one of the judges.

Nevertheless, I felt my body tighten a little as she took the stage. I tried to relax, knowing Sallie and Joel were so excited to see their mom. They cheered her on as enthusiastically as the packed live audience at the studio did.

"Kari Thompson, everybody," hostess Portia announced as Kari—looking completely her performer and not ragged, drunk self—did a glossy smile at the completion of one of her classics.

And then those tense feelings I felt rose tenfold. I watched as she walked over to the judges' table and kissed Ryan. Kissed him … on the lips … and not simply a quick peck. Then the camera cut to commercial on the crowd's collective "awww" and Kari's seemingly all-American-girl sweet smile.

The text from Ryan came in almost immediately after. *U OK?*

No reference needed. He knew I would be watching the show. He also had to know the answer to his question. Was he crazy? No, absolutely not. I was not okay.

But I didn't type that back. I didn't text anything at all. I was lucky I could read and comprehend his text. The world around me was in a black, closed-in cloud called fury.

Trust me … I had no idea she was going to do that. That second message came through a couple minutes later, and I watched via the television set as he put down his phone.

And then he had to be present and focused on the poor contestants as they fretted about their fate. I walked away. I didn't need to be witness to any more disappointment.

I knew the show had ended. The kids, remembering what I had told them, found me in the kitchen, putting a later-than-usual dinner on the table. I had made everything ahead of time for the "Sloppy Joels" on a baked potato. As they laughed at the creation, I heard my phone chime again. That time it was an actual call from Ryan instead of a text. My response was the same, though—nothing.

"Bethany, please answer. I need to talk with you. Call me," was his voice message when I retrieved it.

Again … I did not. I couldn't. I was afraid of what I might say. I was afraid of how much I was hurting. I was afraid to hurt anymore.

***

The ache was still clinging to my heart when I heard the garage door open about an hour later. I had remained stoic and rational for the kids, but I knew I wouldn't be able to with Ryan. I knew no matter what we ended up saying, it was going to be emotional and heartbreakingly true. Because I had enough.

"Bethany! Betha—"

He stopped in the middle of calling out my name once he spotted me. I had decided to wait for him in the breezeway that connected the garage with the house's main residence. I wanted to talk with him without innocent little ears around.

I adjusted the bag on my shoulder and, in a straightforward way, gave him the details that any good person watching someone's children would do. "The kids did their school stuff, ate dinner …" And before the last item on my verbal list, I made a point of exaggerating my eyes. "Watched their dad kiss their mom."

He dropped his leather jacket on the bench and sagged his shoulders. "That's not—"

"Since you're home, I'm gonna call for a ride—"

"Bethany, you saw what happened when *I* jumped to conclusions."

That only infuriated me more, and I belted out as I had never done with him before. "Jumping to conclusions! Jumping to conclusions? I didn't kiss an ex … or get even close. It's not jumping—" I stopped myself with a much-needed breath. "There's national video proof. It's trending for goodness sake."

His grumble was pure frustration. "I know you got my texts. You need to give me a chance."

Something about the ache in his tone and the pleading in his word choices made me at least not move any further or take out my phone to get an Uber. A lot of me, after all, didn't want to leave. A lot of me wanted to listen. But there was still a part of me that didn't want to be broken.

That Bethany was the one who was mentally reaching for the doorknob.

Most likely figuring my silence was better than an alternative, he spoke candidly again. "Do you really think I had any part in that? Bethany? After all you've seen, after all I've talked with you about, after ... us?" It was amazing how intensely he could look at me.

The fact was, I didn't think he had any prior knowledge or desire for the kiss with Kari. I knew that deep down. But there was so much more tied into it.

"I don't," I admitted and tried to put into words what I was feeling. "But I'm not going to tell you it doesn't hurt, and I ... Ryan? I don't know how much I'm supposed to put up with." Darn it, I could feel the tears burning beneath my eyes ... the ones I had been holding bravely in until then.

"Okay. Listen." He was calmer. "What *isn't* trending—but would be if anyone was privy to it—is how I went absolutely ballistic on her afterward ... at her car. She was just going to leave because she knew I was going to be mad. I have no idea why she is acting the way she is—all these ups and downs—but I've had it. No, you shouldn't have to put up with any of this crap, and neither should I. I pulled her aside and gave her the ultimatum right then. We either came up with a date to announce the divorce or I was marching right back into the studio, finding any press I could, and telling them right then and there."

That was a little more to take in than I had expected. "And?" I cautiously got out.

"She scoffed, but then she talked with Voight."

I tilted my head a little toward his in anticipation of an answer. "Mmmm-hmmm?"

"May fourteenth. She already has interviews set up for her album release. She'll do it then. The right angle and it will probably add to sales. I don't care. Just so it's done."

And while it was news I most definitely wanted to hear, I had also learned my lesson before about counting chickens. "Are you for sure this is legit?" I asked. "I mean she ju—" But I didn't want to think of what had led to our topic of discussion.

"She seemed resigned to it. Actually, oddly mellow. And I talked with Voight, too. Like he told me before, he had just been waiting for her to say the word." Ryan was still walking on eggshells because he knew my heart was just as fragile. "I'm sorry, okay? I'm sorry I let her even kiss me. I wasn't expecting it, and I'm asking you to please believe me and know it actually turned out to be kind of a good thing."

My mouth creased on one side. Having your boyfriend's ex kiss him was never a good thing in my book. I had learned that the hard way, too.

"Two weeks, okay?" he cited the momentous Monday the fourteenth date, only to be interrupted by me looking at my chiming phone. "Bethany, come on, whoever it is, it can wait."

"It's my sister. I called Garrett for his birthday, and he wasn't picking up. So, I texted her to see what was going on."

I hadn't wanted to phone my parents, knowing, if that was the case, I would be in for a lengthy conversation. I figured I could get a quick text response from Ella. Since it was already the first of May, I knew she was busy studying for her collegiate final exams. She was doing that at my parents' home, having moved back early from the nearby campus to save money for her own apartment and to concentrate on graduating with good grades. At least she was finishing college better than high school.

"Uh-huh." Ryan seemed distracted, but I knew it was only because he wanted to get back to the topic at hand.

BDay boy crashed early. Too much cake. Or maybe he's tired from all the smooching w/ the new girl at school. When are you going to get some, BTW? All those beach bods out there. Mmmm. My sister's text was followed by a GIF of a shirtless man on the beach.

Ella played her role as middle child to the classic hilt. She liked to be portrayed as the woe-is-me girl who never got any attention because she had two sick siblings. That was far from the truth. First of all, my allergy was quite manageable. And Garrett only got sick a few years before. Plus, Ella actually had her own medical drama, which was serious but short-lived and had no real long-term ramifications.

The truth was, Ella was ... Ella. She got her attention in all the bad ways. She was the one who cut class, drank underage, and was lucky she was even in college after a poor report card her senior year of high school. All of which, for the most part, she managed to hide from our parents. And even though she was good at keeping quiet and we had a true sisterly bond—that wasn't just our same colored hair and similar eyes—I didn't want to risk her incidentally blurting out my secrets. That was why she didn't know anything about Ryan. Maybe when she got serious about someone, she would understand.

I only relayed the part about Garrett to Ryan. "Ella said he crashed—went to sleep early. What kid does that on his birthday?"

"How old?"

"Turned sixteen today."

"Geez, I slept through most of my teens ... growing pains with growth and hair spurts, voice changing ..."

"For real?"

"Yeah."

"Good to know."

"Bethany?" Ryan said my name with a mixture of caution and hope.

I was actually glad for Ella's interruption. It gave me a chance to process and accept. "Two weeks and then no more secrets." I said it as a statement. Although, the insecure, pull-the-carpet-out-from-under-your-feet part of me still had it as a question.

"Yeah."

"I have one request."

"Okay …?"

"Kiss me better than you kissed her."

"Put your bag down, Miss Negotiator."

I didn't lose his eyes as I let my bag drop to the floor. He first played with my hair cascading loosely along my face and resting around my shoulders. Then he traced his finger along the side of my cheek where my freckles resided and gave me the most serene, peaceful smile. Before he even pulled me into his torso—which I noted was covered with a black T unlike the one he had worn on TV and kissed her in—I knew, without our lips yet touching, it was already a better kiss. His look and touch alone were more. And he could have stopped right there, but, the soft, magical feathering of his lips just sealed the deal.

***

"Hello?" I answered the phone after the first ring. After all, it was already in my hands.

"Hey, there."

"Hi." I was trying desperately to focus on Ryan's voice. "I thought you said you were going to be in meetings all day. It is Friday, right?"

"Yeah, it's Friday. And I am."

"Oh." I didn't get much more out. My cluttered mind was in complete contrast to the brilliant sunlight beaming into my tiny dorm-like room.

"Meetings." Ryan grumbled. "Hate all the committees and jargon. I'd rather just do it. How about you? Is everything all right? You good?"

"Uh … is everything …? Uh … truthfully? No," I stumbled out my words.

"What's up?"

"You have a couple minutes to talk?"

"Yeah. It's fine. They'll wait. What's wrong?"

"Those growing pains of my brother's?"

"Yeah? Sleeping a lot—"

"Yeah, and now his foot is swollen out of nowhere. My mom talked with his pediatrician. They're concerned. They're setting up appointments with all kinds of doctors again."

"The cancer?"

Ryan knew all about the scary time a couple years before when, at thirteen years old, Garrett got extremely tired and couldn't finish his middle school football practice. He was always a kid who kept going from one thing to another. Until he didn't. Since then, my parents only allowed him to shoot noncompetitive hoops in the family driveway. All because of his diagnosis and the desperate time it took to find a bone marrow match for him … especially since neither of us siblings was one.

"Yeah … yeah, maybe," I answered. "I mean, they don't know. They want to run some tests. I just got off the phone with my mom."

"You were talking with her right now?"

"Yeah."

"Remember they don't know anything yet. What's that saying about worrying?"

"It does no good?"

"Yes, but no. There's an actual quote about a rocking chair. I'll find it for you. I'd tell you not to worry, but I know that's not really possible."

"I know. That's exactly what I told my mom. There's not a chance in you know where that she's not going to worry, though. If there was an award for worrying, she would win hands down, even with anxiety meds."

"Well, good thing she takes them, then. A lot of people need to. If something happened to Joel or Sallie, I might, too. I can't imagine what your folks are going through right now."

"Yeah. We were all pretty much a mess last time. My mom was freaking out about everything. And my dad was praying a lot. I felt helpless being away at college … at least I could drive in every so often to visit. And once Garrett got out of the hospital and things went well, I got the offer to come out here after graduation. I debated because him getting sick made me truly realize how far California is. But then it also made me realize how quickly things can be taken away and to live for the moment and all that." I took a second to reflect and then knew I needed to refocus. "Sorry. So, why'd you call me in the first place? Simply to get out of your meeting?"

"Ha!" His voice seemed a little lighter at my joke. But then he turned more subdued again. "No. I … You want to hear something weird?"

"All the time." I was trying so hard to be myself.

"I was sitting in this meeting, and I had this sudden pang-like thing. I knew something was going on with you."

"Wha …?"

What? Like ESP? Like what? He just knew?

"I know … weird." He did the slightest of chuckles at himself.

"Huh." I was still trying to process that one.

"I mean, it could be the raspberry chocolate donut I had."

"Ry …"

"That was probably it." He kept talking. "The weirdness, though—" He stopped himself and then seemed to go off in another direction. "It gives you something to do but never gets you anywhere."

"What? The weirdness does?"

"No. That is the Erma Bombeck quote about the rocking chair and worry. It gives you something to do but never gets you anywhere."

"Ah. Yeah. True."

It was true. But it still didn't matter. If we cared about someone, we would rock the darn chair twenty-four seven. Plus, it seemed we would call out of the blue because of a "pang-like" thing.

"Hey, I should get back. I mean, I was actually the one who asked for this meeting. But if you hear anything or need anything, you call." I liked the kind, concerned, and confident way he spoke.

"I will," I agreed and then knew I needed to add one more thing. "Ryan?"

"Yeah?"

"Thanks for thinking of or panging or whatever me."

There wasn't a chuckle that time, but I felt like I could sense his smile. "Uh-huh. Talk soon."

***

Even though I was on the internet looking up scary, medical things I knew I shouldn't be, I was in a little lighter of a mood later that afternoon. For one thing, I was further removed from my mother and the anxiety she would exude when fretting about one of us. For another, I had talked to that insightful, dark-haired man … who appeared to be calling again.

"Two phone calls in only a couple hours' time?" I answered Ryan's call. "What? Did you eat another donut?" He had decided to make light of his pangs, so I walked that comfortable, joking line, too.

"There she is."

"Huh?"

"When you answered the phone so generically last time, it just confirmed to me that something was wrong. You are never a standard hello."

"Hmmm."

Dang, he was killing me with his Bethany insight … in all the good ways. Or was I just predictable? I mean, how I typically answered the phone was the creative side of me. I had grown up being taught to answer our landline as if it was almost a business—"Opala residence, Bethany speaking." I realized it was a polite, proper way—just like ladies wearing dresses—but it was one of the things I rejected once on my own.

"Anything more about your brother?" he asked.

"No. We won't know anything for a while."

"Do you want some good news?"

"Is there bad news, too?"

"No." He chuckled, and I imagined him shaking his head. "No quarter needed."

"Definitely. Lay it on me, then."

"Can you get off work the twelfth and thirteenth … and the afternoon of the eleventh?"

I was mentally trying to picture my calendar in my head. But it didn't matter. If Ryan was requesting it for personal *or* professional reasons, I would make it happen. "If I need to. I already have off all that time for Carolina, though."

"You need to," he said definitively.

"Why?"

"We never got that picnic at the beach."

That sure was the truth. Just recalling how Kari had dramatically interfered on our beach date and then again on the show revved my temper up. But I decided to take a deep yoga breath and not let him note the agitation.

I went with lighthearted sarcasm instead. "We're going to picnic at the beach the whole weekend?"

"Napa," he answered immediately and then, with even more enthusiasm, continued, "Well, just south of … but really get away. What do you think?" I didn't realize I hadn't replied until he prompted me. "Geez, I hate when you don't answer me."

I loved, wanted, and needed a getaway with him so much. I don't think I truly knew it until he proposed the idea. Trying to mask the sudden tears, I came up with a sassy response for my hesitation. "Sorry, I was looking up what to wear in wine country." Then, with even more excitement, I exclaimed, "Yes! Let me see what I can finagle at work. I might need to bribe and switch with some people, but I'll make it happen. That sounds so great, Ryan."

I could hear the joy and ease in his voice, also. "I'm glad. I totally think so, too. Off to another meeting. Call or text me when you get things worked out."

CHAPTER FIFTEEN

Those next several days were exhausting for both of us. I managed to trade days and hours at the coffee house so I could have off for the weekend away and still go to Carolina almost immediately after for a week. But that meant I was working almost every shift if I wasn't watching Sallie and Joel. And Ryan? He never stopped between the show gearing up for the end-of-the-month finale, his manager job, and the kids. Yet, despite it all, everything was somehow better and more at ease. Falling asleep in each other's arms on Monday and Tuesday and knowing that Kari's announcement was taking place directly after our weekend away, our natural bond was growing even stronger.

I was downright giddy on the Friday afternoon we drove to the Napa region, and, in a way, I know my lightheartedness and excitement helped Ryan. While he wanted the time away with me, there was slight apprehension about leaving the kids. Kari, of course, was going to have them. Not only was it the weekend, but it was Mother's Day weekend. Since we would be gone, she agreed to stay at Ryan's house so there was less disruption for the kids. And another good thing was, there hadn't been any more extreme incidents like the daycare pickup scene or even the on-air drama. Kari had remained pretty neutral, even-toned, and quick when exchanging the kids. But Ryan had never left Sallie and Joel. He had been with the kids—or at least in the same city—consistently since the breakup.

So, when we were en route to wine country, I proposed a humorous Ryan-Bethany way to get his mind in the right mood. "Road trip game. Name a song that has the word 'wine' in the title or has to do with wine."

He turned slightly from his driver's side and squinted at me. And then in true fashion said, "You first."

"Why am I always first?" I bellowed with a laugh.

"I'm giving you an easy point. I'm older and know a lot more songs."

"Phew!" I spit out.

"I'll even give you a two-song start."

"I don't need it, but fine," I boasted. "'Red, Red, Wine' and 'Strawberry Wine.' Go!"

"I have ninety-nine of them."

"What?" I balked incredulously—ten additional years of life did not provide him with that many more songs.

He started to sing, "Ninety-nine bottles of wine on the wall, ninety-nine bottles of wine. Take one down, pa—"

I literally smacked him. "That does not count as ninety-nine! Plus, I think it is bottles of beer."

He turned his head and did a smirky, sexy smile in my direction. "Thanks, Lenay."

"For what?" But by the way he softly and appreciatively looked at me, I knew he was very aware of my true intentions with the song game. "You're welcome. Now, help me not be so nervous about meeting your family."

We weren't just going to some B&B or chalet in wine country. We were going to stay in Ryan's brother's house. Dylan and his wife were traveling with their only child to a weekend soccer tournament a few hours away. They were letting us use their house at the winery they owned if we would take care of their dog. The vineyard manager and staff would have everything else in order. I loved that Ryan and I could truly be alone together and out of the spotlight of LA. Even more so, I loved the fact that I was going to meet part of his family—that he *wanted* me to meet Dylan, and that I obviously wasn't a secret to those close to him.

I didn't need to be nervous at all, though. All three of the northern California Thompsons were very welcoming. They peppered me with noninvasive, but really wanting-to-get-to-know-me questions throughout the tour of their home. The house was very rustic with wood elements and stone fireplaces, which reminded me a lot of the farmhouse roots of Ryan's home, although on a smaller scale.

When Dylan showed us the guest room—which was more like a suite—his wife and son started loading their car for their trip. As Ryan placed our bags on the bedroom sofa, I examined the soaring ceiling and then noted the photo on the table. There was a teenager in a red and white tank top and cutoff jean shorts. He was flexing his muscles on the back of an older blue pickup truck.

I gave it a second glance and then, holding the photo in his direction, practically shouted, "Ryan, is this you?"

Ryan turned from the bags to see what I was referencing and, after a frowning of his eyes, shoved his brother who was standing next to him. "Unbelievable."

Dylan laughed. "Dork personified."

"Yeah. Uh-huh." He grabbed the photo from me and turned it upside down on the nearby chair. "Can't you ever cut me a break?" He looked at his older sibling.

"Nope." Dylan smirked. "That's why God gave us you, Ryan." As Ryan shook his head, Dylan said, "Besides, I still owe you for the toast at my wedding."

"That was a long time ago, and that debt has been paid in full … and then some."

"Paid in full would be if I had done it back to you. But you, chicken-shit, went off and elop—" Dylan stopped midsentence and looked at me with a wash of guilt streaking across his face.

"Good job, dumb ass." Ryan rolled his eyes at the mention of his wedding to Kari in front of me.

In the milli-second of awkward silence that filled the air, I broke it. "You were ... are married, Ryan? What?" I mocked and then smiled.

"Well, I can see what you see in her." Dylan looked at his brother with a smile and then turned to me. "But what the heck do you see in this chum?"

A thought suddenly bombarded my brain, and I literally blinked before resorting to something sarcastic instead. "Obviously, his fashion sense." I flipped the photo back over. "And there's also the brawns over brains."

"Thanks, Lenay. Just what I need—another person to pile on the 'let's harass Ryan bandwagon."

"I thought it was a pickup truck," I teased.

Dylan started laughing, and Ryan pulled me into those truly strong arms of his. But it wasn't the muscles that turned me on. It was the most content smile on his face. I could already tell that being away and reconnecting with some of his family seemed to put a calm in Ryan that I had never been witness to before.

"Dad, let's go!" Levi called from the downstairs of the house.

"All right, I am being summoned. Try not to burn the place down or lose the dog."

"Try not to be the nerdy soccer dad." Ryan wrinkled his nose at his brother. "Oh, too late."

"Uh-huh. Later, Ry. Nice meeting you, Bethany."

When the trio left, we explored the expansive property, which included the beautiful vineyard. We brought a few bottles back to enjoy with some light snacks on the deck, complete with firepit. There we talked about Garrett and the worry that hung over my family. My brother's appointments wouldn't happen until a few days later and, hopefully, I would have news of the results while in

Carolina. We also talked about Sallie and Joel—whom Ryan resisted contacting since he wouldn't have normally called any other weekend. However, because of an alert on his phone, he did know his house security system was set for staying-in at quarter after seven, which greatly reassured him.

It was a nice, quiet, relaxing way to end our day. So much so, we fell asleep right there. I woke up once because of the chilled middle-of-the-night air. But then I curled myself deeper into Ryan's protective arms. Feeling his body's warmth and listening to his rhythmic whistle breath put me into a peaceful sleep once again.

***

The following day, we went into town. I loved all of it—the slow pace of the streets, the quaint restaurant we had lunch at, and the unique little shops. But there was something else I loved even more. Midway through our excursion in town, Ryan had taken my hand and claimed it with his own as we freely walked the sidewalks. We were far from Hollywood, media, or anyone who would personally recognize us. And although there was still a risk of Ryan being identified, it seemed slim since he was dressed casually and had sunglasses on. Besides, what harm could really happen when the divorce announcement was just two days away?

After we finished a late dinner back at the house, Ryan joined our hands again but this time to pull me into his embrace. His mouth found mine in the most delicious way, and it wasn't just because of us sipping cabernet. It was because of the natural ease and pull of our two bodies. When he slipped his hands into the rear pockets of my jeans, tugging me that much closer, I thought I moaned, loving the touch and togetherness.

But it might not have been me. It very well could have been the dog, whom I felt nudging between our legs. I

193

tried not to laugh as Ryan, most definitely, grumbled at the goldendoodle, who obviously needed to go out.

"Geez, Vino." He broke our hold and petted the mop-headed dog. "Okay ... okay. Way to ruin the moment for me, man." Vino barked, I laughed, and Ryan pointed toward the door where Vino's leash hung. "Door," he directed the dog.

"Think of it as your exercise. I know you love going to the gym at your office building."

"Love and need are two different things. Can't wait to tease you when you're thirty-something and the pounds don't come off as easy." He pecked me quickly on the lips. "I'll be right back." Slinging his jacket over his shoulders, he pretended to kick the dog before the two walked out into the night.

***

I was finishing brushing my teeth when Ryan rejoined me not too much later. "Damn dog," he teased with a smile before saddling up behind me, pulling my hair to the side, and kissing my shoulder, exposed by the simple white tank I was wearing.

"Joel would love to take the dog out."

"Don't I know it." He shook his head and went for his own toothbrush.

Sitting on the edge of the old-fashioned tub, I was watching him brush his teeth when he called out my name. "What?" I questioned.

He did a slight chuckle. "I said your name twice. What were you thinking about?"

I hadn't realized I was so deep in thought that my auditory senses had failed me. I did, however, know what I was thinking about. It was him—him and the thought that had sprung into my brain the day before when his brother had questioned me. And it was also his teasing comment about still knowing me when I was in my thirties—years away.

"Lenay?" He was leaning against the sink, staring at me.

"Nothing."

"Nothing?" It wasn't just the sound of his voice, it was in the way he scrunched his face that told me he doubted the validity of my white lie.

"Just wondering what the plan is for tomorrow." I mean, I did want to know.

He blinked quickly and then held his hand for me to take it and get up. As I did, he proposed his idea. "What do you think about fishing?"

"Fishing?" I repeated.

"Mmmm-hmmm," he replied as we walked into the adjoining bedroom. "Ever been?"

"No."

"I think you'd like it … quiet, solitude, peaceful. It's for the thinker in you." He emphasized the word "thinker" surely still wondering what my lost-in-thought mood was all about. As we both sat on the red floral bedspread, Ryan continued, "There's a place not even an hour from home. We can leave here as soon as big pain-in-the-ass bro returns." He stood up and removed his jeans, leaving on only his boxers and T-shirt.

"You fished growing up?" I returned to the original topic.

"Yeah … the whole Thompson clan."

"I just can't picture you outdoorsy."

"Still the mean, no-frills judge from TV, huh?" He sat down again.

"Not." I poked him on his side. "At." And again. "All. Take me fishing. I think I'd like to try that."

"Yeah?"

"Yeah."

"Can we bring them back to the house for dinner, or are you going to be a catch-and-release girl?"

"Awww, Ryan …" He shook his head at my pouty face, and I questioned, "You hold onto them, don't you?"

GREA WARNER

"Yeah, usually."

"But if they're going to be hurt, you should let them go."

"Betha—" He stopped himself with a little devious smile. "How about heads or tails?"

I legitimately laughed. "That's kind of ironic."

He laughed back. "It is. What are you calling?" he asked and did an extremely sexy sweep of my body with his eyes. "What do you want to be ... heads or tails?"

Knowing what his sexy question was really asking, I pushed my lips together and took off my jeans before saying, "I want to be heads."

He smiled again, brought his hands to the bottom of my tank top, and lifted it off before going to my hips and gliding me onto his lap. "You got it, and the fish coin flip will wait for later." His soft feathering of kisses stopped momentarily. "You sure you're all right?"

"Yeah." I still couldn't completely get my mind off what I had been thinking about, and I'm pretty sure Ryan could tell by his question. In reality, though, it had to do with him and being with him, and there was nothing I wanted more. "Yeah," I reiterated and brought my hands underneath his black shirt right to his heart.

"Yeah? Good." He touched my lips before kissing me again. "I'm so glad we came here. I can't imagine anything more perfect than right now."

My internal and external happy sighs merged. "Ryan, me, either. For real."

"For real." He smiled.

***

Our day of fishing was in a lot of ways like our lovemaking the night before. They both were pleasurably long, serene, and different from any other time. I didn't want the weekend to end, but I at least knew it had the promise of a new beginning with Kari's press announcement happening the following day.

"It was a great weekend," I concluded as we were once again in Ryan's car driving back to his house.

"It's not over yet, baby. We have fish to cook!" Ryan was still in his free-living mood.

"Poor Nemo." I pretend pouted.

"Nemo? More like Moby."

I blew out a burst of air. "Not even. I still can't believe I let you hold onto the fish."

"Tails won," he taunted his actual coin-flip win.

"I know," I conceded. "Regardless, I didn't think we were having them tonight."

"Yeah. You're coming home with me, right?" His voice was more serious then. When I didn't answer, he swerved his head in my direction. "She's leaving right away," he said softly, and I knew—without me actually voicing it—that he had accurately assessed my concern of dealing with Kari. "I want you there." That time he had some hints of Judge Ryan in his voice.

Of course I wanted to stay. But before I had a chance to say that, Ryan's phone started chirping like a bird being attacked by a mad farmer. "What's all that about?" I asked, looking at his phone resting on the console between us.

"I don't know," he started. "Oh, geez, I bet there wasn't reception out there on the lake. I kind of remember that now. The phone is catching up."

"It did seem odd that your hip attachment wasn't alerting you of something."

"Ha! Ha!" He rolled his eyes, but it was pretty true that Ryan had to stay connected to his phone for his multitude of responsibilities. "I promised you peaceful, didn't I?"

"You did."

"Can you check it?" he asked. Because we were in his classic sixties red Mustang—one which would impress my dad—there was none of the modern technology, hands-free, connections like the BMW featured.

I turned his upside-down phone over. "It says you have

six missed calls and voice mails."

"Nuh-uh? In that short amount of time? That's even a record for me." He seemed as astonished as I was. "And it's Sunday—a holiday. No one calls. It's probably one—or both—of my sisters reminding me to call Mom for Mother's Day, like I'm not a grown adult who can remember to—"

"I'm afraid we do that to Garrett, too," I admitted and then read off the first caller's name. "Dylan."

"Oh, geez, what did we do? Not put a dish in the right spot in the dishwasher or a pillow needed fluffed? He definitely has the first-born role mastered."

I swung my head in his direction. "Hey, I'm a first-born."

"Yeah, but I can overlook the few little tendencies you have because I like looking at you in general." There was his sexy smile again.

"My tende—" I shook my head but grinned. "Maybe you'd like to listen to what your brother was actually calling about and quit digging yourself in deeper."

"Go ahead." He tilted his chin up at me with another smile. "Put it on speaker. You know the code."

"I don't."

"Same as the house."

As I went to do as I was told, I couldn't help but internally beam. Ryan didn't hesitate when it came to me knowing his passwords and listening to the messages. I guess I shouldn't have been surprised. He already trusted me with the most precious thing in his life ... his children. But it still made me happy.

"Hey, bro." Came the voice I had learned over the weekend as Dylan's. "Wanted to let you know, already heard back from the breeder. She's gonna have one of Vino's relatives for you soon."

Vino? The dog? Breeder?

My mouth dropped open as I turned not only my head but my entire body toward Ryan. "For real?" My voice pitched in excitement.

"It's time." I think he was trying not to smile but wasn't being quite successful. Ryan would try to deny it, but he loved playing with Vino during our stay. "Shhh, though. It's a surprise for the kids."

We missed part of Dylan's message during our conversation, but I think it was about the details of when to get the new pooch. I did *not* miss the next part of his message, though. And if the first part made me happy, the second part topped it.

"And Bethany? We like her," Ryan's brother proclaimed. "She's a good one. Don't mess it up."

"Pfff! Ha!" I spit out and let go of some of the anxiety that still remained over meeting his family.

Ryan shook his head. "You can delete that one."

"Already saved it." The day really was turning out beautifully—I actually enjoyed the sport of fishing, Ryan and I were in unison, his family more than accepted me ... "Ry," I said, looking back down at his phone. "There are three calls from your house ... your landline."

"Hmmm." His voice sounded even, but I could tell the little swish of concern that accompanied it by the way he turned his head my direction and his eyebrows lifted ever so slightly. "Play them."

"Daddy? Daddy?" Sallie's voice soared through the phone, and Ryan's head jilted even more so.

"That's it?" he asked.

"Yeah," I confirmed.

"Go to the next," he urged, and I knew why ... Sallie's two words—her dad's name—were far from calm. "Are you playing it?"

"Yeah." But we only heard a few seconds of fuzz. "That was it."

"Keep going." Ryan swiveled his head back and forth from me to the road quickly and, if I wasn't mistaken, was driving a tad bit faster.

"Daddy?" Sallie's voice had the same fearful inflection.

"Mommy's not acting right. She's hard to wake up. I don't know what to do. Daddy? I don't … Where are you? I need you. Daddy!"

"Oh, God. What?" Panic struck Ryan's voice.

And I couldn't blame him. That message … those words … her scared little girl sound … I was one hundred percent on alert, too.

"What does that mean? She's not waking up?" He turned to me, and I had a hard time looking in his eyes, not wanting to see the true terror of Ryan as a scared father. "That's from the house, right?"

I looked back down at the phone, but I knew it was the truth. "Yeah, that's what it says."

"Crap!" If I wasn't sure before, I was then—Ryan was definitely driving faster. "Call the house and give it to me."

"Ry," I tried to remain calm. "There's still another couple calls on here … from an Irene?"

"Oh, God. Okay. Yeah, play them."

He brought his right hand up from the steering wheel to swipe at his eyes. He wasn't crying, but I knew there was something daring to break at the surface. And since I had never been witness to it before, the reality of the situation frightened me even more.

"That's Kari's mom," he identified the caller as I pressed the button to allow us to hear the message.

"Ryan, it's Irene. I'm taking care of everything … of course." Her nasal voice seemed to punctuate every word, especially when boasting her own self-worth.

It made me instantly detest the woman but almost immediately feel bad about it. I was brought up to have more compassion than that. The woman's daughter was obviously having some kind of crisis. I closed my eyes and tried to think that way, but her next words made me feel very unchristian toward her.

"Ed and I have the kids," she continued. "Whenever you get done doing whatever you think is more important than answering your daughter's calls, you better make it over to the hospital."

"Oh, my God." Ryan rightfully seemed more concerned about the actual message than the cruel way it was delivered. "Call that number back," he directed me.

Knowing Ryan needed me to be calm and rational, I put my own panicked feelings aside and said, "There's another one. Let's listen, okay?"

I took his nonresponse as an affirmative answer and clicked on the next message from Irene. "We're all at Sinai. It's a good place for … Oh, Jesus, Ryan, where the hell are you?"

"Is that it?"

"Yeah." I did a double-check at his phone. "That was the last one. It was only ten minutes or so ago."

"What happened, Bethany? What the heck happened?" He didn't swipe at his eyes that time but his throat needed to be cleared.

I know he wasn't expecting me to give a legitimate answer. I didn't have one, obviously. I could only guess. And my mind wasn't even really focused from the whirling switch of moods that transpired in the car so quickly.

He did need me to speak, though. He needed to hear my voice. He needed me to be there and to try to just get him through. I understood that much.

"I don't … We're not that far from the hospital." I settled on what I thought should be a calming fact. "It's closer than your house."

"We gotta get there. Dang it. Where exactly?" He was tearing down the freeway.

"I'll pull it up on my phone."

"Yeah, no. I … I know where it is. I'm …" He let go of a breath he must have been holding in since his daughter's first cry for help.

"I know." I breathed, too.

"Sallie sounded so scared." He vocalized his stress.

"I know," I repeated, not wanting to lie. "It sounded like she knew what to do … to get help." I offered some optimism.

"She's the best little girl."

"She is," I agreed and smoothed my hand on his shoulder. "You're a good role model."

"Don't feel like—" He cut his self-loathing off and asked for my GPS skills. "Turn here, right?"

"Yeah, this left."

"Call Irene back for me, please. Keep it on speaker." I did, but when it went to voice mail, Ryan grunted and left a message for his former in-law. "I'm on my way. I'll be there soon, Irene." He nodded toward me, and I understood to hang up. "I need to know how my kids are, Bethany."

"I know." I was starting to feel like a broken, useless record. "I'm sure they're—"

"And Kari? What the heck?"

We sat in silence for a few more minutes and a few more turns. He could have kept asking question after question, but I didn't have any of the answers, and he knew it. Talking about it was not getting us anywhere. Right then, he needed to just concentrate on the road.

"There it is." I spoke of the hospital that was finally within sight. "Turn here. Parking is—" I literally held onto the edge of my seat as Ryan squealed the car tires dramatically into a tight parking spot … one of only a couple left.

He barely had the car in park before opening his door and exiting it. I watched as he started immediately marching toward the emergency room doors. It was a good few steps before he swiveled around to reclaim his eyes on the car with me still in it.

His face looked like it was compressed with a vice as he resorted to walking back to my side of the car. "Bethany, let's go. What are you doing?" he asked after opening my door. "We need to get—"

"You want me to come with you?"

"Yes." His voice was slightly abrasive from the obvious

stress. "Why not?" He tilted his neck for a particularly loud crack. "Oh." The reality of our situation came crashing violently back—Toto, we weren't in Napa anymore. "No," he denied. "I need you with me. Come on."

I took his hand only for a second and then knew to keep a respectable distance from him as we walked alongside one another toward the hospital. I was glad to be included ... that he wanted me with him. But I was nervous. I didn't know what to expect on any level—how dire Kari's situation was, who was going to be there to greet or confront us, what the physical and emotional state of the kids were, or what role Ryan expected me to play. I tried to push that aside since it wasn't about me ... at all. It was about all the other scared souls who were in one way or another connected in the unexpected detour of our day.

CHAPTER SIXTEEN

After temporarily giving up my purse and his wallet so we could go through the metal detectors, Ryan beelined directly to the main desk. I was about two steps behind but could clearly hear him asking the attendants the same flurry of questions he had asked me in the car. That time, though, he was bound to get more accurate answers. In turn, I was darting my eyes around the waiting area. With the kids nowhere to be found, I realized I was also looking for media or for anyone recognizing Ryan. That was what my world had become … and, sadly, I was used to it.

The hospital personnel were not saying much. They denied that Kari was even brought in, which I was sure had much more to do about her celebrity status than normal patient confidentiality. Out of frustration, Ryan shook off his blue baseball cap and rummaged through his dark hair, saying he could show them his ID. But the hat removal turned out to be enough of identification, I guess, when you are on television two nights a week. They proceeded then on telling him the basics of Kari's admission and where to find her.

"An overdose?" Those magnificent blue eyes I always loved gazing into looked even darker as he whispered those words and we headed down a corridor. "They said overdose."

Yes, I had heard it, too. I knew he was in a minor state of shock, considering not only the panicked call from Sallie but the latest revelation of what caused the call in the first place. Admittedly, it floored me a little, also. Then again, I was getting used to the drama that seemed to surround all things Kari.

"That doesn't make any sense." We turned onto another hall, getting deeper into the hospital and hopefully closer to where Kari and the kids were. "She's not ... she doesn't ..."

"I mean, we saw her at the daycare." I spoke quietly, not knowing how Ryan would take my recollection. I knew he wasn't in total denial of his ex-wife's issues, but would he believe that Kari had gone as far as what the hospital personnel said? When he shuffled in his step, I offered a kinder alternative. "When they say OD, could that mean pass out from drinking too much?"

"Uh, I don't kn—" he started, only to be cut off by a guard who physically stepped in front of us to halt our advancement in another hallway.

It took a moment of convincing again. Jeans, worn boots, and a plaid shirt had been very appropriate for our fishing date but not when needing to be identified as Mr. Mean TV persona. But Ryan was once again cleared—due to his actual ID. And I'm sure the stern, concerned look on his face probably helped, too. We were told there were only three rooms beyond the guard. Kari was in one. The other two were empty. Without saying it, I gathered we were in some special wing for situations just like Kari's—celebrities or public figures who needed the privacy and protection. When I been in that same hospital not that long before, I was in a crowded, curtained-off hallway rather than a room. That pretty much said it all.

Ryan was about to approach the nurses' station when we both heard his name called out. I was kind of impressed that I already recognized the voice. After all, I had only heard it once and it was via a phone recording. The same crassness was very evident, though, even in just one word.

When we simultaneously swiveled around, no introduction was needed. Kari's mother was standing up from her seated position in the small waiting area. Her salt-and-pepper hair was askew, but the rest of her was completely made up as if she was attending a ball. She wore a lot of eye makeup and her red lipstick matched her shawl trimmed in black. The glare she gave Ryan was just as dark.

But if Ryan noticed, he didn't comment. "What's going on?" He stepped toward his ex-mother-in-law. "How's Kari? Where are the kids?"

"We need to talk … in private." If the look she gave Ryan was evil, the one she had for me was demonic.

Taking both her words and look into consideration, I started to take a step away. But Ryan lightly brushed my arm. And if it wasn't a glare back at Irene Hynes, it was definitely a strong impression.

"She's not going anywhere," he said firmly. He blinked once in my direction, and I stopped turning for his sake, even though I didn't necessarily want to be a part of the awkward conversation. "Tell me, Irene," he prompted.

She did a little huff but proceeded on answering, nonetheless. "The kids are fine. They're with their grandfather. Ed has them. They needed the bathrooms and hadn't eaten."

Upon hearing her words, Ryan's body seemed to ease a little. He then lowered his voice. "What the hell happened?"

"You didn't answer your damn phone is what happened." Her suddenly slanted eyes shifted to me.

"We were at the lake. There wasn't reception," he started to explain. "I … damn." His body tensed again. "What happened? Was she fucking drinking again … with our kids at the house?" Ryan rarely swore, but if he did, you knew he was beyond upset. "Did she pass out? I thought that was a one-time thing. She told me—"

"Sallie called us after she couldn't get you. From what I gathered—in the middle of our race over there and Ed calling 9-1-1—" Geez, Irene was drama queen personified. I was sure she was scared and all those things happened, but the dramatic pauses, slight tilt of her head and arch of her eyebrows were pure exaggeration. "What we gathered," she started again, "was that Kari had been complaining about pain and was sleepy. And also, she was upset about the photo of you and the little gold digger here." In case no one in our intimate setting wasn't aware of who the "gold digger" was, she waited half a beat and then jerked her finger in my direction.

While I wilted a little on the insulting lie, Ryan asked, "What photo?"

"What photo? What photo!" she screeched.

"Yes, what photo?" He was more animated that time.

I was trying to piece the information together as it was coming at me in rapid-fire pace. Besides Irene's obvious detest of Ryan's relationship with me, there seemed to be some kind of visual evidence of it. But Ryan and I had never taken a photo together. Our relationship didn't need digital proof. Yet, it appeared someone had it, nonetheless.

In the time it took for me to process, Kari's mom had her phone flipped around and was pointing it at Ryan. When I leaned slightly in his direction to view the screen, I saw the damning image. It wasn't two separate headshots or even a screenshot of when I was on the show. But it *was* the two of us—holding hands as we strolled the streets of northern California. It didn't seem to be a professional shot—probably a camera phone—but it was clear enough to see how happy and content I appeared. And so did Ryan, who, despite his sunglasses, had, unbeknownst to us, been recognized after all.

"Crap." As he scrolled through the tabloid page—

complete with a closeup of our hands—I tried to see what was written in the short article. But Ryan handed Irene back her phone. "We're making the statement tomorrow. I wish we could have done that before the photo got out."

"Your God damn statement is going to have to wait," was her less-than-attractive reply.

"Irene." He said her name with a breath, which I recognized as trying to keep himself in check. "Let's get back to what happened. She was drinking?"

"No. Well, a little." I thought maybe Irene seemed a little more subdued until she concluded her thought with a dig at me. "*She* is not family."

"Stop it, Irene. She's not leaving."

Ryan's adamant rebuttal finally wore her down. "It's prescription drugs," Kari's mother explained. "We found them in her purse."

My mind went straight to an unkind place. Wasn't that little tidbit ironic? I did a quick glance at Ryan. It wasn't me he needed to be worried about having drugs in a purse. It was his ex. It was his kids' mother.

As soon as I let those mental flood gates open, I closed them just as quickly. I was being petty. I was not being the compassionate person my parents had raised. We still didn't know Kari's condition. But it had to be bad for all of us to be standing where we were. I should not have sunk to that level, but at least I had only done it internally. And that was probably just because I had spent the last so many minutes being harassed and raked over the coals by a person who obviously did not know the power of being kind.

"She's been taking them since the attack on tour … because of the headaches after the concussion," Irene further explained.

"She had a concussion?" Ryan shifted his feet and eyebrows.

"Yes." Her tone was once again dismissive … at best.

And it pissed Ryan off. "Dang it, Irene, how was I

supposed to know that?"

"She didn't tell *anyone*." On just that last word, Kari's mother seemed the tiniest of bits fallible, but then she snuck in another dig. "And you two are separated."

"Divorced," he clarified instantly. "We're divorced … and for a while now." He looked at me then, almost as if I needed the confirmation, too.

I didn't, though. I wanted him to know that. I wanted to reach out and hold his hand again, but I couldn't. Because even though I knew, and Kari knew, and Irene knew of the dissolution of marriage, the world didn't. We were in a public place with the possibility of hospital personnel approaching at any time.

"Okay," I practically whispered instead.

"Well, there you go," she sneered.

The tension between all three of us was immense, and I once again wondered if my presence was making things worse or needed at all. But he wanted me to stay. He had repeated it numerous times. So, I did.

"Between the physical pain and seeing you move on," Irene continued, "she was taking more than she should and mixing it with her anxiety meds and the occasional drink or two—"

"I got it." Ryan closed his eyes and reopened them. "Is she all right now? She's okay?"

Gosh, I thought. After all the nasty nitpicking with one another, would we finally get to the real issue at hand? Please.

"Thanks to a hit of Narcan."

"Oh, crap." Ryan's instant response to Irene came at the same time my breath did a quick vocal hitch.

Kari legitimately could have died. An actual shiver streaked through my body. In a flash of seconds, I thought about how Sallie and Joel must have felt and even what fear Irene and her husband must have gone through. And … Ryan.

He looked at me … his face twitching just the slightest

to make the connection to me. I reflected back with the softest of closed-mouth smiles, and he closed his eyes in appreciation. Right then I knew not only the reason he wanted me with him in the hospital but that I had, indeed, helped.

"The doctor is with her now … speaking with her privately. But we're talking about possibly getting her help. You know what I mean?" She did a sideways look at me, as if she was talking in code.

"Rehab," Ryan stated blatantly.

After a slight *hmmmf*, Irene confirmed, "Yeah, but she seemed fine this morning when she called to wish me a happy Mother's Day. She's a star and she's tough like me. So, she can power—"

"She needs it."

I turned in the direction of the deep voice that said those words. A hearty-sized man in a royal blue button-down and suspenders was suddenly beside us. And so were Sallie and Joel.

"Daddy!" the two little ones yelled in unison.

"Oh … Sallie, Joe-Joe, you guys all right? Come here." Ryan bent down to engulf them in a hug.

"Mommy's sick," Joel stated what was obviously foremost in his mind.

"I know, Joe." Ryan's voice lost all of the animosity it had held when speaking with his ex-mother-in-law. Instead, it featured the soothing, strong, caring tone I was most familiar with. "I'm gonna see Mommy in a minute. Want to make sure you're okay, first."

"I'm okay," the mini-macho man replied, as if seeing your mother rushed to a hospital wasn't a big deal.

Ryan flopped his blue cap onto Joel's head and then turned to his daughter. "Sals? You all right?"

"Where were you, Daddy?" she asked and then admitted, "I was scared."

It was not only her words but also the brave way she tried to speak, despite her obvious fear, that practically broke me. I had come to know those kids so well. I understood the vulnerability and the wanting-to-always-do-right who was little Sallie Thompson.

Ryan, of course, understood her more than anyone. And the recognition of what his little girl went—was going—through affected him immediately. He pushed his lips together for a second and then said in an even calmer voice, "I know. I'm so sorry, Tink. My phone wasn't working for a while. But you were so brave. You knew what to do—to use the programmed numbers and call me and call Gigi and Grandpa Ed, right?" Ryan looked up at whom I had pretty much concluded was Ed Hynes.

"Yeah. You told us that."

"I did. And you did great, Sallie. Great." Ryan smoothed his daughter's hair and then quickly stood up.

His eyes were misty ... even more so than when we had been in the car. To that point, he had surely been running on adrenaline. But seeing that his kids were safe and knowing that Kari was going to be all right, he needed the release. He looked directly at me, and I watched as his eyes showed me everything in a matter of seconds—embarrassment over his vulnerability, comfort that I was there, and a plead to divert the kids. He said all of that without any words. I knew him. He knew me. I was never more aware of our connection than in those few seconds in the hospital.

I took the step forward, purposefully touching Ryan's hand and allowing him that moment to turn away. "Hi, guys." I tried a smile at the Thompson kids.

"Hi, Bethany." Joel was pure Joel while Sallie softly smiled.

"Ed Hynes." The elder, with hair color similar to his wife's, stuck out his hand to me.

I accepted it, thinking how in just a few words I knew he had a lot more class than his quote, unquote better half. "Hi, sir. I ..."

I ... What *I* did was stumble. I was glad to meet him?

Really? No. And no matter how cordial, I knew he had to feel the same way about his daughter's ex's girlfriend. Because, for sure, he knew who I was.

"Ed." Ryan managed to collect himself, turn in our direction again, and bail me out.

"We … Our little girl could use your help, Ryan."

"We're *all* going in to talk to her," Irene interjected.

"To be as honest and frank … whatever it takes."

The interaction between Ed and his wife was quite interesting to observe. Irene was a fierce woman who could put anyone in their place. But her husband seemed to at least be able to bring her to a pause.

"Yeah, uh, of course," Ryan responded to Mr. Hynes. "When?"

"Soon. We're waiting for Maks," Ed spoke of his son.

"And the doctor is bringing in a mediator or specialist or something," Irene added, making me assume they were talking about some sort of intervention.

"You sure it's a good idea that I'm a part of this?"

Irene's mouth clamped straight and long, but Ed replied, "It will make a difference, Ryan."

"Yeah. Okay," Ryan agreed. "But the kids shouldn't—"

Joel was kind of bouncing around. But Sallie had been carefully listening and observing all of the adult conversation. And both Ryan and I knew it.

"Ry," I interrupted gently. "Can I talk with you for a minute?"

"Uh, uh, yeah." He looked at Kari's parents and the kids and then walked a couple of solid steps to the corner of the room with me. "I'm sorry." He was the first to speak.

"For what?"

"Geez, I don't know. All of this. For involving you." He rubbed his hands violently on his face.

"You want to stay, right?" I asked. "You want to help with the intervention or whatever."

"Yeah, I mean, I should. She's my wi—" He stopped

himself at the same time I did.

"She's not your wife." I was firm and swift with my reaction, even though I knew I should have held into account all the pressure he was under.

"Oh, man, Bethany, I'm ... Please don't make more out of that than needs to be. I'm just used to saying it. I've had to keep saying it," he pleaded. And when I didn't speak, he continued, "She's the mother of my children. The thought of them being in some kind of danger today? I was losing my mind when I had no idea what was going on. I don't know if you can understand the guilt I feel for leaving them when she obviously isn't stable."

"To be with me." I sighed.

His shoulders dropped. "I didn't say that."

"I did, and it's the truth." And *I* felt guilty.

"No ... yes ... look ... ahhh." He blew out frustration. "Yes, I do think I should stay to see what is going on. I want to make sure she gets whatever help she needs. Because, let me tell you, if she doesn't and I have to get lawyers back into this, I will. I will protect those kids no matter what."

Okay. Okay. That was why I had pulled him aside in the first place. Everybody's emotions were so high, no one could have a simple conversation without arguing. And I didn't want that to be us.

"Stay," I said simply.

"But—"

So he didn't need to worry anymore about what to do or even how I was feeling, I gave him my solution. "I'll take the kids back to your place."

"Bethany ..." I think it was his natural inclination to say no. He didn't want to trouble me. But the other parts of him disagreed. The part who knew he needed the help ... that the kids needed security, safety, and comfort. And the part of him who knew by then he *wasn't* troubling me. "Yeah?" he asked. And when I nodded the confirmation of my offer, he said, "Thanks," and we walked back to the kids and their grandparents. "Hey, kiddos. I'm gonna stay with Mommy. She's okay. Just want to make sure she gets her sleep."

"Like Sleeping Beauty," Sallie offered.

"Yeah, Tink," Ryan agreed, surely happy that Sallie still had that fairytale innocence. "But it's getting late. So, Bethany's gonna take you home, okay?" He glanced at his watch and grumbled once more. "I doubt I'll be home before bedtime. If you put those pjs right on, though, she might get you a snack or play a game with you."

Joel seemed nonchalant, but Sallie, who normally wouldn't have questioned, was a bright girl. She knew the merry-go-round their mixed-up day was on was not normal. She seemed slightly smaller then as she peered up slowly at all the adults surrounding her.

"Sals?" Ryan questioned.

There was the slightest of hesitations from his daughter before she reached for a hug from him. "Okay."

"I love you, little girl."

"I love you, too, Daddy," she said and then walked right to me, taking my hand.

I only had a second or two to relish the feeling of being someone's safe place when a tall doctor, with completely symmetrical circular eyeglasses, emerged. He scanned our collective crew with his eyes before landing on Irene. Whether it was because he already met her or he just somehow sensed she was the force to be reckoned with, I wasn't sure.

It was on her nod that he did speak, though. "Well, no immediate ramifications, but what we talked about earlier should happen."

"Her brother is on his way," Irene confirmed and then added an additional stab, I'm sure, just for me, "This is her husband."

"Ryan," he said with a slightly corrective tone and then reached out his hand to shake the doctor's.

When the man in the white coat had a look of concern

at Sallie and Joel, Irene clarified, "The kids are going home." She swung her head in my direction and gave me a dead-on sneer only I could see. "The *babysitter*"—there was a gallon of emphasis on that word—"is here. She is going to take them."

Ryan stomped his boot-covered foot in anger, but I closed my eyes to subtly shake off his urge to say anything. His response was a controlled, low moan before turning on his good-daddy voice for the kids. "All right, Sals and Joel, give Grandpa Ed ... and GiGi"—I appreciated the way he used his own dramatic pause to finally include Irene—"a hug, and thank them for helping." Even in distress and not really feeling the truth in his words, he showed good manners around his children. As the kids did as they were told, Ryan turned to me. "Bethany, are you sure?"

"Yep." I pursed my lips together and then added, "Should have left those fish go."

He grumbled but kept a positive attitude. "Keep them chilled. We'll get them later. Here. I'll get a cab back." He placed the car keys in my hand and purposefully squeezed to interlock our fingers for a second or two. It was all we could say or do.

***

Admittedly, I was a little bit of a pushover. I gave the kids a snack *and* played a game with them. And it was a little later than their normal bedtime when I suggested they go to sleep. I was a pushover because I knew they needed some happy things to place in their minds rather than the traumatic ones that had previously occupied them.

But I was also guilty of allowing them those perks because I wanted to keep *my* mind occupied. Playing games and talking with the kids kept me from scouring the internet to see if there were any other articles and/or photos of Ryan and me. It also kept me from thinking—or overthinking—what he was doing at that exact moment. He was with *her*—his ex-wife, the mother of his children, the woman he had professed love of before—and it had to be an emotional scene. I was pretty sure you weren't supposed to yell or get angry with the person at one of those things. You were to say how you felt and how it would be without them in your lives, right? I tried not to picture Ryan's face as he said words like those. I tried to realize how important what he was doing was. I tried not to feel jealous. I tried.

I did text him when the kids needed to go to bed, though. Putting them to sleep was new territory for me but, even more so, for them. It wasn't, I'm sure, that they didn't trust me. It was just another strike that their world wasn't quite right. But then again, no one's seemed to be at that moment.

Can you call? Kids want to say good night.

"Hey," I answered when his ring came almost immediately after I sent the text.

"Hi," he said right back, and I wondered if he noticed my greeting was once again not my typical Bethany self—everything was too heavy.

"Sorry to bother you."

"Bethany, gosh, no. How are the kids?"

"They're … they're okay. I mean … obviously what they saw is going to affect them," I spoke the truth.

"Yeah." His sigh was more tired than I ever remembered hearing from him. "Did they talk with you about it?"

"A little. Joel, I think, might want to be a paramedic now." On Ryan's welcomed soft chuckle, I continued, "With Sallie, I reinforced what you told her. I didn't want to say too much."

"I trust your judgment, Bethany," he said reassuringly, and I appreciated it. Just hearing his voice made me feel better.

"Other than that, it's all about the art of distraction.

You know ... babysitter tactics." I couldn't resist.

"Sorry about that. Irene can be such a witch."

He didn't need to tell me. I had been a witness and victim for a long enough time to realize Irene's true colors. I tried to keep the fact that her daughter was in such distress in mind. But I imagined—pretty much knew—that even without that factor, Irene Hynes was who she was.

"Here." I changed the subject back to why I had asked him to call. "I'll let you talk with the kids. Do you know when you'll be back?"

"Sorry. I don't. Everything is going to be fine, but there's a lot of stuff. If you need me, though, I'll leave right now."

I wanted to tell him *yes*. Of course I needed him. Our wonderful weekend had the plug so abruptly pulled out of it, I felt like *I* should have been the one at the hospital with paddles up to my heart to keep on ticking. But that was selfish, and he was under enough stress.

"No. No," I denied. "We're fine. Do what you need to do." And there was a weird pause. Thank goodness I could pass the phone off to Sallie.

***

The security system let me know when Ryan got back to his house later that evening. It was strange hearing him enter through the front door instead of the garage ... as if he was the guest and not me. In a lot of ways, I no longer felt that. I felt welcomed every time I visited and comfortable entering his house to wait for the kids on show days. But that night seemed to spin the wheels in reverse for a little way down the road of life.

While I couldn't hear his exact movements in the expansive house, I imagined he glanced into the living room and then went upstairs. That would obviously be where his slumbering offspring were. And he would have to figure, because of the later hour, that I had found similar refuge in his room, too. But that was not the case.

Since his body was silhouetted by the hallway light, I couldn't tell the features of his face when he did eventually find me. But his words were definitely riddled in concern. "Hey. Everything all right?" He sat down next to me, and I could then see the weariness.

"Hmmm," was what I managed.

"Why are you down here? Why didn't you go upstairs?"

I sat up in the guest room's bed and answered, "It was crowded up there."

"What?" More confusion from an exhausted mind.

"All her things," I mentioned the multitude of products in the master bath.

And then he understood. "Oh. Geez, there are how many bedrooms and she was staying there?" A frown erupted on his face at the thought of Kari boarding in his bedroom those couple of nights. "I'll take care of it. She—"

"Ryan?" I had enough of Kari for the night. It was my turn. "Do you mind if we don't talk about it? She's all right, right?" I added when that do-good-to-others thought also entered my brain.

"Yeah … will be."

Okay. "Do you think maybe you could just lay here with me?"

His shoulders sagged, but it wasn't necessarily in a negative way. It was in a way that I knew, in particular with the slight brush of his soft hand to my face, that he needed to let things go, too. He shed himself of his jeans and plaid shirt, lifted the comforter, elongated his body next to mine, and did exactly as I had asked. Those arms felt heavy but so secure as he wrapped them around me and brought me onto his chest. When he kissed the top of my head, it was so sweet I wanted to cry. And by his slightly vibrating movement, I knew he did, too.

"Lenay …" My name out of his lips seemed serene, needy, and sad all at the same time. And we laid there for a moment or two in silence before drifting off to sleep.

CHAPTER SEVENTEEN

"All right. Sorry, just toaster pastries this morning. No time for special chocolate oatmeal. We all slept in a little late." I could hear Ryan talking with the kids in the kitchen as I was making my way down the hall.

"I want simaman."

"Cinnamon." Came Sallie's corrective sister voice.

Which prompted Joel to whine, "Daddy!"

"Sallie, he's trying," Ryan said, followed quickly by, "Uh, uh, uh, no. Don't stick your tongue out at your sister."

I stifled a laugh, picturing what was going on. It truly was Americana … and so removed from the other aspects of their life—the glitz, glamour, and stages. The kitchen scene was the side of the Thompsons I knew and liked best.

"We got cinnamon," Ryan continued. "How about you, Sals?"

"Cookies and cream, please. Where's Bethany?"

I paused my feet on her question, wondering if she asked it because she knew it was late when they had gone to sleep. Or, was she simply used to me sleeping over? Still unseen, I leaned against the wall and waited for Ryan's answer.

"Getting dressed. She really slept in. You two must have tired her out." I could hear the teasing in his voice.

But Joel didn't. "We did not!"

"Daddy did." Sallie gave her own theory, and I almost laughed again. Maybe even more so when she concluded with "fishing."

"Yeah, maybe." Ryan went along with that theory. "Did she show you the fish we caught?"

"Yeah. That one was soooo big!"

Ryan and I had caught a few fish. But none of them were even close to being big. Well, except maybe to the eyes of a four-year-old boy who wanted to be just like his dad.

Ryan did an actual chuckle. "Here you go. Drink your juice, too." I heard the clank of a couple of plastic cups and was ready to approach when Ryan spoke again. "I'm glad you like Bethany so much."

"She's pretty," Joel commented, and I stopped and secretly listened once more.

"She is." I could almost hear the smile on his face.

Sallie added her own set of adjectives, as if she just had to outdo her little brother. "She's smart and funny and … skinny."

As I shook my head, Ryan agreed, "She's all those things, too. So, remember what I said? Bethany has to work and then is going to see her mom and dad. GiGi is going to pick you two up from school, and you'll stay at their house until tomorrow night."

"Not Mommy," Sallie said it as a statement, but it came out a little as a question.

It was for me, too. Since I took the weekend off and was heading to Carolina for Ella's graduation, I was working an extended shift at the coffee house and couldn't be there for the kids those two days. It had been okay, though. Kari was going to take them. But, obviously, that all changed. I guess Ryan had made similar arrangements with Irene.

"No, babe, we talked, right? Mommy's—"

Sallie's interruption of her father seemed to be almost a recitation. "Tired from her tour. We'll see her soon."

"Yeah. I love you, guys." I could hear the emotional tug in Ryan's voice before he tuned it right back up. "Come on. Grab your bookbags. We have to catch the school van, and I have to let the front gate know to let Bethany's ride through in a little bit."

"What about Eli?"

I was wondering who Joel was talking about and what Eli had to do with their scheduling, when Ryan answered, "I got it packed, buddy."

And then I remembered. Eli was Joel's stuffed toy dog. How did Ryan think to do all of that, especially when he had so many other things on his mind? I closed my eyes in silent appreciation and listened as they made their way to the front door.

After grabbing my own cinnamon pastry, I went into the living room. I should have felt rejuvenated, having done a yoga pose and being freshly clothed for the day, but I didn't, and I really couldn't put my finger on what exactly had me feeling that way. I think maybe because it wasn't just one thing. It was a number of things all tied into knots together. And the silence in the house, without two active children and their dad, made the feeling settle in even more.

I heard the front door announce Ryan's reentry before he found me sitting on the sofa. "Hi, beautiful."

"Don't forget funny and smart and … skinny." I tried to perk up my ominous attitude and admitted to my eavesdropping. "Those kids …"

Dressed casually since it was a show day instead of an office day, he smiled and replied, "You have some fans."

I kicked the instant, self-depreciation thought of *No, I didn't. I was a coffee barista, not a superstar* right out of my mind. Because, in truth, I knew what he said was right. I knew those two fans were the best anyone could ask for.

He sat down next to me. "Thank you for taking care of them last night and for, I don't know, just dealing."

His kind words only made me want to cry, though, because I realized how much he meant them. But I also knew … suspected … feared … that there was going to be yet something else to deal with. And I already felt like I was teetering on a breaking point.

"I don't know that I am, Ryan," I said honestly.

"Tell me."

"I guess I need to know everything." Need was a lot different than want but, alas, it was the truth.

He sighed slightly and then began, "She's being settled into the … resort. We're calling it a resort. That's what I told the kids in case they say anything to anyone." He confirmed that the previous night's end result was a rehab facility—surely the best, exclusive one where all the stars went. "Hopefully, it won't be long. She's never had issues with drugs or alcohol before. They're blaming it on a combination of things—exhaustion from a long tour, the trauma physically and mentally of being attacked, the scripts interacting with her pills …"

Irene's comment at the hospital about the anxiety pills was something I never knew about Kari. But then again, there was no reason I should have. It made sense why Ryan talked about so many people needing them when I had told him my mother took a similar prescription. Never would I have thought my stay-at-home pastor's wife mom would have anything in common with a world-renowned singer. I guess we're all just people struggling through life.

"At least this bizarre behavior since coming back makes sense now."

"What did Kari say to you?" I had to ask. It had not only bothered me the whole time he was gone, but it had also filtered into my sleep with visions of the two of them together.

"We had a good talk. She knows we're over. But with

everything that happened and now having to face it, there is a lot of guilt and remorse and jealousy."

"She hates me," I summed up. It wasn't too hard to come to that conclusion since the few interactions we had with one another were nowhere near civil.

"No, she … It's more about the kids. She hadn't seen them in such a long time, and now when she does, she hears about you."

It was my turn for my shoulders to sag, and it wasn't a good feeling. "What am I supposed to do about that?"

"You're not," he immediately reassured. "You're fine. It's fine. It's her problem, and it is exasperated by all the other issues. She needs to get some therapy, and it will be fine."

"And? But?"

I knew there was more. I could see it in his squirming face and narrowing eyes. Even more so, that weird feeling I had since waking up wouldn't let go.

And then came the blow—the one I somehow knew was coming all along. "We have to hold off on the statement about the divorce and anything else."

My entire body instantly got tense, and I rose from my seated position. I breathed out a gust of air and closed my eyes. I couldn't do or say anything for a moment. I was completely frustrated. The fact that the whole world didn't know they were divorced from the beginning only partially made sense to me, but I had learned to accept that. But, no. Just no. I couldn't any longer.

I didn't even try to think of others. I just blew out my exasperation. "What does it matter?" It was somewhere between a yell and a cry. "It's done. The divorce is done. It's over. It's been over. Nothing is going to change that."

"I know." He was trying to remain calm as he joined me in an upright position. "It's just not the time. For one thing, we don't want to draw any more attention to Kari and, most certainly, where she is. We got her there without incident last night, but the press is obviously going to be looking for her for a comment about the photo. We just have to keep silent and hope for the best."

"Until when? Days? Weeks? What?" I know I was putting pressure on him, and it was something he absolutely did not need. But I simply didn't care at the moment. I was tired of the whole secrecy and coverup.

"I don't know, Bethany!"

It was the first time he had ever significantly raised his voice at me. I had seen him disappointed and determined when he thought I was a drug user. I had seen him tentative and leery when he saw me with Andre. I had even seen him pleading when I had been witness to that kiss on television. But our current situation was different. He was upset. And it was directed toward me with probable cause. I was pushing him.

I managed to contain my voice a little better as I offered, "So, you're not putting out any statement and just going to ignore the questions? Or are you going to lie and say the photo was doctored, or I am just a friend?"

"Yes. No. I don't know." To further demonstrate his stress, he popped his neck and took a breath. "There are people working on halting what is out there, okay? For one thing, the media can't even positively identify me."

I rolled my eyes. "It's you."

"But, as you know, I didn't use my cards anywhere. We only paid cash. We didn't say who we were, and besides the essential people, no one knew I was even out of town. There's no proof. And the really good thing is, I haven't seen your name anywhere. It's just mystery woman."

Yes, I was astutely aware of all that—the precautions taken and my name status. The article that Irene had "so kindly" shown us at the hospital had identified us as "Ryan Thompson and mystery woman." I had, indeed, scoured the internet after the kids went to sleep. Besides some reposts and tag-ons of that article, there weren't any additional ones. But even though my name was still unknown, the image of me was fairly clear. The good part was, I was a nobody songwriter who had faded into the press sunset as soon as my show episode aired. That definitely helped me not being recognized right away. But it probably wouldn't take long for someone to connect the dots.

"And, Bethany, it would be a good idea for you to take down any photos of you on your social media. I know you don't usually post them, but—"

"Yeah. Fine." I let out a gargled sigh, shut my eyes momentarily, and then continued, "Forget the media. There are people at work and where I live. What if they see the picture? They know I was on the show and a few know I am working with you. I'm pretty sure some of them will know it's me, even with sunglasses on. What do I say? I don't want them thinking I am a—" I couldn't even say home-wrecker even when I wasn't. "And what about my family?" I knew the likeliness my mom or dad would see the photo was slim to none, though—they frowned upon the lifestyle that was portrayed in such magazines and television shows.

"Tell your family … who you trust. You know I have mine."

"My father … my parents … won't like the deceit. *I* don't like the deceit."

"Just so we're clear, I don't like the deceit," he said firmly.

"It feels—"

"Bethany, I get it. I get it. I do." Frustration and pleading were rolled into one. "Like I said, I'm being advised to wait and give it some time and space. Let the professionals work on it … try to minimalize it. I promised no comment about anything."

"Who? Who is exactly advising you?" I was realizing that not only did they get Kari to commit to treatment the night before, but there had been a lot of other conversations going on, too—like decisions on what to do with the kids and how to handle the ramifications.

"Lawyers. Her team."

I don't know why that was the final straw, but it was. "Fine. Then, that's what I'll give you—time and space." I grabbed my phone and bag from the coffee table and started past him.

"What? No." He followed. "Geez, that's not what I meant. That's not what I need at all."

I adjusted the strap on my shoulder and made it into the hall before turning around. "Maybe I do."

I wasn't sure that was the case. But I couldn't stand there and listen to the myriad of words that were all saying the same thing. Nothing was changing. Nothing was going to change. It was supposed to. I was told it was going to, and then, once again, a different decision was made.

"Ah, man, Bethany. I … I don't know what to do. I know what I want. But I have to think of the kids, and I have to think of you … and, yes, Kari. The other thing is, in the state she is in, they don't think she can handle everyone knowing about the divorce right now. She'll think everyone will think she is a failure, and it could hinder any progress. She needs to find her way, and then it can all come out. It won't be long. Everyone …" He emphasized the word and made a point to look directly into my eyes. "Everyone can be—will be—happy."

I knew and was even sorry that Kari was hurting. But I hurt, too. "I hope so. But right now? What's going on isn't … I can't get the rug pulled out from under me again." He knew me enough to know what those words meant and how I had been scarred in the past. "I want to believe you, Ryan, but that's not what it looks like right now. It's like I said before—sometimes everything seems so fake."

"We … are … not … fake."

I loved that he was determined to let me know our situation was not what he desired and that he had faith in us. It mellowed my good-bye heart for a beat and allowed me to tell him what had been pounding in my soul for days. "Do you remember when you asked me what I was thinking about that last night at your brother's? Gosh, Ryan, that was just over twenty-four hours ago."

So much had happened. So much had changed. Yet, so much had not.

"I know." He sighed. He got it. "What?" he asked a little more calmly, surely recalling our lovely evening. "What were you thinking about?"

"Number four. You are number four," I admitted.

"Four what? Stars? Are you playing judge now?" He was, obviously, trying desperately to bring some levity to our conversation.

But I was too emotional and ready to tell him something I couldn't keep inside anymore, and it really was the worst timing. "No. Four," I answered seriously and somehow managed to look him in the eyes. "You're the fourth man I've been with." I counted the mutual hand job I had with a guy friend of mine before Hutch. An experimental first for both of us, it still, in my brain, was sex. "And I swore—I had made this secret pact with myself a while ago—that there would be no more than six … like the six strings on a guitar. I know it sounds weird. But in Napa I thought I wanted to change that to a four-string guitar. And now … now …" I was used to writing my feelings in fictitious lyrics. But saying them out loud to the person I wanted to the most? It was new and scary territory for me. But I was determined. "I'm worried that isn't the case or at least, the string broke." Admittedly, it was a stupid, immature, girly, got-my-heart-stomped-on-a-couple-times pact, anyway.

"Bethany …" I knew I had caught him off guard by the way his voice emotionally trembled my name.

"I don't want to be hurt, especially—" I stopped myself.

"What? Especially what?" he coaxed in the same serene mood I was suddenly in.

And then I went for it because I had pretty much already said it with my guitar analogy. "Especially when I know I love you." I brushed his hand after saying those three words and looked down at my phone, which had been vibrating. "My ride is here. I have to get to work." And I opened the front door.

"Bethany, wait. Geez."

I knew from the volume of his voice that he had stepped out to the front porch after me. But I didn't turn. And I knew he wouldn't follow me to the Uber. We didn't need anyone else as a witness to our connection. We didn't need any more photos in the press or someone quoting what we were saying to one another. I even instructed the driver to take the private exit out. Looking through the back window as the car pulled away, the last image I saw was Ryan shaking his head and starting to close the door.

***

He tried calling me shortly after I left. It was as the Uber was pulling up to the coffee shop. I'm sure he planned when to time his call—at the point between when I wasn't entrapped in a vehicle with a stranger and the few minutes or so before I actually had to start my busy day of coffee and pleasantries. He also should have been intuitive enough, though, to realize that it didn't matter. I was not going to pick up the phone.

I listened to his voice mail message as I went to the back room and put on my apron. His words were simple, urging me to call him back ... he wanted to talk. I did not—call him back or want to talk. I needed as much of a break from the Thompson saga as I could get. Luckily, the customer turnover was steady enough to keep my mind otherwise occupied. And when there was a lull in activity, I took the opportunity to sing a few songs—sad ones—for the customers who were there.

For a while, I kept an eye on the door, half-expecting Ryan to make an appearance. But he didn't, and I was glad. The coffee shop wasn't the place for our next conversation—not only because of the nature of our talk but because of the implications of the public around us.

Gracie was the only one who mentioned the photo to me. At first, I started to deny it. But then I stopped. I shouldn't. I couldn't. I wouldn't. It was me in the photo online. Not only did Gracie know I worked with the music manager, but she recognized my medical alert ring on the enlarged photo of my hand intwined with Ryan's. As my boss in a job that dealt with food, she was very familiar with the ring. Not wanting to lie, I pushed the truth around a little and admitted to the authenticity but brushed it off as one of those camera-angles, out-of-context kind of situations. She said she took my word for it but voluntarily added that she wouldn't give up my guise to anyone. I wondered if that was because she didn't believe me and had lived in the false lights of La-La Land too long. Or, was it her relating to hiding … as she felt she needed to with her sexuality in certain situations. Either possibility was simply cry-worthy to me.

Ryan tried calling again after my shift. But, when I didn't answer, he did not leave a message. And I knew he wouldn't try again—at least not for a while—since he was preparing to go on live television.

When I eventually walked into my room at the apartment house, my feet were heavy and my heart even more so. It would have been a smart idea to have stopped at the building's dining hall first, as I hadn't eaten since the toaster pastry in the morning … but I didn't. I just flopped on my bed and pulled my dark hair out of the messy bun it had been in since I thought someone at the coffee shop had been looking at me a little too long. It could have been for a multitude of reasons besides a scandalous photo online, but I had decided to at least try to create a mini-disguise.

I took out my phone and started checking my social media. During the Uber ride from Ryan's house, I had eliminated the very few photos I had on my sites, but I wanted to make sure there weren't any comments or posts about the "other" photo. Relived that there weren't, I had just started to search the web when there was a knock on my door.

My sigh and greeting were the exact opposite of my next-door neighbor's exuberance as she bustled into the room. "So … who do you think is going to be the 'it' performance tonight? I like that Tisha. She has the lungs and the confidence. What does your man think?"

"He's not my man." I partially grumbled and made an effort to sit up.

She blew off my denial. "Whatever you want to call the reason you are never around here anymore. I'm just psyched to actually watch it with you tonight."

I couldn't take it anymore. I had been holding it all in. Not only that morning and the gut-wrenching admission I made to Ryan but the dramatic night before and, heck, pretty much since we first met. I brought my hands up to my face and began to downright sob.

"Crap, Bethany." Willow's voice instantly softened, and I felt her sit next to me. "What's wrong? Is it your brother?"

"No." I pushed out a puff of air and removed my hands from my face. "We haven't heard anything yet besides the foot isn't broken, so that isn't what is causing the swelling. Sad when you want a foot to be broke."

"What's this all about, then?" She looked at my tear-stricken face.

It wasn't a broken *foot* … it was my broken heart. "It … I … it's … it's Ryan," I managed to tell the truth.

"Oh." She paused. "Oh. I know you've been quiet about everything, and these situations don't usually …" She had no idea what the real situation was, but I knew she was going to finish her aborted sentence by saying "end well." And I feared, even if I wasn't the mistress of a married man, what she was predicting was true.

"You haven't seen or heard anything?"

"No." Her answer slightly reassured me that the photo wasn't completely wide yet and maybe Ryan or Kari's "peeps" had been able to slow it. "What? What would I have seen? Can you tell me?"

Ryan had said to tell whom I trusted. Not only was Willow someone I did without a doubt, she knew most of it, anyway, and I really needed to talk. "Ironically," I started, "I think you'll like him a little more if I do. Do you mind if we don't watch the show, though? I don't want …" Gosh, to see him … to ache for him … to wonder if what I had said was the right thing to do.

"No problem."

"I don't even want to be in this room." Suddenly, my living space felt even more claustrophobic than ever.

"You want to get out of here? Yeah, let's really get out." She made up my mind for me before I even had a chance. "I'll drive. You do whatever you need to do to release—talk to me, have a tear in your beer …" Patting me on the leg, she stood up. "I'm gonna get changed into some fun clothes. You?" She smiled a tease. "Well, do what you can."

CHAPTER EIGHTEEN

Putting my hair up once again and getting out of the clothes I had on all day did help reenergize me a little. Not usually much of a makeup gal, I even refreshed my face with some lipstick and highlighter and popped my brown eyes out with complementary shades of green and brown. Having the windows rolled down in the car further lifted some of the heaviness from my body. And the couple of beverages I immediately started with at the fairly empty bar, admittedly, coated the hurt a little, too.

Willow acted as the smart sidekick as she drank only diet soda, ordered us appetizers, and listened as I discretely—not using names because of our public setting—filled in some of the missing blanks of Ryan and Bethany, hashtag the truth. She heard it all, including the divorce, the winery, and the photo. But I stopped there. I did not feel comfortable telling her about Kari's incident or where it had landed her. And I also didn't tell her about the exact words spoken between Ryan and me that morning. But she knew I was at my breaking point and needed something to change. Because, really, that was what it came down to.

When we got to a point in our conversation where

nothing else could be said, Willow changed subjects, mentioning an event taking place at our apartment building. "What do you think of that social thing on Friday?"

"I don't know. It's—" I started to mention the building's anniversary party.

"It's not 1950!" she interrupted with a boom. "They're moving backward instead of forward. A social? First of all, who calls it that? Second, a social definitely involves guys. We already practically live in a convent."

I couldn't help but do a soft chuckle. "It's still a nice idea."

She rolled her eyes. "You going then?"

"No, I'll be in Carolina."

"Great excuse," she scoffed.

"It's actually great timing."

"To put some distance between you and Mr. Mean."

"Ryan."

"I know what his name is. I thought we were using code. I guess he's not totally mean. But he is a little bit if you are hurting so much."

But I hadn't been correcting Willow with her choice of names for Mr. Thompson. I was making a new statement … acknowledging his presence. "No. Ryan." I subtly nodded in the direction of the bar door—the one I was facing and Willow was not.

It was then, when Willow turned from her bar stool, that Ryan spotted us. His eyes opened wide for a split second and then seemed to go sad and remorseful in an even quicker motion. I managed to keep watch on him, but I think it was only because I was in shock from actually seeing him there.

He wasn't alone. There were a few others surrounding the entry, and I recognized them all from the show— Portia, the other two judges/artists, and other producers or execs. When Ryan was pulled away with them to an elongated table at the side of the room, Willow's voice directed me back to her.

"What do you want to do?"

I took another swig of my fruity concoction and tried not to look again at the table full of television and music professionals. But it was hard. I wanted to know what he was doing … how he was feeling. I didn't answer my friend, though, because I didn't know the answer. But then, just as suddenly, a very Willow-esque plan popped into my mind.

I called over the bartender—the hunk with a killer smile, squinty eyes, and bulging biceps—and leaned a little closer than I had all night. I wasn't flirting. Neither was he. But Ryan didn't know that. Then, not only did I order another drink, but I made a request.

Moments later, "Landslide" started blaring from the establishment's speakers. I mouthed a "thank you" to the bartender, took a sip of my new drink, and worked really hard on not turning to see Ryan's reaction to the song. I didn't need to see him, though, to know he understood not only how the song came to be on at that particular moment but also how I was feeling. I knew because a text from him came through to my phone almost immediately.

What R U doing?

Drinking, I texted back, feeling both oddly nervous and proud of myself … clearly a result of those said drinks. *What are YOU doing?*

Exec Prods BDay. Last min after show celebration, he answered just as straight forward. When I looked at my phone but didn't reply—and I knew he had a seat where he could watch me straight on—he texted again. *I want to talk w/U.* Another follow up came when I ignored the text. *Meet out back.*

I flipped my phone over so I couldn't see the screen. Willow, who had not spoken a word since questioning me about what I wanted to do, bit her top lip and made her eyes grow wide at my actions thus far. She was totally latching on to the vibe.

"What is he doing?" I asked, refusing to give him the pleasure of turning myself.

From her position at the bar, Willow could get away with the partial turn much better than I could. "Looks like he is making conversation, but he's not," she noted. "He keeps looking over here, and his hand is on his phone. Now he's texting or something." When my phone vibrated another incoming text and I didn't even turn it over to read it, she added, "Well, now he looks mad."

"You should be a play-by-play sports announcer," I teased and felt for the first time that night a little tipsy. I wondered if it was all purely alcohol or seeing him that had caused the ultimate effect.

"Ha! Ha!" she joked back. "Yeah, I have a radio voice. Not the face."

Hollywood—the dasher of dreams for all of us, I thought, and then commiserated, "Like me—I can write them, just can't sing them."

"Cheers, sista." Willow raised her soda glass and then brought it abruptly back down. "Oh, well, he's, uh … he's coming over … here."

And then, there he was, standing right next to me. I could see him out of the corner of my eye, but, even more so, I could feel him—the heat vibrating from his tall, built body. And I could smell him—the musky vanilla scent that was so Ryan. I waited for him to speak to me or touch my hand or acknowledge my presence in any manner—and he definitely could have since Willow and I were the only two at the bar besides one other couple at the opposite end. But he didn't.

Instead, he called over the bartender, and I silently cursed myself as I turned the slightest of bits to see the interaction completely. Ryan slid his credit card and a piece of paper to the bartender and said, "I'm buying a round for that table over there." He did a nod in the direction of the crew he was sitting with. "And that, too." Ryan barely gave the bartender a second to look at the credit card and read whatever was on that paper before asking, "You understand? You're good with that?" His tone was pretty sharp and a little condescending—very un-Ryan like … more Mr. Mean.

"I've got it, sir," he replied in a tone where I knew he recognized who the music rep was.

And then Ryan turned to me before I could glance away. "Out back." His blue eyes were deeper and more direct than I ever remembered them.

And it made me nervous … and giddy … and bold all at the same time. "Well, hey, look, Willow, it's Ryan Thompson." I looked from him to Willow, whose eyes seemed to grow ten times at my sassiness.

"Please."

His one word, which started out in the same firm tone, somehow ended a little with a plead, and it got to me that time. I'm not sure if he knew it, though. Bringing his hands up to massage the back of his neck, he glanced over at the table of his cohorts and so did I. No one seemed to be looking our direction and/or, thankfully, putting gossip photos together. But when Ryan put his phone up to his face—and I knew it had neither rung nor had he called anyone—I understood what he was doing. He was making an excuse for stepping outside, which he did with one last blink of a look at me. It was sad that I knew the tricks of deception.

I exhaled sharply as Willow said, "He's intense."

I found myself giving Ryan an excuse … albeit a legitimate one. "He's stressed."

"I didn't say it was a bad thing." My best friend winked and pretend-fanned herself, not knowing how much her being there and keeping things light helped me.

"I … I'm gonna go see him." I hadn't made up my mind until it came out of my mouth.

"Sure?"

I couldn't help the sigh. I *wasn't* sure if it was a good or bad decision. But I had made it. "Yeah. Rescue me, okay?

You *are* my wing girl tonight, right?"

"I got you," she reassured.

"Not long, Willow," I warned, not knowing how well my emotions—especially in my alcohol-induced state—would hold up.

"I'll pay the bill. We're done, right?" Again, she made the decision for me. "Yeah, we're done. Then I'll get the car and pull it around back for operation rescue. Does that work?"

"Yeah. What do I owe?"

"We'll settle it later. Settle whatever with Mr. Mean first."

I didn't argue. Willow and I were tight enough that we didn't have to worry about who was paying and when we would even things out. Besides, I couldn't concentrate enough to split a bill right then even if it was just one dollar. My stomach felt like it had two sides attempting to constrict and meet in the middle to form a fierce knot. And as I slid off the barstool, I wondered if talking with Ryan would help untie it or create a few thousand more.

***

When I walked out to the deserted alley, the first thing I noticed was the mystical look and feel of the setting sun. The next thing was Ryan. He was standing against the far wall simply staring at me. I immediately stopped and let him take the necessary steps for us to be close enough to talk.

As he did, I was thinking it was only that morning when we had been joking about the description the kids had of me. But it was also only that morning when I had walked out. It felt like years before. We, somehow, seemed like different people. And it made me so sad.

I pushed all those thoughts aside and tried to regain my strong-woman mentality. "All right, Ryan. I'm out here."

"What's going on, Bethany? What are you doing?" He

definitely had let down his bravado.

"I told you … drinking." And the knots turned to swishes in my stomach just to confirm my answer.

"Uh-huh. How much?"

"Enough." In all honesty, I wasn't sure, but it wasn't as much as I was probably giving out the vibe for—nerves, sadness, and anger were aiding that. "You know, I kinda had a crappy morning."

His body contracted on my words, as if he was the one with the knots. "I want to talk with you about that. We need to talk about all of it. I want to tell—"

"No," I interrupted. "I've heard it all. I need a break." I really, truly did. Even though my heart pitter-pattered seeing him there in that bar … in front of me … I just needed some time removed. I knew I was almost in tears when I reiterated, "I just need a break. I want to forget for a moment."

"Let me drive you home," he offered. "We can talk—"

Even though it didn't outwardly advertise it, I knew the shirt he had on was the one he bought during our getaway. And that alone almost got me to give in to him. But then I saw something else he was wearing. It was something he wore all the time. It was something he shouldn't be. It was—

"No." I backed up a step, glaring at his lie-of-a wedding ring.

There was a little sigh before he said, "You shouldn't be drinking. Tell me you're not going to have any more. I'm worried about the choices you make when you—"

"Worried I am going to eat something wrong for me or *do* some*one* wrong for me?"

Ryan fiercely squeezed his eyes at the crudity of my words. I shouldn't have said them. It was an instinctive, couldn't-get-hurt gut reaction that I, indeed, would have never said had I not been drinking. I felt immediately sorry for saying them and tried to make a little bit of amends when he reopened his eyes.

"I'm …" But I couldn't quite say I was sorry. I did, however, acknowledge his concern. "You don't have to worry. Willow is pulling the car around. She's sober. We're going back home. And Ryan …" I breathed in. Darn it, if I wasn't going to speak the truth to him again. "I wouldn't do that. Sober or drunk, God help me, you are the only one. I … well, you know."

If my own self-preservation of not wanting to be hurt didn't stop me from telling him I loved him again, Willow's sudden presence in front of us did. "Car is on the side. Couldn't pull around." She looked from me to Ryan to me again.

"I gotta go." I gladly took Willow's entrance as a perfect exit and walked right past him and to my savior friend.

"Bethany …" He semi-sighed. "Bethany, please." But I continued to walk. "Willow?" I looked at Willow when Ryan said *her* name that time. "Willow, can *you* stay for a second?"

I had no idea why Ryan wanted Willow to stay … what he wanted to say to her. I just knew *I* couldn't remain there. When Willow lifted her eyebrows at me, I shrugged, gave a slight nod, and walked to the other side of the building. It was where Willow's car was. But it was also just out of eyesight—but not earshot—of their conversation.

It was Ryan's voice I heard first. "I'm glad we're getting a chance to meet. Bethany has mentioned you quite a few times." He sounded so polite—not that he wasn't normally, but it wasn't the same natural way he talked with me.

"Don't believe the hype," was her typical witty Willow comeback.

"I won't if you won't."

"Well, about …"

Oh-oh. Was Willow going on attack? I had wondered if the reason she decided to stay back was out of curiosity or to play protective mama bear by confronting the man who had made her friend cry.

"Ryan … can I call you that?"

Good grief, Willow. Please, just don't call him Mr. Mean. He normally would have found the humor in it but not right then. I steadied myself against the brick wall.

"Yeah. Ryan."

"She needs a little bit of space." My friend echoed my sentiments.

"Did she tell you everything? I know you had your suspicions, and I told her—"

"Yeah, but really only now because she is so sad and she needed to talk."

"I don't want to see her hurt. That's not …" His voice hesitated, and I think it was more out of emotion than indecision, although I couldn't see him to know for sure.

"Let her be for now." Willow sounded like a wise, old fortune teller. "She knows where you are."

"But she doesn't know what I want to say." There was a pause before he spoke again. "Tell her something for me. What she told me before she left this morning? I one hundred percent feel the same way. But I want to tell her in person … face to face. She needs to give me that chance."

"Okay." Willow didn't know I had told Ryan I loved him, but I was pretty sure she could deduce my feelings by everything else I had said that night.

It was interesting that Ryan didn't say the actual words either, and I wondered if the reason was that he somehow knew I wouldn't tell Willow that intimate of a detail, or he truly just wanted to tell me in person. But the fact was, he wanted to tell me, and it beautifully lit me up. Yet, at the same time, it brought me straight back down. I wanted to hear those words from him, but not then … not like how we were … not when I knew the situation around us was still not going to change. To hear him tell me he loved me would only make it hurt that much more.

After Ryan thanked Willow, she changed the conversation topic in another typical Willow way. "You know, this look suits you." I reimagined his worn jeans and light green T-shirt as my friend continued her fashion critique. "That's what you should be wearing on-air—not the open jacket and slick shirt. So yesterday."

I think I heard Ryan actually do a half chuckle before he told her something I already knew. "Yeah? I'll tell the show's wardrobe people. They are in charge of it. Congrats, by the way, on your graduation."

Admittedly, I swooned a little, hearing him personalize his comment to Willow. That was the Ryan I had totally fallen for—no matter what distress he was under, he cared. He cared about me. So, he cared about what and who I cared about. And Willow, I knew, would hear and see that, too.

"Thanks for being such a good friend to her," he added.

"It goes both ways," she replied. "I better be that now and make sure she didn't decide to start walking. We know how she likes to do that."

I shook my head and, if I would guess, Ryan probably did, too. It was kind of weird hearing two of my favorite people talking with one another and teasing about me. It was nice. Too bad it wasn't under other circumstances.

"You'll tell her what I said?"

"I will," Willow reiterated, but that time her voice was much louder since she had begun walking and was then almost next to me. Surely not surprised I had been there the whole time, she silently took my arm and practically dragged me to her car. Once we were secured inside and the car was started, Willow immediately gave her review. "Scum ... Mr. Mean ... bastard ..."

"He is not," I replied quietly.

"No, darn it," she admitted as we pulled onto the main road. "He actually seems pretty nice ... and so into you." I couldn't help but sigh as she continued, "You heard everything, right?"

"Yeah."

"What did his message mean?"

"I've gotta keep something private." I brought my side window down, needing the air more than ever.

"Does it change anything?" She poked at my ambiguity.

"Yeah. It makes my heart twist around even more." The sighs were becoming a melancholy habit.

"Good God, girl. Maybe we *should* just live in a convent with 1950s socials. It would be easier."

"Truth." I managed a laugh before remembering about my monetary involvement in the evening. "How much do I owe you? What was the tab?"

"Nothing."

"Nothing?" I tilted my head and curled my lip at my neighbor. "Willow, I drank more, and it was pricier. I am going to at least pay my fair share." I was definitely not going to let her pay for the night, especially when it should be the other way around. I owed her for just being there for me.

"I didn't pay a thing," she said.

"What? You skipped out on the bill?" I almost shrieked. "Are we like Thelma and Louise now?"

"Yeah, let's go find young, cowboy Brad Pitt." When she went along with my idea, I realized she was taking it too casually to have really skipped out on the bill.

"Will—" I started again.

"It was covered."

"What? By wh—?" I didn't finish the last word because I had figured it out. "No. No. No. Tell me he didn't pay it."

"*He* did. Bartender said everyone sitting at the bar, but you know it was for you."

"Oh, no."

"What? Why? Had I known, I would have ordered something better."

"Oh, geez, he shouldn't have. Why did he do that?" I

know I was getting more animated again, thinking of Ryan footing our bill.

"Didn't we just have the conversation about how much he cares for you?"

"But—"

"Let him. Let him, Bethany. Know he is looking out for you, and he feels some guilt. Those are two good qualities."

I got my friend's point. And I appreciated it. Besides, it wasn't like Ryan hadn't paid when we did things together before. But that was just what I feared ... *Were* we together?

***

Since I went to breakfast later than usual and just before it closed, I had my toast and tea in solitude that next morning, which was probably for the best. I didn't need any more noise or questions from women in the apartment who may have connected me to the photo. Although, thankfully, there was nothing new online.

Just as I pressed the elevator button to go back to my room and finish packing, Ziva—a.k.a. Ratched—called out my name. "Miss Opala." Her full hips shook in her mop of a dress and she semi-huffed, as if whatever she had to say was a huge inconvenience. "A package just arrived for you."

I looked at the smaller than paper-sized bubble envelope she was holding. "Oh. Okay. Thanks."

"You *did* stop your mail for the week, didn't you?" She practically hissed while handing over the package.

While her unnaturally black hair and excessive amount of foundation, red lipstick, and eyeshadow attempted to disguise her age, her wrinkled hands with dark spots were a giveaway. I didn't know her backstory, but I figured it had to be sad for her to be so miserable. Was she someone who had come to the city seeking fame and fortune and never found it? And this is where her life had led her?

"Because we can't keep shoving gossip magazines in your box every day. They won't fit for a whole week."

"I don't—" I started to deny that I received such materials—which I did not—when I got a better look at the envelope.

There was no return address—just the messenger service. But I recognized the handwriting. I knew Ryan's Gs always had an extra swirl, and he put a slash through his zeros and Zs. Gosh, what did he send me?

Ziva broke into my internal guessing game. "And you know you are responsible for rent this week, too. We don't give free passes for traveling or illness." Her dark eyes pierced.

"Yes, ma'am." I inhaled in through my nose and exhaled through my mouth, determined to remain courteous as I had been taught. "Thank you for all you do."

Not knowing how to take it, she mumbled an "mmmm-hmmm," and I stepped onto the elevator.

I didn't open the package until I was securely back in the solitary setting of my room. The more I thought of it, the more I decided it wasn't going to be anything business-related. It was going to be something personal … especially with the non-return address. And it lightened and scared me at the same time.

I tugged at the sealed flap and, once open, shook the contents out of the package. A miniature white envelope attached to a small, gold foil, square box fell onto my bedspread. I sat beside it and opened the card first. My mother had always taught us that it was proper etiquette to do so. And even though I wasn't in front of the giver or *any* guests, I abided by those rules.

Once again in Ryan's handwriting, but without a signature, the card read, *I hope Willow gave you the message. Please let me tell you in person.*

I closed my eyes and did a cleansing breath. He didn't

have to write a lot to get his message through. And it only made me more curious as to what the contents of the flat box would bring.

I peeled the two pieces of transparent tape from the sides and lifted the top off. Cushioned in a bed of cotton was a silver charm. It was shaped like a wine bottle with the word "Napa" inscribed on it. I knew exactly where he had gotten it. I had been admiring the charms at the same store he had bought his T-shirt. I had no idea he had even known I was looking at them, but, obviously, he had. It was becoming ever so apparent that we were connected in so many ways. Except ... for the one string that had become severely frayed and in risk of tearing us completely apart.

Nevertheless, I reached out to him. I texted my thoughts ... however brief. *Beautiful charm from a beautiful place. Thank you. & also for the message.*

His reply back was so immediate, I wondered if I had even sent mine first. *In person Lenay.*

I'm finishing packing and need to leave soon, I texted the excuse. It was extremely legit, but I also knew my heart was scared to hear his voice or see him in person and hear those words. I wasn't ready. I knew it was good that I had taken a stand with him, but that didn't mean it didn't confuse and hurt me that much more. *Slept in later than I planned,* I added before sending the text.

His text back wasn't quite as fast, but it was caring Ryan to a T. *How R U feeling?*

Dull pain, I admitted.

Take good old-fashioned aspirin.

That will help the head.

For as business-oriented as he was, Ryan was also a creative soul. So, he understood word choice, and he completely understood me. I didn't need to add a broken heart emoji to paint the picture.

When he didn't reply, I sent a follow-up text—one I probably should have sent the night before. *Thank you for picking up the tab. You really didn't need to.*

He ignored my thanks and continued with his own agenda. *Don't want U to go w/ us like this.*

It's for the best. Time to think. I did legitimately believe that.

Don't OVERthink, was his reply, followed quickly by, *U already R. Delete "Landslide" from your playlist.*

My face mimicked the teary-eyed emoji I did send that time. "Landslide" had been drumming through my head since first waking up. I was afraid it was the *only* song on my playlist.

GREA WARNER

CHAPTER NINETEEN

It took me a while to get to sleep that night—between the excitement of seeing my family whom I hadn't seen since Christmas, the time change, and getting reacquainted with sharing a room with Ella and her constant sleep mumblings. Plus, of course, I was thinking of Ryan, who seemed so desperately far away. I had arrived in Carolina as the show was airing, but the evening had brought a bustle of family activity. So, while I didn't watch it, I had pretty much imagined where Ryan was and what he was doing the entire time.

When I *had* finally drifted off to slumberland in my childhood bedroom, I guess it had been both soundly and deeply. Because, when I woke, it was to a sisterless room and midmorning sunlight streaming through the window. I suppose my body needed that recharging meltdown.

After brushing my teeth and changing into comfy clothes, I grabbed my phone and started down the creaky original wooden stairs of our red brick home, which was over one hundred years old. Boasting pure Southern charm, it had housed every pastor's family of my dad's church since it was first built. I loved the large rooms, multiple fireplaces, original ornate wood fixtures, dormers, and the fact that there were three stories—although, the third floor was a small guest room for any waywards who needed my father's help.

I had just started down the main floor's hall when I saw the text on my phone. It had been sent the night before, obviously after I had managed to go to sleep. The message, from Ryan, stopped me in my tracks.

Hope U got in OK. The resort news has already been leaked. Ignoring everything.

Shoot! That didn't take long. I took refuge in my father's home office, not yet wanting to continue to the kitchen and family room areas where I could hear the voices of my sister and mother. I needed to further investigate Ryan's message. I needed to search online to see what exactly was out there. I was curious for sure and felt bad that Ryan was having to deal with one more thing. But I was also fearful that there was a connection to me—us—because of it.

Most of what I found was speculation. It was reported that Kari was exhausted, and/or had a mental breakdown, and/or was abusing drugs or alcohol. Her manager put out a generic statement, saying she was taking some time off and would come back stronger than ever. And as Ryan had suggested in his text, the press said Mr. Thompson had no comment.

But the photo of Ryan and me did reemerge in connection with some of the articles. Comments like, *Is this the reason for Kari Thompson's downfall?* and *Ryan Thompson days before his wife's break* and *Who is she?* surfaced on the less reputable but, nonetheless, well-read sites. And while it made me ill in my stomach, I at least rejoiced that my name was still a mystery to the public.

I hadn't been able to sit in my father's tall leather chair. I was a bit too worked up. So, instead, I was leaning against the filing cabinet when I called Ryan. The irony that he didn't pick up—when talking with me was what he wanted all along—made an airy grunt escape my mouth.

But his non-answer was probably for the best. I had not given myself a chance to stop and take it all in yet. And I needed to do that. I hung up and decided to text instead.

It wasn't much, but it said all I needed it to. *Saw it. What about the kids?*

Sallie and Joel were not mentioned in the articles, which I found extremely courteous of the press, especially when they knew they could get emotions rolling with the mention of the Thompson offspring. Perhaps they didn't want to risk a lawsuit, because I know Ryan would have gone *loco* on anyone who harmed his children. Then again, citing two little kids wasn't necessary when gossipville already had a superstar in rehab and a possible fling on the side.

While my father did church things and Garrett was at school, my mom, Ella, and I went shopping and ate lunch at one of my favorite local Carolina eateries. Seeing my mother anxiously watch me as I chose menu items and stopping herself from completely asking the waitress about allergens was like stepping back in time. I felt sorry she put so much stress on herself when I was completely competent with making the decisions. And if something happened, it could be handled. Just being around her drew the stress into me. And that was something I really didn't need, especially with the added pressure of waiting for something else in the press to drop … and the fact that Ryan had yet to text me back. I tried to remember he was being bombarded with so much. But it hurt that I wasn't more on top of his priority list. Then again, I guess I hadn't given him much reason to think he was on mine, either.

So, when his text did come through, I felt a little relieved just to hear from him. *Kids don't know a thing. Glad. Thx for asking.*

Of course, I replied right away, grateful his text arrived just after we finished dinner so I could slip into the hall while my parents cleared the dishes.

U R safe, too. Nothing about who U R. The fact that he was thinking of me and that he responded immediately reassured me.

I know.

I also realized from reading the articles, how insanely protective Kari's fanbase was. They were one hundred percent on Kari's side, with posts for her to *feel better soon … take her time to be healthy … remain the beautiful soul she is … be strong … fight.* It didn't matter that if she was in a place like she was, it was most likely for a nasty addiction. She was a heroine in the public eye. Because of their loyalty, Kari would always be the embattled one. Understanding Kari and her insecurities a little better, I did believe that what Ryan said was true. Her recovery would take a hit if everyone knew of her failed marriage. She needed to feel successful. She needed to be liked. And in order for her to get well, she needed that more than ever. Ryan was in a no-win situation, and so was I.

Have you talked with Kari? I asked but wasn't sure I wanted the answer.

No, he answered immediately. *She is supposed to have a few noncommunication days. But I don't plan to … not my place. Her team will do what they need to.* When I didn't reply, he asked a question of his own. *Anything about your brother?*

I looked across the room to Garrett, dark-haired just like the rest of us. He was bringing desserts into the family room and fighting with Ella because he had just given the last crumb of something to the dog and not her. Sixteen and twenty-two years old. Siblings never change.

I decided to bring some levity to our texting since, besides the fact that his foot swelling was dissipating, there wasn't any news about my brother's health, and both Ryan and I needed a break from the heaviness. *Well, he somehow managed to get three railroads already and is taking most of my money.* I mentioned the game my family was mere minutes from resuming. I tacked on *#MonopolyIsNotMyGame* at the end just for fun.

Ryan took an extra moment and then hit me with two texts in a row—both of them tugging strongly on my tattered heartstrings. The first was, *#TwisterIs* followed by, *God I miss U.*

My heart skipped. I missed him, too. How did everything go so wrong ... so fast?

To make things worse, I didn't answer him. I stared at my phone so long it resorted back to the dark screen. The action made me regain my thoughts and try to think of what to type as a reply. I knew I needed to—whether it was witty, emotional, or just a conclusion. While I pondered the options, the Opala clan started calling out for me to join them in the family room.

In the time it took for me to make a decision, Ryan sent another message, reaffirming what he said and giving me an out. *I do. But kind of glad U R away from all of it right now. Got a lot going on. Talk tomorrow?*

I didn't hesitate that time. *Yeah.*

I wasn't sure if I would be any more prepared to talk with him that next day, though. Because, the truth was ... it didn't matter how much he missed me or we missed one another. Nothing had changed, except for the fact that it might be even worse with the "breaking Kari news."

"Yes! Ha! Ha!" Garrett called out.

"Bethany, he just took the Pennsylvania railroad, too!" my sister whined. "We're screwed!"

"Ella Opala!" That was my father's voice.

I closed my eyes. It felt as if all the trains at all the railroads were barreling through my brain. They were painfully loud and picking up speed. I didn't know how to stop the inevitable crash.

***

Lunch out with friends the next day was, thankfully, refreshing and relaxing. While we talked briefly about my fifteen—more like less than five—minutes of fame on

Singer Spotlight, that was it. They didn't seem to know about any winery photos or, consequently, my current connection to a certain tall, handsome man. Thank goodness everyone's lives didn't revolve around every bit of gossip and entertainment. Far from Tinseltown, they were instead occupied with new jobs, engagements, and even a pregnancy, and I was more than happy to talk about them.

I had just gotten back to my parents' home when a video came into my phone from Ryan. I sat on the front stoop and pressed play, not having any idea what to expect. But when I did, I legitimately laughed out loud.

First on the screen was Joel ... and a bunch of piglets. "Grammy, Pappy, they like me!" he squealed, standing in the midst of a ring full of the pink mammals.

Since he was the obvious videographer, I could hear Ryan but not see him. "That's because they think you are one of them."

"It tried to kiss me!" Both Joel's exaggerated high voice and the way he was squirming around even more than usual caused a wide smile to erupt on my face.

I was trying to figure out where they were when Sallie's voice came next. "Daddy, look!"

Ryan's camera phone swiveled, and then I saw an image of Sallie sitting on a white horse. A slightly plump, tall man with white hair and similarly-hued beard stood next to her. Sallie wiggled a cardboard cone shape on top of the horse's head.

I heard Ryan's laughter right before Sallie called out, "Maybe Bethany can write a song about Unicorn's farm adventure."

"That would be nice, Tink."

The video ended. I took a moment to close my eyes, breathe in, and think of the silliness of Joel and the thoughtfulness of sweet Sallie. Then I read the text from Ryan that followed the video.

I'm not the only one thinking of U.

An immediate warmth spread through my body, and I texted him my reply. *Where are you?*

Got last min flights yesterday. Iowa. Needed balance.

He was home. He went to his roots ... like me. And although I had not seen his face on the video, I could tell it was already the right choice for him, just by the lightness in his voice when he spoke with the kids.

I was also putting together the timeline. On top of the media circus, he had been making travel arrangements, packing, and flying the day before. He had written the plural version of flights, too. The reason he hadn't contacted me right away was starting to make more sense.

The phone ringing in my hand startled me. My eyes shut again, immediately recognizing the caller. He was right there ... one button-push and we would be connected voice to voice. And while it seemed like the most natural thing to do, I liked how things were in that moment. Answering, I feared, would bring the heaviness back.

I waited for the ringing to stop and then for the alert to tell me I had a new voice mail message. The laughter of seeing Joel and Sallie was gone, and the warmness of knowing Ryan had found a safe home base had faded. Sadness, nerves, or a combination instead took their place. I already knew Ryan's message wouldn't be full of pure enthusiasm, simply because I hadn't answered. And he obviously knew I was next to my phone. I imagined his reaction being similar to the one when I wouldn't answer him at the bar that night before I left. There was only one way to find out for sure, though.

"I want to hear your voice, Bethany. Even more so, I want you to hear mine ... my words." He sounded as I had expected ... disappointed but confident.

I knew the words—those three precious little ones—he was referring to, and, if I was honest, that was what stopped me from picking up the most. I didn't want to hear them. My heart couldn't handle confirming we both

257

felt the same way and, yet, couldn't live those words openly. And even though I was trying to understand, it still wasn't fair and I couldn't risk being hurt even more.

Enjoy this time with your family. Tell the kids I said Hi, I texted.

The hesitation in his text back was surely the length of his sigh. *I will & I'll call again.*

I put my phone down, wiped at the tears I had allowed to run down my face, and looked up to see my mother in the open doorway. I knew her well enough to know she had been keeping an eye out for my return from lunch. It wasn't just my allergens that caused her anxiety. It was being a mom—wanting everyone to be safe and happy … and knowing there was no way to guarantee such a feat.

***

My face was waffling with hot and cold waves as I felt my blood pressure try to regulate in light of the latest news I had just found out. At the same time, I was attempting to follow the contrasting jovial conversation around our dining room table full of family. We were celebrating Ella's impending graduation and my homecoming. Garrett's hopefully good news would have to wait—test results pending.

My father's glare was direct and to the point. He knew what my sideways and downward glances while sitting at the table were all about. There ought to be an official name for the art of discretely looking at one's cell phone. It was one I, obviously, had not mastered.

"I'm sorry," I apologized. I meant the comment for just my father, but the whole table stopped talking about Ella's career options and instead looked at me. I imagined my cheeks having a bright pink tone, despite not wearing blush. "I …" I couldn't sit there any longer. It wasn't just my face. My whole body felt like prickly fire pins. "I'm sorry. I need to make a phone call. It's important. I apologize, Paw-Paw and Maw-Maw."

"It's fine, honeybun, go ahead," my mom's father replied.

My father continued to watch me as I rose from my seat, but he didn't say a word. I'm sure it was a sign of respect to his elder and my mother. He would do anything for my mom.

"Ella's gonna be a garbage truck driver or work for a porta-potty service," my brother luckily jumped right back into the previous conversation, teasing our sister.

"I just missed making assistant manager of the cookie shop, thank you very much," Ella repelled back. "And there's the possibility at the real estate place …"

Her voice faded as I went toward the back door with an eager, dark brown Newfoundland hound on my heels. He needed the back yard as a place to do his business and run. I needed the air and privacy to follow up with Ryan's text.

I really need U to call me. He had written. *Your name is out there.*

I had known instantly what he meant. And my instinct was to, indeed, call him right away. But first I scoured the web for articles with my name.

It didn't take long to discover what Ryan had said was true. A couple of publications were citing a "source" who came forward to identify the woman who was holding hands in the Napa region with Ryan Thompson. The dramatic writing made it almost seem like there was a crime scene and I was some type of murderess. Not only did the source say my name was Bethany Lenay but also that I was from North Carolina. Plus, I already had a nickname—Twitter Girl. They had connected me to my *Singer Spotlight* audition and the conversation Ryan and I initially had on the social media outlet. The clincher—as if there needed to be one—was the source said the affair had been going on for a few weeks or so. Of course, it was longer than that, but someone knew for a while at least.

As if Ryan's text wasn't disconcerting enough, the additional facts that were out there were stomach-knotting, vomit-worthy worse. I was going to have to tell my family for sure. They had to be prepared, and they deserved to know from me before hearing it from anyone else. Because, after all, there is no finer gossip than Sunday church gossip. No matter the whole truth behind the stories, it was bound to be disgraceful for both my father and mother. The only slight upside was, my real last name wasn't used.

When searching any further online was only going to aid in a potential future ulcer, I cut myself off and did what I had said I was going to do. I called Ryan. All previous reasons not to talk with him were thrown out the window. I *needed* to talk with him. I needed to hear his voice. I needed whatever reassurance he could possibly provide.

"Hi," was his solitary, solemn answer.

"Hi," I echoed back with the same delivery.

"You looked online, huh?"

"I did."

"I'm so sorry."

"I know." I also knew it wasn't him who needed to harbor the blame.

"Where are you?"

"Home. Everyone is here—even my grandparents. I stepped outside. Ryan, what ... what should I do?"

Our back yard wasn't big, but it was wooded. I felt as if the trees were absorbing my pain. And I wondered how much sadness they had seen in their long history.

"Beth—" Hearing my desperation, he broke on my name before recollecting himself. "If this helps, no one is going to get your number. They're not going to get your family's number. Your last name is not out there, and the show is strict about not releasing any of that." He said it to be reassuring, but there was still too much that *was* already out there.

"I'm glad it will be hard for the press to contact me.

But a lot of people—real people," I emphasized without deliberately trying to be spiteful, "know me by Lenay, not Opala. Or, they know both. Ryan …" His name came out of my mouth like a plea for help.

His sigh that time showed his pure frustration over our entire circumstance. "I will respect any decision you make about who you tell and how much you say. I'm not saying anything, though. If I even pick up the phone by mistake—no comment. I have a call into the team. They'll give some advice on how to proceed." Even though he couldn't see me, I nodded, and he spoke again. "We were lucky no one connected you until now. I think besides the sunglasses, it was because of your hair. Your hair was so different on the show than it is now."

"You didn't know what happened to that short-cropped blonde when I showed up at your office." I recalled our first meeting and, for a moment, my heart warmed with the memory.

"Yep." I think his did, too. "And that is the only real physical reference anyone had of you since you don't really post photos or took the few down. They didn't make the connection."

He had been right. He had been smart. He did know the crazy media world. But there was still a hole in the plan.

"So, obviously, whoever leaked my name is someone who knows me on a more personal level. But who would do that? And who knows that an affair has been going on for a while? No one. No one, Ryan! Who do you think the source is?" The possibilities had been feverishly circling around in my head since reading the story. "It's making me sick." I practically cried, and I swear the trees moved without even a trace of wind.

"I don't know. I'm trying to figure it out, too. I know you are …" He hesitated but then went for it. "It's not Willow, is it?"

"No." And I reaffirmed with a second confident,

"No."

"No, I don't really think so either." His voice had remained calm if not sad. "She has your back for sure."

I did an internal chuckle at the flashback of my friend defending me that night at the bar. It, without a doubt, was not Willow. Really, though, who else knew about Ryan and me?

Like a thorn in my side, I came up with an alternative possibility. I struggled for an adjective I could live with saying out loud, especially at my parents' house. "What about Kari's ever-so-pleasant mother?"

I knew Ryan agreed with my characterization of his former mother-in-law, but he denied the possibility of her being the nark. "Irene definitely doesn't want it out. She wants to still pretend in the fairytale. She's living her own failed Hollywood career through Kari. And the pretense of a healthy marriage? She does that with her own, too."

I found that interesting and sad all at the same time. But it was not, by far, my top priority. I wracked my brain for people who not only knew what I looked like but also knew my singer name.

"Ryan?" A new option popped into my mind. "How about Anamaria?"

"It's not Ana. When the initial photograph went out, I talked with her. She had no idea. I had to tell her everything because she is taking a lot of the heat via the office right now. But she is completely loyal. She has proven that time and time again with numerous client issues in the past. I completely trust her."

The idea of Anamaria made me think of others in his world. "Morrison?"

"As much as I would like to blame him since he was playing Mr. Huggy with you, anyone in the business would not do that ... at least anyone who is reputable and wants to keep working. And Morrison is top-notch. Look, we could go through a bunch of names ... people ... and still not figure it out. And believe me, Bethany, I'm upset. I'm pissed. If I can do anything about it, I will. I just don't want you making yourself sick over it."

"I already am," I admitted.

"I know. I know you are." In a weird way, his voice sounded both worried and reassuring.

"Ry, I have to tell my family everything. I don't want them blindsided by it."

"Absolutely."

"Blindsided by what?" I practically jumped on my sister's voice—I hadn't heard or seen her come outside at all. "Oooo … what gives?"

"Ella!" My mom's voice was even louder. "Where is your sister? Where's the dog?"

I first looked at Ella, who had the spill-the-secret gleam in her honey-brown eyes. I then directed my attention to the open door where my mom was crossing the family room. "I gotta go." I spoke into the phone.

"I know. I hear," Ryan answered back.

"Bethie!" my dad called out, and the four-legged furry creature bounded toward the open doorway as if my name were his.

"Call me." Ryan's voice sandwiched my dad calling out my and my sister's name.

"Ella!"

"Oh, goodness, girls. Get inside." My mom brushed her graying-before-its-time hair away from her face and waved us in from the family room's doors.

"Good night," I managed to Ryan before hanging up.

"What is this blindsided business?" Ella whispered.

"I'll tell you later."

"Tell me now," she verbally bounced back. "I'm going out."

"What?" I jerked my head. "You're leaving now? Everyone is here."

"For you. For your homecoming."

I heard the jealousy in my sister's voice. But the funny thing was—and she could never see it—I was, in a lot of ways, jealous of her. Growing up, she was the one who got to do everything without restrictions or fear. Did she push those boundaries when she shouldn't have? Absolutely. But she had that freedom.

"I'm home for your graduation," I justified.

"Bethie! Ella!" We both semi-turned toward our father's voice.

"Tell me," she prodded.

"I will later if you promise not to say anything right now."

My sister followed up my plea with a negotiation tactic Ryan would have appreciated. "Cover if I come in late, then." It didn't matter that we were both over twenty-one, our parents still had rules.

"Yeah, okay." And I walked into the house.

I managed to make it until after dinner before looking at my social media accounts or searching the web again. There weren't a lot of comments, but the ones that were there weren't kind. And I was sure they would only grow.

As if knowing that was exactly what I was doing or because he was looking at them himself—both equally likely—Ryan texted me. *Make your accounts private &/or turn off comments.*

I will :(

I'm so sorry. Clear your mind. Get some rest, please.

CHAPTER TWENTY

The only one of Ryan's requests I was able to fulfill was switching my accounts to private. Clearing my mind? Impossible. Resting? Forget it. I did neither that entire night, not only worrying about what people who didn't know me thought of me but also anticipating what my family would.

I decided to delay telling them until morning because there were just too many around well into the night. I wanted to tell my parents when it was only the three of us. Garrett had long since taken the bus to high school. And Ella—whom I had put off by feigning sleep when she got home in the middle of the night—had just left for her shift at the cookie shop. I knew my siblings would need to know, but I simply didn't want too many voices and opinions in the initial conversation. It was going to be hard enough without excessive Opala chatter.

For as good as I was at connecting words to convey messages in a lyrical format, I did a horrible job relaying exactly what was going on with Ryan and me. I stumbled. I restarted. I showed the photo. I looked down.

I wanted their approval. I wanted their advice. But what I got was what I feared the most—their disappointment.

My father's voice even elevated, which was a rarity. "My daughter—the daughter we raised—is involved with a married man? And someone in a power position?"

Yikes! Oh, no. I totally failed trying to describe my relationship with Ryan.

"No ... no," I began to explain. "First of all, we're more like partners. You know we wrote some—"

"Oh, my gosh!"

All three of us swiveled to spot my sister at the entry of my dad's home office. We must have been so involved in the incredibly awkward conversation that we hadn't even heard her return. But there was Ella—a combination of surprise and interest decorating her face.

"Ella, what are you—" our father started.

"Hmmm ..." My sister smiled a smirky grin at me. "You *did* get some beach bod. Married ... really? And this power thing? What exactly does that involve ...?" She purposefully let her comment fade, and I looked at her with eyes and mouth wide open.

"Oh, sweet merciful." Our mother gasped, and I was even more mortified, thinking she may have actually understood what Ella was referring to.

"Kidding, Mom. Relax." Ella lifted her eyebrows at me.

"You three know how to take turns on your mother's and my nerves. I'm going to lose even more hair." My balding dad made me feel even worse, knowing I shouldn't be "taking a turn" since they were already so worried about Garrett.

"Yeah, but I never—" Ella stopped herself and looked at me with what I swear was a little bit of awe. "Whoa. So, who's the dude?"

"Caye ..." Our father looked to our mom for help.

She tried. "Ella, why are you here?"

"I forgot the shirt." My sister was very organized with some things, but when it involved homemaking and finance ... not a clue. "You know we have that special promo one tha—"

"Yes, yes. I washed and hung it up. It's downstairs. You are going to be late. Get it and go," our mother replied. "We need to talk with Bethany."

"Yes, ma'am. I'll even go out the basement door." Ella saluted me and said as she left, "Scoop … later."

Later, I thought, I will be regurgitating the little bit of breakfast I had managed to eat before the big reveal. Later, I thought, I will be disinherited as part of the family. Good luck finding me. Later, I thought, my world will spin me completely out of control.

Ella's interruption didn't help matters. I think, if anything, it only added to my father's frustration. At least, he did move on from the power comment.

"Okay … you wrote together. He's helped you out. But this Ryan guy … what kind of guy does that to his wife?" The second part of his dialogue—the question—was slow and deliberately to the point, just like most of his sermons. It was also riddled with disgust.

"Daddy, you didn't hear everything. It's not like—"

"I don't know you." He actually turned from my direction.

"You *do* know me." I almost cried.

And my mom tried to play peacemaker. "Barry …"

"Where did we go wrong?" He looked at his wife and then turned back to me. "Thou shall not steal … though shall not commit adultery … though shall honor thy father and thy mother …"

I could recite all of that, too. And I noted how he was being selective in his choices and how he rearranged the order of the commandments. "I know you're disappointed in me. But I didn't do any of those things. I promise." Besides maybe coveted the Thompson house, but that was not at all the issue.

"All right, Bethie." Strangely, in dire circumstances, my mother's anxiety seemed to flip and she could be the rational one in charge—it's that mom lifting a car off a

267

child thing. When it's over, though, she lets the anxiety crumble to an extreme. "Let's sit. We all need to sit." I think *she* needed to sit.

They listened as I managed to get the whole story out a little more fluidly. I even told them the part about me telling Ryan I loved him and knowing he felt the same way but not wanting to hear it. I was pretty much in my no holds barred state of mind.

My father was going to interrupt a couple times, but my mom gave him a look. It's funny. I had seen him counsel so many others—with situations worse than mine—and he was always so calm. But when it came to his first-born baby girl? Nope. Not so much.

Toward the conclusion of the tale, they were both much calmer and more receptive. But that didn't mean they didn't have concerns. Heck, so did I.

"He's how old?" my father questioned.

"Thirty-three." I knew the age difference was a strike, but there was a twenty-year difference between them and Ryan, so they were old enough to be his parents, and in relation to everything else they feared …

"He's divorced." That was definitely one of them. "The bible—"

"Daddy," I interrupted immediately. "What about the immorality and adultery? Yes, I listen in church." He couldn't help but smile a little, and my mom did, too. "It wasn't *him*. He, in fact, has been loyal to her. Even in the decision to keep the divorce a secret."

"All right, Bethie girl, but he already has kids," was his next point of concern.

"He does." Fact.

"You'll want your own. You're young," was his counterpoint.

"It doesn't always work that way," was mine.

I looked from him to my mom—they knew that. And I'm sure it really wasn't a major bone of contention with my parents. Their concern was for my well-being.

"What I wanted even a couple years ago," I continued, thinking of the life-goals conversation Ryan and I had, "I am finding out it isn't what I want now. And if he makes me happy …"

"Are you?" my mom questioned. "You don't seem to be. You're crying—"

"I—" But I didn't know what to say.

"Bethany, you know I saw you yesterday on the front stoop. And I didn't say anything because I know you will tell me if you want to talk. You have a pride in you," my mom added. "Daddy and I have noticed how tired you look. And you said you're not even answering his calls."

"*Are* you happy, Bethie?" my dad tagged in.

Oh. Oh, geez. Why did they ask that? Why were they making me think about all those things? When it was listed like that, I wasn't happy … at all. Yet, when I thought about Ryan … when I thought about the time spent with him … about nearly everything besides hearing one more time we couldn't be the real us, I was happier than I had ever been. Ever.

What then? Why? Why couldn't I just be happy? I knew his feelings, but I wouldn't let him say them. Was it that I was simply holding onto stubbornness from an argument we had when we were both beyond exhausted from being up with Kari's drama? Or was it all the lying? I realized he never, ever demanded that of me, but I took it on myself. I believed him when he said the divorce would be revealed soon. I did. But was there still that part of me afraid of being rejected one more time?

After my parents gave me the time to internally ponder their simple but yet so complex question, I tried my best to explain. "Honestly, I don't know. I don't know if I am. I think so. I think what it comes down to is principal. It's what you raised me on. I want it all from him, and I know his hands are tied."

"Bethie, you should consider staying here," my father suggested. "I know the music thing is good, and at least this Ryan situation isn't as bad as it seemed. You—"

My phone, resting on my father's wooden desk, started to chime. My dad was still talking, but I was only focused on the ringing and Ryan's name on the screen. How ironic. I scrunched my eyes shut. I was so confused—Stay in Carolina … Ryan … crying … love … angel … devil …

My stress level reached a higher peak when I reopened my eyes to see my father not only answering my phone but putting it on speaker. "Daddy, what are you do—"

"Hi, there." His voice seemed deeper and more pronounced than usual.

In contrast, Ryan's was not as secure. "Uh, hi. I was calling for Bethany."

"Figured as much. This is her father." As he spoke, I looked at my mother who was shaking her head. My dad was a patriarch in so many facets. "Ryan, I presume."

"Yes, sir, Mr. Opala."

It was funny listening to him. I thought I had heard and seen all versions of Ryan Thompson. First, the mean judge on TV. Then, the creative lyricist. The caring father. The thoughtful friend. The passionate lover. The in-charge exec. But shy guy was something new.

"Ryan, she doesn't want to talk with you right now." My dad was looking at the phone as if he was actually staring Ryan down.

"I understand." He sounded so defeated.

"After how you treated her on that glorified television show, I don't know why she ever even talked with you again."

"Daddy!" I belted out.

I was shocked he went that route … that he even mentioned the show. I had barely brought it up. It was of zero concern to Ryan and me. But maybe it bothered my parents, and they had never said anything to me.

Ryan didn't react to my dad. He reacted to hearing me. "Bethany …"

"Yeah, you're on speaker. Sorry. I didn't know he was

going to—"

My father continued right on, citing what I think was one of the major issues he had with both Ryan and, honestly, me. "We've told her to stay here where things are honest and right and not covered with half-truths. I did not raise my girl to be a liar, and I'm at least grateful she knows she doesn't need to do that with her family. I'm glad she told us everything."

Whew ... wow. He was laying it on thick. He had finally seemed a little more at ease about everything until Ryan actually called.

"Sir, that is not who I am. I understand your concerns. My family has those same beliefs. I was raised in a church-going, heart-helping family. Still am."

A soft smile accompanied my body which was relaxing the tiniest of bits. Ryan was holding his own and speaking honestly. And it dawned on me then that my father might be giving Ryan a little test—man-to-man. I don't think he ever did that with Hutch. But Ryan was not Hutch. I had never told my parents I loved someone before. And even though I was upset when Hutch and I broke up, I think they could already see that Ryan was different.

"It's good to know." My father did a one-nod. "But you have to understand this is my daughter ... my daughter we are talking about."

"I do understand." Ryan sounded a little more like his confident self every time he answered my dad, and I think that was because he was so confident of his feelings. "I have a daughter of my own. I would lay down my life for her ... both my kids. I am glad Bethany told you everything. I hate the lies." He directed his comment to me, then. "Bethany, you know that. And you know I don't lie to the people I care about."

That was enough. As much as I loved my parents and I appreciated that they listened and supported me, my phone conversation was not theirs. It was mine. It was private. I hoped that someday they would meet Ryan and they could have a much more amicable conversation but not then … not then with all the confusion floating around.

I grabbed the phone and took it off speaker. "Ryan …" I started to walk out of the office.

"Betha—"

"You're off speaker." I opened the front door. "I'm going somewhere private."

"It's fine. It didn't matter. I'm glad you told them." I could hear his voice change to one of concern as I walked down the slope of the front yard. I didn't have any shoes on, and the grass was dewy from a late-night rain. "Bethany, you're coming back, aren't you?"

"I … I don't know."

It wasn't even a consideration to stay in Carolina until my dad brought it up right before Ryan called. And now it was in my mind. Did it have some validity? I didn't know. I think it just added another wrench to a terribly cluttered toolbox.

"Wha …" He didn't even say a complete word, and I knew he was devastated by just the possibility of me not returning to California.

"It depends on Garrett and …" I was trying to rationalize on the spot. "If I do, if things are still …"

I couldn't even say it. How much longer would things remain as they were, and how would that change us? *That* thought devastated me. Staying sheltered in Carolina seemed like the safe thing to do, both as protection from the press and from heartache.

Legitimately not knowing the answer, I changed topics. "How are Sallie and Joel?"

I heard his mini-sigh, but he had been around me long enough to know to go with the flow of my conversation. "They're loving farm life and sad we have to leave tomorrow already."

"I'm sure. It's a different world, huh?" I asked in an "ahhh" kind of state. "Tell Sallie I'll work on that song for her."

"We miss you."

And just like that, my heart fluttered. Gosh, I missed them, too. "Ry …" But it was all I could say.

I heard a bit of a hitch in his breath before he asked, "Nobody's bothered you, have they?"

"No. No press. My social stuff is off. Willow called. That's all. What about you?"

"Ignoring everything. There's nothing else for them to print so … we're hoping it will die off."

"That is still what the team is saying?" I asked in somewhat of disbelief.

"They wanted me to come out and say that you and I are working together and that's it. Refute the word 'affair.'" Did he hear my *hmmmf* before he continued? "But I won't lie … not about you."

That should have made me feel better, and it did, but only a little. "No comment, though. Isn't that the same thing?"

"It was a compromise." He seemed to blow out some air. "Bethany, just so you know, I am not happy about it."

"But you promised … for Kari." How could I knock a man who was a firm believer in keeping his promises?

"For … yeah … for her to feel more secure first. Besides, the source isn't really the most reliable person now, is he?"

I kicked at a random pebble on the street, and I wished I could kick it harder because, yes, I had seen the identity of the person who sold Ryan—and most of all, me—out. I had seen it sometime in the middle of the night when I couldn't sleep. And it made me sick. No wonder my parents thought I looked exceptionally tired. I was. And I hadn't even shared that latest little tidbit with them.

"No, he's not," I agreed.

"He's a—"

"Bastard."

I shook on the thought of what I had let happen

between Andre and me—bastard was way too kind of a word, especially after his press junket choice. The latest updated articles had mentioned his name, that he saw Ryan and me at the cemetery, and that he knew from personal experience why someone would be attracted to me. He hadn't admitted to the two of us actually having sex but, at least in my mind, I think it was implied. I'm sure the only thing that, thankfully, stopped him from going into *those* details was the fact he might have gotten in even more trouble from the apartment, and that wouldn't be good.

"I guess he got the money he needed by selling his story," I continued, and then added, "I'm sorry. I kept blaming people on your end, and here it was my stupid—"

"Stop. This is not on you," Ryan replied firmly. "I thought it was the cleaning people. I terminated the service last night."

"Oh …"

"You know, I'm glad I don't know where this Andre jerk lives, because someone would have to restrain me. I'm sorry he continues to hurt you. I'm sorry *I* continue to hurt you."

"Ryan … don't … no. That's not true. I know—"

The neighbor across the street started to happily wave from her car as she pulled out of their driveway. I could hear laughing somewhere in the neighborhood. And me? I had tears running down my face.

"Lenay …"

I started making my way back toward our house … back to the safety of our home. "I … I'm gonna go. I think I still need to talk with my mom and dad for a little bit."

"Let me just—"

I wasn't sure if he was going to say it. But if "we miss you" and "sorry I continue to hurt you" sent me into a tailspin, I definitely couldn't handle any more declarations. "I gotta go."

I hung up even more emotional. I copped out again

and felt bad I wasn't letting him speak. Because every time—every single time—he only said the sweetest, most considerate, heartfelt things. He ... hurting me? I was pretty sure it was the other way around.

I made my way back to my father's office where my parents appeared to have not moved an inch since my exit. I'm not sure they had even said a word since then, either—it was so silent. I sat down in the empty chair once again. I didn't have much more in me. I wanted to hear from them.

When my mom looked at me, I nodded, and she spoke. "Bethany, listen, sweetheart, I'm not sure how your conversation went. No matter what, we will always be here for you. Always. I understand this is a hard situation. I really do see both sides you are struggling with. And like your father said, you should take this time to think. If, and *only if,* this ... he ... is what makes you happy should you go back."

That cleared up nothing. Yet, it cleared up everything. I didn't know exactly what or how I felt, but my mother's advice allowed me the chance to take the time to figure it out.

Still, there was another person's opinion I wanted. "Daddy?"

"He held his own with me," my dad stated, confirming what I predicted his demeanor had been about when talking with Ryan. "And he sounded so truthful with what he was saying. Like I told him, though, you are my little girl. I don't want you hurt. I want you happy."

I gave them both a hug. I had needed to tell them. I probably should have told them all along. It helped lift part of the weight off my shoulders. In a weird way, even having my name out in the public and not waiting with fear of when it was going to happen felt good.

Something else I decided I needed was a shower. I wanted to start the day over again—afresh. Besides, my feet were semi-green. It made me think of Ryan walking in his bare feet all the time, too. I made my way upstairs and was in my bedroom when his text came through.

I know U know how I feel. Let me say the words that when U said them to me meant so much. & know that I am trying to do the best for everyone. I promise YOU that I am working on making this right.

I didn't cry. I just read it once again and tried to sum up the courage to reply back and accept his truth. But before I could do either of those, he sent a photo.

The image was perfect. As if I had any doubts, it confirmed he listened to everything I talked with him about. The photo symbolized us. It symbolized the hope I was desperately holding onto. It symbolized that he felt the same way … even if I wouldn't let him say it.

Four strings with a heart, I typed back, referencing the image of the guitar with a heart instead of a hole in the center.

The ONLY kind. Pls tell me that hasn't changed.

I didn't stop and overthink. I just sent back four heart emojis. I had followed my heart with the text, and it felt right. If only everything was that easy.

CHAPTER TWENTY-ONE

Do you happen to be awake? I sent the text.

Lying here panging like crazy w/ thoughts of U.

For real? I don't know why I didn't believe him—his text came in seconds after I sent mine.

FOR REAL, he replied, and only then did I realize I had used our tagline. *It's pretty late. U OK? Is there a reason for my pangs?*

Just the normal fretting about the mess my life suddenly seemed to be, I thought. I couldn't sleep. I had been lying there for hours, thinking, composing lyrics in my head, and watching Ella murmur dreamily. I needed something else. I needed my partner ... my friend ... and just that.

If I call, can we just talk ... about anything and nothing. Not about us?

Call me, Ryan replied.

I hesitated, both with the amount of time I took getting back to him and then with the eventual word. *Promise?*

He didn't get back to me ... via text. Instead, my phone rang. My face jerked a little since I was anticipating a visual indicator, not an auditory one. I swung my feet out of bed.

"Tell him he better be worth waking me out of my dream with Bachelor Number Sixty-Nine," mumbled my sister, who was normally notorious for being hard to wake up.

"Ella …"

"Answer the call, Bethie." She pushed some of her dark hair away from her face and rubbed her eyes.

I pressed the button to connect to Ryan. But I didn't talk. I was still waiting for …

"I promise." I needed those words because I knew they meant something from him. "Talk to me."

"Ella has decided to become a nun."

"She what?" Ryan had never met or talked with my sister, but, regardless, he knew that would have been the shock of the century.

Ella threw a pillow at me. "Go talk mooshy-mooshy with beach-bod somewhere else. This is not a conversation for my virginal ears."

"I'm sorry … your what?" I jested back.

"But deets later," she whispered.

I mouthed "You got it," because once everything had come out, Ella had actually been a very good listener.

"I'm guessing the nunnery is not really the truth." Ryan's voice was soft like mine as I quietly shut the door behind me, not wanting to wake my parents.

"Not even close. But then who knows where she will end up." I started climbing the staircase to the third floor. "She doesn't have a plan or direction. She got a generic degree off of a sports scholarship, but she's not professional athlete material."

I opened the door on top of the steps. The guest room was musty and needed some fresh air, but it was as remote of a space indoors as I could find. And I realized I felt as lost as some of the people who had stayed in the room before.

"I'm sure she'll find her place eventually," Ryan offered. "Sometimes it happens under the most unexpected circumstances."

I sat on the edge of the bed, covered with a white down comforter. Looking out the dormer window, the sky seemed void of any stars. Everything was as dark as dark could be.

"What else? What else you got to hit me with at one-fifteen in the morning?" His voice soared across the line.

"Two-fifteen here."

"Right."

"What are you going to name the dog?" It was the first normal, easy, erase-my-racing-mind question I came up with, and it reminded me of the last truly happy moment I had with him.

He didn't miss a beat. "We have a little while yet until we go back to Dylan's to get it, but I should let the kids choose the name, huh? Although, they'll each end up picking the name of their best friend and arguing about it or then hating their friend and the dog …"

I smiled. "Our dog's name is Moses. Guess who picked that?"

"So, you're saying dads get final vote."

"On some things," I answered, in case he was thinking of my dad's influence if I remained in Carolina or not.

Luckily, Ryan stayed on the lighter topic of puppy names. "Well, I better get thinking then. The dog is a relative of Vino. So, wine is *their* business. Maybe something about music? Ideas?"

"Hmmm, I like that. Let me think." When Ryan started humming the *Jeopardy* theme, I legitimately laughed.

"That laugh …" I could hear the smile in his voice.

"It's been a while," I admitted and then shot out an idea. "How about Lyric?"

"Much better than Rhapsody."

"Geez … yes. Is that what you came up with?"

"Well, I *was* playing the theme song at the same time, too."

"Excuses, excuses," I teased but thought about how it

was just another example of what a great team we were.

He *tsked* but then agreed. "I like the name Lyric. Guess what my folks named their pigs?"

"Do I want to know?"

"There's Bacon and Hambone and—"

"Oh, my stars! No!"

It was Ryan's turn to laugh. "Oh, yes."

I think it was because we were talking so carefree—as we used to before ex-wife drama monopolized our lives—that I completely flipped on him emotionally. Out of the blue, I blurted out one of the true emotional holds on my heart. "I'm so scared for Garrett, Ry. He can't go through that again."

His exhale was strong but so were his words. "I know you are. I'm sure everyone is."

"But it's hard to talk with them about it, especially because there's nothing to go on yet."

"Because you're used to problem-solving, pleasing others, and doing things on your own."

"I don't know about all of that."

"Yes. You are so independent and confident but in a kind way. It's a good thing, but, when you need s—"

"I want to talk with you."

Absolute truth. Not a doubt. Not having that—even if it was my own doing—severed me.

"You can." He spoke with his own confidence.

"It's just like it was before," I went on. "My dad is stoic. He thinks God will take care of it. And my mom is going to have a nervous breakdown." My news probably didn't help that. "Ella is just Ella. And Garrett? Who knows? He's a typical moody teen."

"And you're not going to change them or any results that come in. Don't rock on that rocking chair. Talk with me in the middle of the night if it helps. It's more than okay with me."

I swiped at my nose and eyes a couple times. "I so needed to hear your voice ... to talk with you."

"Bethany, I ..." He did a disgruntled clearing of his throat. "Dang it. I promised you I wouldn't."

I dabbed at my eyes again. He had stopped himself and, for the first time, I wondered if I wanted him to. I needed those three words right then but, at the same account, didn't want to be an emotional wreck when he said them.

"Song? Song for right now?" he changed the subject.

"Oh, Ryan ..." I didn't know if I was up for that game.

"Song." He was attempting to get his voice and mode back to our beginning banter.

My answer didn't help. "'Hole in the Bucket.'"

"No, no, no ... no."

"Yes. I feel like there is a big hole and nobody can fix it."

"Oh, man. I think I would have preferred 'Landslide.'"

"At least there is some humor with 'Bucket.' What? What's yours?" I turned the tables on him.

He was prepared and hit me with an emotional, non-funny one. "'Get here.'" And he loosely quoted some of the lyrics to confirm the meaning. "'If I had my way, you would be closer ...'"

"Thanks for not making this easy," I said with only a smidge of sarcasm.

"I never promised you that."

"When are your flights tomorrow? I mean, I guess, technically today."

"Afternoon/evening. And you? Ella's graduation and then the retreat on Sunday, right?"

I spit out a puff of air. "Yeah, the Sunday church retreat is a whole day event. No electronics. We place them in a basket and then they are put in a quote/unquote safe place."

"You know, some artists use that tactic to freely, wholly create."

"Yeah, that's kind of the idea—let all things go." I really could use it creatively and interpersonally.

"Geez ... so, with our schedules, I probably won't talk

with you for a couple days."

"No," I confirmed. "I'm glad we did now, though."

"You and me both. I hope next time it's in person."

"Mmmm." I couldn't say much more, because I still didn't know the answer to that. "I hope you found your balance."

"Almost. I hope you find yours."

***

It was true. We didn't speak with one another after that late-night chat. Post-graduation and lunch out, I texted, asking him to let me know when they got back to California. I had a deep-seated need to know he and the kids had arrived safely. I guess there was a little bit of my mom in me. He complied by sending a photo of a sleeping Sallie and Joel in the back of a cab heading to the house. I had already been asleep myself but was glad to see it when I woke that next day—Sunday morning. I was able to get a smiley face and ZZZs off to him before turning in my phone for the entire day ... for the "greater good of all humanity."

Of course, I knew Monday was going to be a crazy time for him. Every Monday was with the live shows. In addition, it was the first show since news of Kari's *own* retreat and the Twitter Girl affair broke. So, it was bound to be even more stressful for him. I also wondered how the kids were going to adapt to being back in school after a few days off and who was watching them. Was it Cruella Irene again? I bet that irked Ryan to no end to have to rely on his ex-in-laws.

Because of my schedule, I wasn't able to respond to his text earlier that day telling me things weren't the same without me and to call him. And I actually didn't even get to see the show until almost the very end. When I did, Portia, in a striking deep blue pantsuit, was on stage introducing one of the contestants—Tisha Chrisley. And irony of ironies, Miss Chrisley was going to sing one of Kari's hits.

Dressed in slender black slacks and a lengthy top with zippers—which would make Willow proud—fresh-faced Tisha came onto the stage and addressed Ryan. "I hope I can do your wife justice."

All eyes, including mine, of course, were then on Ryan. I'm sure everyone else was watching the tight grin on his face and wondering even more so about all the rumors. But I … I was noticing everything else *around* his lips. He was clean-shaven! What happened to his beard? What happened to the rule that he had to keep it until after the finale? When had he done that? And … why?

That thought swished around in my heart and brain before more elements on the stage connected. Tisha was smiling broadly at Ryan, and I suddenly became freakishly possessive. He was mine. Don't you dare look at him that way, Tisha Chrisley. But then my emotions flipped again. He wasn't mine. I wouldn't even let him tell me how he felt. And the world still thought, just as Tisha had said, that Kari was his wife.

Then Tisha belted out an absolutely beautiful rendition of Kari's "Outta Here." It was perhaps, dare I say, even better than the original artist herself. I wondered if Ryan felt the same. Of course, the other judges—Jorja and Calvin—deferred to him to give the critique.

"First of all, Tisha, you more than did it justice. Your tone is impeccable." He agreed with my assessment, and I swear Tisha looked as if she was going to faint because Ryan didn't give out compliments easily on the show. Mr. Mean was still a part he played. "Second," he continued after a slight pause, "Kari is not my wife. We've been divorced for six months and apart for over a year now."

The gasps and wide-eyes from the crowd were almost cartoonish. The same could be said about the *Spotlight* personnel. It was all a complete surprise to the world who thought they already knew all the gossip out there.

Ryan was continuing to talk, and if he hadn't had my attention before, he had it completely one hundred percent then. "I like how you mixed the song up a bit, too. It was creative and reminds me of one of the contestants we had in the early stages of the competition. She is a spectacular songwriter. This show didn't change her life, but she sure did mine." It was only on that last part of the sentence that I realized he was talking about … "Bethany Lenay, since you won't let me tell you in person, I'm gonna tell the whole world. I love you. Please make your next lyrics be our song."

My stomach dropped. My mouth went dry. My heart flipped and flopped and turned inside out. The strongest, largest of clamps wouldn't have been able to shut my gaped mouth. He had put it all out there—the divorce, his love for me …

The gasps from the audience had become downright murmurs. It was hard for Portia to get the normally perfectly timed show back in some kind of semblance. But when she did, I somehow got all my body parts to work correctly, including my hands. I found my Twitter page, changed my settings, and typed a message for Ryan. It was the first time we communicated that way since our initial online correspondence. And despite my instant nerves, I managed to find exactly the right words.

@RyanThompsonMusic for real?

As they were cutting to commercial break, I saw Jorja, who was sitting next to Ryan, nudge him and then show him her phone. I then looked at my phone again. And there it was—a tweet back from him.

@Bethany_Lenay For real. He kept up with our original banter, which was quite impressive since I was sure if *I* was feeling the pressure of his big on-air revelation, he was feeling it double. *Let's meet up.*

I backed up against the wall, trying to focus. People were talking to me, but I was thinking. I had been thinking all weekend. And what was happening changed nothing.

What happened to your face? I privately texted that time.

He switched formats also and reacted instantly. *U like?*

You know I do.

I will never reject U.

I closed my eyes. He had done it for me. His connection and thoughtfulness were almost unnatural. Even when I had all but pushed him away, he was committed to us.

And then another text came in. *Song U R feeling right now?*

You first…

Whether it was the time constraints he was under or the fact that he already had his, he didn't argue with me as he usually did. Instead, he offered, *"Truly."* I was humming it in my head while looking at his follow-up text. *Yours?* And then a moment or so later, *Come on…U know I hate when U don't answer.*

But I didn't. I couldn't. For one thing, I was too emotional. The last two minutes or so were only then catching up with me. Wow, all of that just happened. For another, there were too many people talking to me. And the texting was going to have to stop soon, anyway—the show was returning from commercial break.

"We have one last performer." I was listening closely to Portia since I was so very invested for all kinds of reasons.

Ryan, obviously still waiting for me to respond, looked up from his phone. "What? Who?" His eyebrows furloughed slightly. "Everyone sang. I thought we were just doing wrap up and previews."

"New twist for today's episode," the hostess continued. "We're bringing someone back."

The studio audience sure were getting their fill of surprises that night. I watched as they looked from one another once again with wide eyes and mouths. The judges looked equally as shocked. None more than Ryan, who was trying to nonchalantly glance at his phone. My dad would have given him a good glare.

But I couldn't think of that. I was too busy trying not to shake … trying to focus … trying to walk. And then saying, "Hi, my name is Bethany. This is an original song, and it's how I am feeling right now."

The multiple lights above my head felt so warm. The stage so immense. The crowd so darn loud. I hadn't come to do any of that. Yet, there I was.

I had just wanted to talk with him … to see him again. When my plane had landed in LA, I knew I didn't want to wait until that night when he got home. I had made up my mind, and I wanted it to be then. I had the cab driver take me straight to the studio, hoping the laminate pass I had tucked in my wallet for months was still eligible for a free entrance into the show. At first the guards had not given me access, saying the seats were taken and I should have called ahead. But then I pulled out my second "card." I used the name Ryan had told me was his studio code word, in case I was ever watching the kids and there was an emergency. It wasn't an emergency, but my heart *was* hurting. And I was even more grateful the show's producers honored the request and kept me backstage. The plan had been to watch the final part of the show there and then see him once the cameras had stopped rolling and he was alone. It was a bit risky, knowing the *Singer Spotlight* crew made the connection and even more speculation could get out. But Ryan had said they were under strict policies, and I was trusting he felt the same way about seeing me.

And then when he made that announcement to the whole world, the producers had rushed to my side, coming up with the mad-crazy idea of getting me onto the stage. There hadn't been much time to make a decision and, had I been given more, I most likely would have chickened out. But Ryan had put everything out there, and I wanted to, too. I wanted him to know how much I appreciated not only those words but what being with him meant to me.

Even though the crowd was stirring with mumbles and

motion, I focused solely on him. His deep blue eyes … his clean-shaven face … his look at me. While first it was of pure shock, it melted rather quickly to peaceful adoration.

"Four-String Love" soared through the raised ceiling of the vast auditorium, and the active crowd became practically mute. I was lucky I knew the words. But then again, I had been writing, singing, and repeating them nearly nonstop for two days. The retreat had, in fact, been very good for me in all kinds of ways. There was no direct identification of Ryan or me in the lyrics, but there was also no question that it was all about the two of us. While Ryan, undoubtedly, could identify the meaning for every single word choice, the viewers would probably be able to fill in some of the subtle blanks.

It wasn't my best performance. I hadn't warmed up. My voice quivered at times with emotion. I would have never made it to the first round, again. But I didn't regret it.

On the last note, the crowd erupted and my legs jittered. I saw Portia out of the corner of my eye start to reemerge from the side of the stage. But Ryan was there first. He was in front of me … beaming … nodding … staring into me.

"You're here," he said, and the crowd hushed.

"In person," I voiced what he had wanted from me from the beginning. As I started to speak again, he removed the mic he had connected to his body, which was allowing the audience an insider's glimpse into our conversation. "You know I was backstage when you made your big proclamation?"

"No, obviously, I didn't." He handed his mic to Portia, who smiled and took my guitar and mic stand also off stage, guaranteeing us at least audio privacy. "I didn't even know if you were in the city or state. It didn't matter. I hadn't planned it, but it felt so right."

"Ry, you didn't need to say all of that. I knew. I was just scared to hear it because of … of everything else. I shouldn't have done that. I should have trusted you and knew that it was going to work out."

He took my hands in his, providing not only my body more balance but my heart, too. "I shouldn't have let other people tell me what to do for so long. Kari is exactly where she should be and has who she needs with her. *You* weren't. You were hurting. You were being hurt because of something completely out of your control. I couldn't let that—"

"You and I were both hurting." I caressed his hands. "And I'm here now."

"For good, right?"

"Yes." I felt the smile erupt onto my face. It made me so happy … happy enough to even tease. "Tails won."

"What?" The slight squint of his eyes showed his concern. "No."

I couldn't let him think for the slightest of moments, though, that I would ever have our love be the result of a flip of a coin. "No," I reassured. "You … you and your pangs won." And my little bit of guilt for leaving Carolina had been erased when I retrieved Garrett's message in the cab, saying he got a clean bill of health and our mom needs to chill with the hypochondria stuff.

"I … love … you."

As he kissed me, the stage lights faded and there were announcements for how the audience should exit the building. The show was over for the night. The official winner would be crowned the following day, but I knew I had already won something much greater than a title, fame, or money.

"I love you, too." I smiled. "For real."

"For real."

SNEAK PEEK AT *TAILS CALIFORNIA*

August 2021

Nearly every woman enthusiastically added a point to their shower scorecard. Aside from how Ryan and I met, how he proposed was the easiest question. After all, it had been shared in numerous media outlets. There had been four roses—three had thorns, but the final one did not. Instead, it hosted a spectacular, sparkling ring with the words "for real" inscribed inside. The proposal definitely personified all we were to each other and all that our future held.

"But tell them what he said right before that." My younger sister, Ella, was far from being a romantic, but she did love my engagement story from three months prior.

My internal smile was probably even greater than my external one. I couldn't help it. When it came to Ryan and our life together, I couldn't be happier. "We were playing a game we sometimes play with one another—naming a song about what we are feeling at that moment. He went first, which is never the case."

During my retell, the church's wooden basement door opened and the man himself appeared. But no one else noticed, since their attention was solely on me. I brought my hand up to my face and smiled the teensiest but happiest of bits.

"He said his song was Train's 'Marry Me.' And, at first, I didn't get it. But then I made the connection to the video's coffee shop girl, and the lyrics, and the title. And I

… it was …" I met his eyes. "He is … everything."

A collective "awww" hummed from the group of women as my mother, looking every bit the part of a matron in her black skirt and red floral top, pronounced, "Speaking of …"

Next to me, Ella quietly growled, "He had one job to do—bring flowers. Geez, men!"

Both my sister and mother had been relentless about my groom-to-be bringing me flowers when he arrived at the end of the bridal shower. Ryan and I had even laughed about it. He had said he would stop by the florist on the way from my parents' house, where he and the kids were visiting with my dad and Garrett. But where was the bouquet? In fact, where were the kids? He was supposed to bring them, too. And why was he so early?

Since he hadn't moved from the entry of the door, I walked to him, ignoring the soft murmurs and looks as I did so. He could broker major talent deals and appeared live on national television, but it seemed he was intimidated by a room full of my female Carolina friends and family. It was only after I said hi and wrapped my arms around his burgundy button-down covered chest, that I realized something was wrong … very wrong.

Fall In Love With the Country Roads Series:

A young woman content with her solitary life.
A rising country music star.
They were friends once ... until their lives took them down separate roads.

Now, years later, when a child volunteers his uncle to sing for a fundraiser, LARA FAULKNER realizes it is none other than her college pal, FINN MURPHY. As the two get a chance to reconnect, Lara reveals to a compassionate Finn details of her shocking past and the traumatic decision she had to make.

Through trust and love, the bond between Finn and Lara deepens as the country singer manages to get an emotionally scarred Lara to let down her self-proclaimed walls. But will secrets, lies, and tragedy cause a bumpy detour on their road to complete happiness?

Grab the whole series!

Available in Ebook and Print at all major book
retailers.

ABOUT THE AUTHOR

There really wasn't any other path. Grea Warner knew from a young age that she wanted to write. She was born to write. First it was in diaries with little metal keys and in written tales that she slipped to friends in study hall. School newspapers, a college television drama, and the soap opera world were next. After producing and writing a local show, she decided to delve into the world of the novelist. When her fingers aren't tapping out her latest book filled with angst and romance, Grea can be found hiking the trails or jamming to her favorite country artists on the radio.

Website: http://greawarner.com/

Publisher interview: http://www.inkspellpublishing.com/grea-w...

Socials:
  Twitter: @grea_warner
  Instagram: greawarner
  Facebook: https://www.facebook.com/Grea-Warner
  YouTube trailer link: https://www.youtube.com/watch?v=yrz9DjROoIM
  GoodReads:

https://www.goodreads.com/author/show/17230140.Grea_Warner

BookBub: https://www.bookbub.com/authors/grea-warner

www.ingramcontent.com/pod-product-compliance
Lightning Source LLC
Chambersburg PA
CBHW061941170626
46813CB00006B/2494